MORE CUMBRIAN GHOST STORIES

TONY WALKER

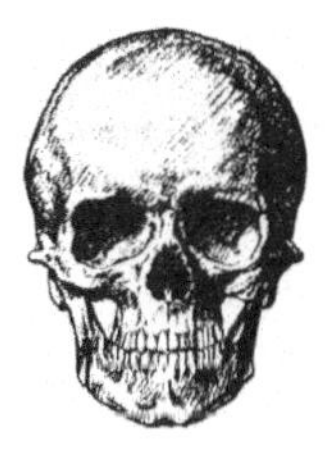

CONTENTS

Introduction   v

1. The Dalston Vampire   1
2. The Netherhall Boggle   11
3. Mabbin Crag   23
4. The High Harrington Horror   42
5. The Butcher of Botcherby   54
6. From Whitby to Whitehaven   68
7. Dubmill Point   79
8. Eachy of Bassenthwaite   96
9. Bella Sheep Head   111
10. The Mole Catcher of Barbon   128
11. The Tricking of Lord Thomas   143
12. A Brief Stop in Barrow in Furness   155
13. The Screaming Skulls of Calgarth   163
14. The Milk White Child of Ravenglass   178
15. The Haunting of Unit 409   194
16. The Shadow Man of Kendal   206

Also by Tony Walker   221

INTRODUCTION

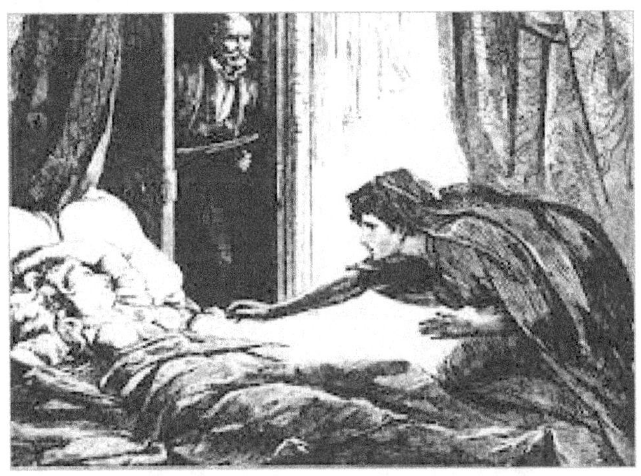

This is my second volume of Cumbrian Ghost Stories, though in truth most of them are monster stories, demon stories and stories of the fey folk.

Some of these stories have their origins in the days of our live storytelling events pre-COVID-19, which are now proving difficult to get back off the ground.

Others were tasks that I set myself during lock-down. I tried to write a story from a different part of Cumbria. I used a location and whatever sparked off in my head. It produced some weird juxtapositions.

When considering individual stories, The Dalston Vampire comes from my association with Dalston Hall during my ghost-hunting days so I am very familiar with the place. The West Cumbrian stories draw on my own local knowledge and some nostalgia for the past though I never went out with Bella Sheep Head. Although, Red, Henry and Howard did often await me in various pubs.

We had a lovely stay at Barbon Inn but never met the mole catcher. I love Ravenglass, and have always thought there should be a ghost story associated with Dubmill Point.

Of course we now have news that Cumbria is to be no more and to be divided into the old-new counties of Cumberland (without Alston and Penrith!) and Westmorland and Furness.

I hope you enjoy the stories. If you do, please leave a review.

Catch me on The Classic Ghost Stories Podcast both on YouTube and on any podcast app: Spotify, Apple, etc.

I hope you get a little scared and I would probably also like it if some of the stories made you laugh, or at least smile.

Tony Walker,

Carlisle, October 2021

CHAPTER 1

THE DALSTON VAMPIRE

It was 1322, and the winter was the longest and coldest anyone remembered. The ground lay heavy under snow long-frozen and the land was locked with ice. Without expectation, the Scottish army came south. Perhaps hunger had driven them, and perhaps cruelty, for Cumberland had been harried and burned by them year after year since the English defeat at Bannockburn.

As the day waned, Lord Henry Dalston stood tall on the red sandstone battlements of his pele tower. The River Caldew flowed through woods and fields to the east of the lofty tower, but it was from the cold north that the threat would most likely come.

He had heard how they crossed the frozen Esk at Longtown, reached Kirklinton and then besieged the great walled city of Carlisle. Most likely, raiding parties would soon come to Dalston. The icy wind blew past. There were no livestock to be seen in the fields as farmers had moved them south already. Lord Dalston had sent all servants but one home to their families. Only Mary remained, a woman of middle years who had no family.

No livestock to be seen, but plenty of black crows on bare tree-tops. Lord Dalston scanned the horizon, and a black figure in the middle distance caught his eye. The figure stood tall in a black cloak and hood against the white snow. He did not move at all, merely stared back at the tower.

Dalston thought the man better seek shelter lest he fall prey to the swift Scottish horsemen on their small grey ponies. Dalston hailed him with a shout and a wave of his arm, but the man did not respond. He shouted again, but again the man did not respond and finally, with a shrug, Dalston pulled up the trapdoor and took the wooden stairs back down into the security of his tower.

In his day chamber with its tapestries of hunting scenes from the Inglewood Forest, its glass windows, its wooden floors, Dalston spoke to his wife Edith. 'Do you really think they will come, Henry?' she asked.

Dalston rubbed his eyes. 'I do. They will scout the area for victuals to take back to the besieging army at Carlisle. Mid winter is a foolish time to start a war.'

'And that's why they caught us by surprise.'

He stroked her hair. 'I think I'll take a glass of wine, even though it is early.'

'I'll ask Mary to prepare food earlier tonight. There are only the two of us. I hope everyone else has got safe home.'

Dalston reached inside his doublet and pulled a great black iron key on a leather thong that he kept around his neck. He smiled gravely. "We are safe inside with the door locked. They won't bring siege equipment on their raids for food. They can take what they wish from the hall below; we can't stop them. But they'll not get into the tower. My ancestors built it secure, and no raider has ever got in once we draw the bolt across the door."

Darkness fell early on that winter night and dinner was served in their bedroom, where they sat quietly in the gloom lit by flickering candles. Lady Edith wore sable around her shoulder and a shawl of wool to keep her warm and she worked at her embroidery, but every now and again looked nervously up to check on her husband. He sat deep in thought, sipping his white Rhenish wine.

She said, 'We have food in?'

He nodded. 'We had plenty in for the winter, in any case. It'll go further if it's just we three.'

After a while, she asked, 'Are you worried?'

Dalston gave a weary smile. 'We've been through it before. They won't spare siege engines from Carlisle for such a little place as we are.'

THEY RETIRED TO BED EARLY, but Dalston slept little. Scenes of fire and pillage troubled his dreams, and then, in the deep of night, he awoke suddenly, thinking he heard soldiers and horses outside, but when he listened, it was only the soft sound of the north wind blowing round the pele tower. He slept again and when he awoke; it was day and Edith was already up.

They breakfasted together and then climbed to the tower roof to observe whether there were signs of trouble from the north. On the tower, a slight breeze blew, but it was cold. The mountains to the south were white, the trees dark, but the ground pale and frozen.

Great palls of smoke rose from where they knew Carlisle to be under attack.

And then Edith said, 'Look, Henry, who is that?'

And there, standing in the same place he had been the day before, was the black-clad stranger.

Lord Henry Dalston said. 'I saw that man yesterday, and he was standing exactly where he is now.'

'Well, he must have sought shelter overnight,' said his wife, 'for he would have frozen otherwise.'

Dalston nodded. 'I wonder who he is. I should call down and offer him shelter.'

But Edith put her hand on her husband's arm as if to stay him. He turned and regarded her. 'What, Edith? You are usually the first to offer succour to waifs and strays.'

She paused. 'He seems so strange.'

'I will go down and see him.'

'If you do, take your sword.'

He smiled. 'If it makes you feel better, I will, of course.'

'It would. I'm sure it's nothing, but he looks so odd standing there without moving.'

Lord Henry Dalston made his way down from the roof and down the spiral stone staircase inside the tower. He strapped his sword to his waist to please his wife, then went down past his room and the room below until he came to the great iron door. It was a latticework of painted iron bars and had been there for centuries. Once it had been the main entrance to the tower, when the tower stood alone, but now it gave entry to the Baronial Hall. He drew the heavy key on its thong from around his neck. The iron was warm from where it had lain pressed against his heart. He put it in the lock and turned the key. The key turned easily in the greased lock.

Henry Dalston walked through the deserted Baronial Hall. As many of the valuables as could be moved had already been put in the pele tower for safety. His boots echoed on the stone floor. He went to the main door and pushed it open. Outside, his feet crunched on the frozen snow. He walked round the tower until he came in sight of where the dark-clad stranger stood in the middle distance. Dalston hailed him. 'Halloo! Stranger, can I help you?'

The man didn't speak. Dalston's hand went to the hilt of his sword, and he went closer. He stopped twenty yards away. The man wore a long black cloak ragged at the bottom. The cloak's hood was up, throwing his face into shadow. He had on a breastplate that looked old-fashioned. He wore a sword on a belt at his side and leather trousers with knee-length boots.

Dalston shouted again, 'Hello there, stranger! I am Henry Dalston, Lord of this tower.'

For the first time, the man spoke. His voice was slow and accented such as Dalston remembered folk speaking in his grandfather's time.

'Lord Dalston,' the man said. 'I greet you. I am Gospatric Map

Belog, Lord of Cadeirleng .'

Dalston recognised the old-fashioned name Gospatric and the fashion of using the patronymic 'map' to show he was a son of Belog, was as the old Cumbrians had done. The names were old Cumbrian too, in the language that no one now spoke. Also, his pronunciation of his home as Cadeirleng was not like the more familiar and modern Catterlen.

Dalston said, 'I am sorry, sir. I do not know you. As far as I was aware, the lord of Catterlen is Herbert de Vaux.'

The dark clad man said, 'I know of no De Vaux, and I assure you I am lord of Cadeirleng and always was.'

'Enough of this, sir. You risk your life here, if you are English, for the Scottish army is abroad and seeking plunder, or hadn't you heard?'

'I am neither English nor Scottish, Lord Dalston.'

'Are you French then?'

'I am not. I am of this place.'

Dalston grew angry at the manner of this stranger who claimed honours he could not possibly have, and what did he mean he was not English, Scottish nor French?

Dalston spoke. 'I was going to invite you into my tower for your own safety, as a matter of common courtesy. '

The stranger said, in his strangely accented voice, 'I accept your courtesy, Lord Dalston. It will honour me to be your guest. At least for a while.'

Now Dalston remembered his wife's misgivings about the stranger; strange for Edith to be so disquieted, but the man also made a strange impression on him with his old-fashioned name and clothes.

He wished he had not made the invitation he unfortunately had just made. But what could he do? He could leave no one to the mercy of rampaging soldiers who would not care who they killed, whether he claimed not to be English or whatever he said.

Dalston narrowed his lips. 'Come then Gospatric Map Belog. I will find a room for you. We have only one servant staying with us, so please forgive my poor hospitality.'

The dark-clad man moved closer to Henry Dalston, almost seeming to glide over the snow so lightly he walked. Dalston, for some odd reason not wanting to be close to the stranger, hurried away and Gospatric map Belog followed him to his own front door.

Mary the maid was found and was told to prepare the guest room on the floor above Lord and Lady Dalston's own room, just below the servant floor where Mary slept. From the way she looked at the man, who stood inside the Baronial Hall with his hood still up, Dalston thought Mary did not care for him either.

Still, hospitality was a duty, and Dalston had made the invitation for the stranger to enter his tower.

Dalston accompanied his mysterious visitor and Mary up the spiral staircase to the floor where his chambers were.

'I'll leave you then, sir. You can rest until it is time to eat, for I believe you were all night in the cold.' Dalston said this pointedly, but his guest's pale face registered no emotion, nor did he reply. He simply went up after Mary, who showed him to his chambers.

'He is a strange man,' Lady Dalston said as they sat in their chambers. Dalston had just come down from the tower's roof. 'He makes me feel very ill at ease.'

Dalston shrugged. Whatever thoughts he had about Gospatric Map Belog, he didn't share them.

'Have the soldiers come, or is there any sign of them?' she asked.

'Smoke from Carlisle. New fires over towards Cardew and Cumdivock, but no sign of the soldiers themselves.'

'That's good, isn't it?' she said hesitantly. 'Perhaps they won't come.'

'Perhaps.'

'But even if they do, the tower is secure.'

Against most things, thought Dalston, but he said, 'Yes, yes, of course. Try not to worry.'

They lapsed into a troubled silence and, as dark was falling, Mary came to light the tapers.

'Is our noble guest settled in his chambers?'

'I think so,' said Mary, a lit spill cupped in her hand.

Lady Dalston said, 'Have you lit the tapers in his chambers?'

Mary shook her head. 'I knocked and asked to come in to do it, but there was no answer. I knocked several times,' she said, as if to reassure her lord she had done her duty.

'He must like to sit in the dark,' Lady Dalston said.

'Perhaps he went out?' Mary said.

Lord Dalston shook his head. 'The gate is locked and I have the only key.'

Lady Dalston began, 'He makes me—'

But Dalston signed for her to hold her peace in front of the servants, and Lady Dalston blushed and fell silent.

'Your dinner will be ready in an hour. I have prepared some pullets,' Mary said.

Dalston nodded. 'You have done well, Mary. Knock again on our visitor's door just before food is laid out. We will eat in the old dining room.'

The old dining room was the room in the pele tower that had been used for eating before they built the Baronial Hall. There was an enormous fireplace, which was rarely lit these days. Dalston had had one of the male servants lay the fire of dry logs and tinder before he left to go to his family.

But when they sat in the red sandstone dining chamber, with its old-fashioned tapestries and tapers held in standing candle holders of black iron, there was no sign of Gospatric Map Belog.

'Did you knock?' Lady Dalston said, as Mary served the meal.

'Aye, my lady, but he did not answer.'

Dalston was tired. The strain of waiting for the Scottish soldiers had eroded his patience. 'We will eat anyway. If he chooses not to eat, then that is up to him.'

Mary filled Lord Dalston's goblet with wine, then went to Lady Dalston, who refused the wine and had clear spring water instead.

The fire burned in its hearth, casting shadows across the walls. Outside, night had fallen and the chill of the winter came through the walls held at bay by the warmth of the flickering flames. They talked of this and that, of happier times and summer and their daughters who were married, and further south, safe.

After they had eaten and Mary had cleared away the platters, Dalston asked if there was any sign of Lord Gospatric. Mary shook her head.

He left Edith to her embroidery and mounted the stairs to the guest chamber. Standing outside, he knocked on the heavy wooden door. No response came. He knocked again, harder this time. Again nothing, so he called out, 'Lord Gospatric, are you not hungry?'

The wind whistled outside, but otherwise there was no sound. Lord Dalston felt the cold come from under the door. No sign of light seeped out. Perhaps their guest was so tired that he had fallen into a deep sleep. If that was so, he would wake hungry for breakfast.

Dalston descended. His wife raised an eyebrow. 'Any sign of him?'

'No,' Dalston said. 'He must be asleep.'

'He must.'

The tapers burned low. Dalston was tired, his limbs felt heavy. He nodded in his chair and then his wife said, 'Time for sleep. Who knows what tomorrow will bring?'

'Who knows?'

'Perhaps they will lift the siege and return whence they came,' said his wife.'

'Perhaps.' He went over and kissed his wife on the forehead. He took her hand and led her to the bed, then called Mary to help her undress.

When Edith was in bed, he dismissed Mary with a smile. 'Thank you for staying, Mary,' he said, and she curtsied with a smile. 'I couldn't leave you, my Lord.'

Lady Dalston fell into a deep sleep. The night was so dark and silent. Only the wind fretted and moaned outside the windows. Then a scream tore through the building. She awoke with a start, sitting bolt upright. Her husband woke beside her. 'What was what, Henry?'

'I don't know.'

'I think it was Mary. Have the soldiers got into the tower?'

Dalston's voice was troubled. 'No, that can't be. I have the key. And besides, they would have to come past our door, and there would be such a noise of them breaking down the gate and mounting the stairs.'

'Then what is it then?' Lady Dalston asked, a terrible fear growing in her heart. 'It was Mary's cry. I know her voice so well.'

'I will go,' Lord Dalston said, rising in his nightshirt.

'Take your sword, ' she said.

It was dark, but he had flint and iron and lit a flame in the tinder from which he kindled a taper. 'Light a candle for me,' she said. Without speaking, he did so, pulled on his doublet and breeches and hurried.

It was raining heavily outside their window.

Lady Dalston watched her husband leave, sighing and trembling, waiting for him to return.

But minutes went by then, quarter of an hour, and still he did not return.

Lady Dalston half expected to hear sounds of fighting or shouts and alarms, but there was only silence. After a while, she rose and went to the door. 'Henry! Henry! What keeps you?' she yelled, but there was no reply.

With her hand to her throat, she fetched a taper and trembled, peering up into the gloom of the spiral stone staircase that led up to Mary's chamber.

'Husband, are you there?' She shouted, but her only answer was the sighing of the wind.

'Henry, please tell me you are well.' She yelled, but her only answer was a flutter of the taper burning in her hand.

'Henry!' she called again. 'Please speak!' But the only answer she got was the pitter patter of soft rain.

With taper in hand, she finally summoned her courage, and stepped out onto the stairs of the tower, the stone cold under her bare feet. 'Henry?' She called, but her voice was quieter now, as if she no longer expected an answer.

Lady Dalston heard someone coming down from above.

Whoever came was not in a hurry. He came, almost silently, down and down, towards her, step by step by step.

Lady Dalston stood shaking. She could not run and she could not stay. She didn't know what to do.

And the footsteps came down, almost in sight now, just round the corner of the spiral stairs.

And instead of climbing, Lady Dalston descended, taper in hand.

She jumped down the steps, hurrying in her panic, and always behind her came the soft footfall descending.

And then, her heart pounding in her chest, she came to the bottom of the tower. But at the bottom was the heavy black iron lattice gate that had stood for centuries keeping intruders out. And stood now, keeping her in.

Lady Dalston pulled at the gate; she pushed at the gate; she heaved at the gate, but it was to no avail. It was heavy and iron and locked against her. Lady Dalston strained and tugged and moaned in her fear. And behind her, someone came round the turn of the stairs.

Lady Dalston held up her taper and screamed.

Lord Gospatric descended the stairs. His eyes were yellow like fever and his cheeks as pale as snow. His lips were red as blood and blood was on his chin, and blood ran over his cuffs and blood was on his fingernails. And as he came closer, Lord Gospatric smiled.

Lady Dalston saw Lord Gospatric's teeth were long and white and sharp.

And even though he had eaten, Lord Gospatric was still hungry.

Lady Dalston shook the strong iron door, but she could not get out.

And, as Lord Gospatric's cold red fingers touched her, she wished her husband had never let him in.

CHAPTER 2

THE NETHERHALL BOGGLE

My name is Mark Irwin. I am—or I was—a local amateur historian, looking up family history and suchlike for people with ancestors in Cumbria. I also do some metal detecting on the side. At at least I used to do all that.

What I am now—what I will be soon—is unknown to me. As I write, it's late at night, and I'm in my attic bedroom, and I can hear it downstairs, but I don't know what's going to happen.

I first got into this case at the records office at Carlisle. I was researching some family stuff for a man in America, and by chance, came across the testimony of a Lily Goodfellow from Ellenborough, Maryport. It was interesting from the first glance. Her story related to an unsolved murder from 1926. I thought it was interesting then, but now I wish I'd never clapped eyes on it.

The note was in a sheaf of papers relating to Netherhall. The Netherhall Estate had belonged to the Senhouse Family for many centuries — originating as a border Pele Tower for defence against the Scots, but now a dilapidated ruin.

Lily's hand was well-formed, copperplate, but childish. The

paper was yellowed and the ink brown. Half of the last page had been torn and sellotaped together — my guess was that was done in the 1970s sometime. I'll say why later.

In her testimony, Lily begins by telling us she was an apprentice to Booth's, a bakery and patisserie in Senhouse Street, Maryport. I understand that in those days, they didn't pay the apprentices who worked. They laboured for free and learned their trade on the job.

I'll quote this in Lily's words.

'I had to deliver the cakes. That was part of my job, and I took some to the big house at Gatesgarth Corner where the main road splits, the left fork goes to Allonby and Silloth, and the right one goes to Aspatria and Carlisle. I never liked that road. It was spooky. It's a very lonely road, and you had high walls on both sides. On the left is empty fields and on the right is Netherhall itself, though you can't see the hall because of the trees.'

Note: This was before they built the school or rugby club.

'I ran all the way to drop the cakes off at Gatesgarth Corner and ran all the way back again, and I was out of puff and stopped right by the gatehouse to Netherhall. The wind was thrashing the trees about, and I thought I saw something down the la'al lonning to the big house. I got myself lathered, but I knew it was daft because my mam says there's nowt there and there's nee sec things as ghosts and boggles any road.'

'When I'd got my breath back, I ran down that dark gravel lonning with them dark trees all the way to the back door of Netherhall, and I gave the cakes to Sally Cuthell, who I was at school with afore she went into Service. I ran back, and I was jiggered and had to stop at the gatehouse. I looked awa t'wall, and I seen sommat in the lonning. It was behind them two lads. It was big, and it moved. It didn't have a proper shape, but it was a queer thing and it moved and heaved itsel' along.'

'Yan o't' lads seen it, and he shrieked out loud. T'other stood there, but the first yan ran off down the lonning ontil t'main road. The black thing went after him, and it was sea fast. It slithered and dragged itsel'. The second lad nivver seemed to see it at aw. I divn't know how he never seen it. But the first lad — he was shouting after his marra to come back and not be sea daft. He was shouting 'Joe! Joe! Joe!' and I thowt I knew him. I was sure t'second lad was Peter Nixon frae Ewanrigg, and I later found out the first was Joe Hardy because his dad works wid mine down Risehow Pit.'

'Joe Hardy louped awa't wall, but the thing pulled itsel' efter him. I nivver seen him efter, but I know the Boggle got him. I never spoke to Peter Nixon at that time, but I did afterwards. That neet, I ran yeam because I was finished work, and I telt ma mam, and she said not to be so soft, but we found out about Peter, and I know I was right.'

I couldn't find anything else about Lily.

I tried to look up the Netherhall Boggle. As a note, a 'boggle' is a word used in the far north of England and Scotland for a supernatural creature. Further south, they prefer the term 'boggart'.

A boggle is not a ghost, though it can be. They are supernatural creatures that were never human. They can often shape-shift. The Reagill Boggle, for example, is at times a gigantic pig, the Mallerstang Boggle is a huge black hen, and the Thirlmere Boggle is a column of sparks or sometimes a heap of earth, while the boggle at Dearham is a vast black shape of no fixed qualities, other than it is a dreadful black. Finally, the Salterbeck Boggle has no form and may be invisible, though it did kill a man on the cliff path between Harrington and Moss Bay in the late 1800s.

But coming back to this sighting. It was taken locally that this was a visitation of the Netherhall Boggle. Folk round about say the Netherhall Boggle is by all accounts made of dark, sucking jelly. Odd.

There are reports of the Netherhall Boggle going back to 1757.

They may go back further, but that is the first record I could find. It's a brief note by Humphrey Senhouse (1705-1770). It says:

> 'and the rural people speak of bogles and other suchlike and sundry creatures that fly by night or creep in the dark. One notable such manifestation is at Netherhall itself, though I must own that I have never seen it.'

— HUMPHREY SENHOUSE, APRIL 1757.

After finding out about the death of Joe Hardy, life went on, and I got to doing other things. Then, one day in the Autumn, I was on Netherhall Estate grounds. I had my metal detector with me, which is illegal, but the site is so rich in remains, and there's still plenty to find there.

I was in the woods near the river where it's boggy. I got a signal on my detector. When this happens, it's usually only bottle tops or buttons, but I started to dig with my little spade. I got down about eight inches in the soft earth, and something oozed out. This substance was halfway between oil and jelly and had a funny sheen on it. I'd never seen anything like it, and I wondered if someone had dumped old kitchen oil or sump oil that had gone bad, but it wasn't either of them. It was more like a black jellyfish, almost alive-looking, and it had roots reaching down deep because when I got the spade under it and tried to lift it, it resisted, and it made a sucking noise and curled round the edges of the spade.

I chopped a bit of this black jelly off with the spade, put it in a collection bag, and transferred it to a jar in the kitchen.

After a day or two, I lost interest. I'd planned to get it analysed by the chemistry teacher at Netherhall School, or maybe throw it out. But I just didn't.

In the days after finding the substance in Netherhall Woods, I had problems with mildew in the bathroom which took a lot of my time. Damp seeped in through the walls, but I couldn't find from where. The mould grew like a black vinegary-smelling rash every-where. I could keep it in check with anti-fungal spray but not get rid of it.

As I stood, trying to fathom ways of getting shot of the mildew, my mind went back to the unsolved disappearance of Joseph Hardy of Ewanrigg on November 7th 1926. Genealogy work was slack, so I decided to investigate further.

I dug my way into the archives of The Cumberland and Westmor-land Constabulary and found a witness statement from Peter Nixon about the events around the death of Joseph Hardy.

It should also be remembered that 1926 was the year of the General Strike. Although most of the miners were back at work by November, the year was economically and socially devastating for the communities of the West Cumberland coalfield. The men and women scavenged wherever they could just to keep body and soul together.

Here's the statement:

'I Peter Nixon of Shiney Row, Ellenborough, declare this statement to be the complete and honest truth.

On the evening of November 7th, Joseph Hardy and I were on the shore up past Bank End Farm collecting sea-coal. We got two good sackfuls, and we were coming back along Fat Lonning. It was pitch black and early, nearly six o'clock.

We cracked away as we walked and were halfway down the lonning with the fields sloping down to our left and up to our right. Suddenly, Joe jumped, and I asked him what the heck he was doing. He was staring at the field above the road. There was a hedge in the way, and in that gloom, I couldn't see anything.'

The next bit is verbatim.

'I says: what's the matter, Joe?

Well, he says, 'nowt', but he keeps looking over his shoulder. He starts talking normal again — I think we were cracking on about his dad's pigeons —and he jumps again, so I ask again what ails him, and he says, 'Did you see that, Pete?'

And I say, 'See what? I nivver seen nowt.'

'It's there still.' He points out into the dark. His hand's shaking like a leaf in a thunderstorm.

And I say, what is?

And he replies: the boggle.

Well, I laughed out loud because there was nowt there, but he kept staring like there was. But he turns and starts off walking fast. I had to hurry to keep up. We were close enough to the end of the lonning now, about fifty yards from where it comes out ontil t' road.

But Joe was gae dathered, I could tell. I heard him gasping, and he was walking that fast as if the divvel hissel was on his heels. He jerks his head round. There was a rumble like a pile of muck shift-ing. Even I heard that, but what it was, I couldn't say, but Joe seemed flate enough and he dropped his sack of coal and hared off into the gloom. I stood dumbfounded, staring after him, because I wasn't yan to believe aw them stories they tell til't kiddies.

But frae't left, the sound rumbled out again, like rocks rolling over in a heavy tide. I was standing, but Joe had disappeared.

I never saw Joe alive again, and what brought him til his end, I divn't know. Mebbe we'll nivver find out.'

— TAKEN UNDER OATH, BY SERGEANT WILLIAM DIXON, MAYPORT POLICE STATION, EAGLESFIELD STREET, MARYPORT, CUMBERLAND ON NOVEMBER 9TH, 1926 AT 11:30 IN THE MORNING.'

Doing my researches, it appeared that Joseph Hardy disappeared totally. Indeed, his body was never found.

Going through the archives, I saw a man called Simon Mayfield had done research on the case in the 1970s. He was a freelance journalist who wote pieces for the Fortean Times. In 1978, he was up in Cumbria. I know because he'd done a report on the Brugh Marsh Spaceman, which I read, and as a footnote, it said he'd done articles on the Croglin Vampire and the Netherhall Boggle. That got my interest back in the case.

I was still having trouble with the mildew, but I didn't connect the two things.

Archive.org on the internet has a collection of facsimiles of the Fortean Times from that period, and I found the article. Most of it was what I knew already. He'd seen the Lily Goodfellow report and the Peter Nixon statement. My guess was it was him who'd sellotaped the Lily Goodfellow page that was ripped.

But he had found something that I hadn't. It seems he'd interviewed Joseph Hardy's younger sister, Hannah.

Both Hannah Hardy—later Mason—and Simon Mayfield were now dead, but Hannah said that Joseph had brought back some strange muck he'd got from Netherhall. He'd been out with the terriers poaching rabbits and was digging out and got this odd substance. Hannah Hardy said her nana said it was part of the boggle, but Joe had laughed at that. Hannah Hardy told Simon Mayfield that her nana told her that the boggle sleeps underground, spreading out and waiting for people. It can sleep for months or years, but when someone digs up a piece, it grows. She says that the boggle hates animals. It strangles rabbits and moles when it catches them underground.

And that made me think of the strange jelly I'd found. I went to my kitchen and found the jar behind the pickled onions and red cabbage. The goo seemed more than I remembered: Now, it almost filled the jar, though I could swear it had only been a third full when I'd first slopped it in. The oily sheen glimmered in the kitchen lights, and when I rolled the jar round, it sloshed about. I turned the jar over, observed it then put it down.

• • •

BIZARRE THINGS STARTED HAPPENING. I heard noises in the house: creakings and movements that I'd never noticed before. The disturbances came from under the floor. When I was alone at night watching TV or I awoke from sleep for some unaccountable reason at three a.m., I felt something in the house observing me—listening, watching, and waiting.

Whatever it was had a presence, and it didn't feel human. It felt old and it felt forgotten.

Moss began to grow like crazy around my house. The first thing I noticed was clumps of it on the pavement outside, where it fell off the roof. I stood outside, craning my neck, and could see it growing over the roof edge. I'd never seen moss grow as fast or as thick as that.

Only a few days after, the taps started running for no reason, and the water was brown and slimy and thick. All over the house, bathroom and kitchen, the taps would just start up. I couldn't stop them. I ran to the bathroom, the kitchen and the shower and turned them off, but when I'd turned one off, the others started again, all pouring out this oily, dirty water with bits of mould and slime in it.

I didn't want to shower in that filthy water, so I called the water board, and they said they'd send somebody. They took weeks.

The next day, a big patch of damp appeared in the ceiling above my bed. I got a man out to look, but he said the roof was fine, and he couldn't explain it and said maybe it was condensation. But why now? I've lived in this house for three years, and it hasn't happened before.

But worse than that, when I was alone, I saw things in the mirror — things moving and shifting half out of sight. I'd catch the movement out of the corner of my eye, flick my head round, and just miss them as if they were watching me watching them.

All the mirrors developed strange stains like something was spreading on the underside of the silver—like something wanted to break in from the other side of the mirror—like something was growing there.

And I became convinced that something was in my mirrors, and something was in my taps and something was in the ceiling above my bed.

The moss grew even more. That was the oddest thing. I couldn't see it grow, but when I looked back at it, it was bigger, thicker, more luxuriant, spreading over the windows like dark green fingers, locking me in—closing out the light.

I managed to get out for food, but I was frightened. I was frightened to be outside, but I was also afraid to be in the house. Something was coming, getting closer with every day, every hour, every breath.

I don't have any family up here or any friends. I told myself it was all imagination. I thought of moving out to a hotel, but I couldn't afford it.

I locked the front door. I retreated upstairs to my bedroom. I pulled the curtains tight to shut out the sight of that growing moss.

The window was blocked by moss now, and it was feeling its way in, green feathery fingers forcing their way into the room, round the edges of the window frame, along the wall, spreading like a net, like a living thing.

I thought I was going mad. I told myself all of this was natural, and anything unnatural merely a product of my imagination.

I tried to watch TV, but I couldn't concentrate. I kept thinking about the Netherhall Boggle.

I lay there at night thinking about the boggle, listening to it watching me, sensing it grow, hearing it come around the windows and under the doors, through the ceiling and up between the floorboards.

I don't know what the boggle is. It's not a ghost. It's not a demon. It comes from below the earth. It's old. Though the stories of it only go centuries back, I think it's been here much longer. It was here when the Romans built their fort at Maryport. Perhaps even back to the Stone Age. When people returned here after the ice retreated, it was waiting for them.

I know it doesn't like animals, and I'm certain it doesn't like people. It doesn't like me. It can't abide me. I woke it after nearly a hundred years of dreaming—dreaming its hatred of the animal world, deep in dreams of the lichen and the fungi and the spores that pre-date even the plants.

AN ENORMOUS NOISE cracks out downstairs, under my bedroom.

My heart pounds away, and my throat dries. I burst out of my bedroom, and I run to the top of the stairs and switch on the light to look down, and I peer and I stare but I can't see anything properly.

I can't see but I can hear. I hear something moving.

I've got to know what's causing that noise for my own sanity. There will be a rational explanation. I've become mentally unwell. I need to find a way back to sanity. I need to ground myself with evidence. So I make my way down.

The living room door is shut, and a weird brown fungus grows inside the front door, spreading wetly over the wood. I try to pull the front door open, but the mould has welded it shut with its green fingers. I gulp. I yank at the door, but it won't move. I plant my feet, shift my weight and drag at the door, but it doesn't budge. I blink. I need to focus. I'll have to phone someone to get me out: the police, the fire brigade.

But I've left my mobile in the living room. I hesitate a long time, but then I tell myself I'm being stupid and push open the door.

As I step in, I gasp and put my hand to my throat. The laminate floor is cracked and heaved open. Something's come up from below. An awful brown and green mass is pushing its way up into the room — a vast shapeless jelly pulsing and slopping like slimy algae.

The light goes out as the living green mass intrudes into the wall sockets and infiltrates the current, drinking it up.

All the windows are blocked with this growth. There's no light. I scream but my shriek is thrown back, dull and dampened by the thick wadding of the growth that spreads and possesses my house.

In the dark, I run up the stairs. The fungus has grown over the treads, making them slimy and soft and slippery. Halfway up, feeling my way, I trip and nearly fall all the way down, but I scramble up on my knees. I reach my bedroom and yank the door shut behind me.

I sit there alone, trembling behind the door that I've wedged shut with a chair.

THEN I HEAR the noise of it heaving itself up the stairs. It's close now. The mould is everywhere, with its damp, vinegary stink, but its mind radiates from the lumps of vegetation outside my bedroom door. I can feel its intelligence and its hate. I can feel that it wants to silence me, to smother me, to consume my animal life.

The door creaks under the weight of it. It's outside now. It presses against the wood. I feel it close by. I hear the sucking movements. I smell the acid smell. The door bows in and the door lock strains to hold, but only for a second, then it gives way

I try to break the window glass. I throw a vase at the window. The glass shatters, but the moss holds it together like glue. I pound at the spongy mass with the splintered glass cutting my hands and forearms, blood running down, mixing with the green ooze.

I can't get out.

An ominous creak echoes above my head.

Looking up, I see the ceiling bellying wetly, groaning with the weight of the oily slime pooling in the plaster above. There's a smell of earth and rot. It smells of things ancient and bitter and implacable.

The bedroom door finally breaks open under the enormous weight of the boggle. The jelly-slime seeps in over the floor like a slow flood. The squidgy goo creeps and moves, feeling its way towards me.

I shriek as the ooze touches my shoe. I pull my foot back, but soon, I'm in the corner, and the slime is all around, feet deep, knee deep, waist deep, flooding in from all sides and thickening, growing, heaving.

And whatever it touches, it digests. Everything it absorbs, it eats, and when it wraps its cold arms around me I feel it thinking. It thinks of the earth, it thinks of the cold, its thinks of food. And slime pours into my mouth, forcing its way into my nose and throat and eyes, and as it extinguishes my life, it shudders in delight.

CHAPTER 3
MABBIN CRAG

Anthony will have to set off driving early the next day if he wants to miss the traffic. It's a long way, but he and Amanda have decided that this is what they want: a complete change, and a new life.

Anthony knows his mother is unhappy with their decision. He goes to see her on his own, to make sure there isn't an argument with Amanda and his mother locking horns about their decision to move, which his mother sees as Amanda stealing her son and taking him to the far north.

In her small but elegant flat off the Cromwell Road, Anthony sips tea out of the bone China cups his mother insists on. It's winter, and the central heating is on, making the room stifling. In the square outside the window, rain-soaked trees huddle beneath the downpour.

'It's too far, Anthony. Just too far.' She holds the cup's narrow handle between finger and thumb and can't meet his eye.

'We've decided—'

'She's decided,' she mutters, looking at the floor.

'Not 'she' mum — Amanda, my wife.'

'Hmm.'

A long pause as the rain drizzles against the window, and he wonders if he's been there long enough for him to leave without causing too much offence. Then his mother blurts, 'You can't trust them, you know — those northerners.'

He sighs. 'Really, mum.'

But she continues her tirade. 'They're not like us. Barely civilised. And those ones where you're going. It's so remote — not civilised at all!' She looks up with her eyes like an old bird's. 'Where is it even that you're going?'

He's told her before, but he'll tell her again. 'Long Sleddale, mum. It's a lovely house we've bought. You must come up.'

'Never. I can't travel that far. I'm too old. You'll regret it once you're isolated somewhere like that. Then you'll long to be back in London, but it'll be too late then.'

'Come up on the train when the weather improves. I can pick you up from the station.'

But she's not listening, muttering instead, 'Mark my words, no good will come of this.'

Anthony puts down his teacup. 'We'll be fine, mum. Honestly, we will.'

THE NEXT MORNING, it's dark when Anthony and Amanda set out. It takes almost an hour before they're out of London and heading up the M40. They pass blue signs for Oxford within the next hour. He's doing well, streaming down the dark road, catching up with red tail lights and passing them like silk. Birmingham two hours after London and then north again. It gets light about Stafford and the rest of the journey, with a break at Charnock Richard motorway services, takes place in the grey overcast light of a January day.

Anthony pulls the car off the M6 at Junction 36 with the signs indicating "Kendal and the Lake District". He can feel Amanda's excitement. She dozed some of the journey. Earlier, she'd offered to drive a bit, but he didn't need her to. When she wakes, she reads her Kindle until she says it makes her feel sick and then they stream *Dead Can Dance* on the car sound system for fifty miles, then she starts to talk as if she can finally believe her dream is coming true.

From Kendal, they take the old road into the mountains. Anthony himself feels excited at the great grey bulks around them covered in greensward grazed short by bedraggled sheep and the stands of dark green trees and eruptions of craggy rocks. This is their new life. So different from London.

The road goes on, climbing and bending. There are few houses to be seen, the odd car, but no people, except once a farmer on a tractor distributing turnips for the sheep.

They turn down a minor road, and after that, an even smaller one signed for Long Sleddale. They're among the mountains now. Huge hills that loom high on either side. The Sleddale valley is like a snake, or a funnel, pointing them down to a dead-end where no car can drive further.

They've been here before, but the weather was better when they bought the house and its five acres of rough ground. That was July. He drives carefully. The road is lined by grey stone walls built without cement, laid stone upon stone, each fitted to the next by the skill of the men who made the wall centuries ago.

The mountain slopes soar up. Amanda begins to quote:

'But huge and mighty forms, that do not live
    Like living men, moved slowly through my mind
    By day, and were a trouble to my dreams.'

'Wordsworth,' she adds. 'From *The Prelude*.'
'I know,' he laughs. 'You've quoted it before.'
Then, glancing up from the driving wheel to the bulk of the mountains on all sides, he says, 'I hope the huge and mighty forms won't turn out to be a trouble to my dreams.'

She says, 'Of course not. They're beautiful.' She reaches and strokes his neck. 'I feel so free.'

He has to concentrate on the road. He's not used to such narrow lanes, and now he has to turn left onto a tighter lane with grass growing in the middle. He brakes and hits the indicator, and the light blinks and ticks, not that there is anyone behind or in front that needs a signal that he is turning.

They travel this small road about three miles until from afar, Amanda sees the house. It's grey—built of slate and stone, and it stands by a group of yew trees, surrounded by its own drystone walls whose moss drips in the downpour. He slows the car as he approaches.

'Elva House!' she says. 'Our new home.'

They park and stretch, only now realising how stiff the long drive has made them. Amanda turns and regards the narrow road they've driven down. 'Don't know how the removal van is going to get down there.'

Anthony smiles. He has the house key in his pocket posted by the Estate Agent. 'Don't worry,' he says. 'They'll be fine.'

The house is cold and empty and echoes until their furniture arrives, which happens the next day. With their things around them, even boxed, turned on their ends or piled one on another, the place begins to feel like home.

The removal man, a Cockney, says, 'Rather you than me, mate,' gesturing to the mountains and steep slopes around the house. 'There's more sheep than people here.'

Amanda smiles. 'That's what we want. There's such a sense of freedom here, away from the rat race, don't you agree?' She's teasing the Cockney removal man, who scowls and says, 'Give me the Old Kent Road, any day.'

But it is remote.

The nearest house is half a mile further down the narrow lane, about ten yards before the road transforms into a track of stones and rubble not fit for cars and barely fit for a horse.

When the removal men are long gone and the couch and chairs pulled into some sort of shape, Amanda and Anthony take a bottle of French wine and some fruit: sharon fruit and persimmons they got at Sainsbury's in Kensington and make themselves known to their neighbour.

After crunching down the road, lifting the rusty black-painted gate off its latch to open the way before them, they knock on the peeling green paint of the cottage door. It takes the inhabitants a long time to answer as if they aren't used to visitors. Eventually, a woman comes. 'Yes?' she says.

She's thin with a nylon housecoat showing faded flowers. The housecoat looks cheap. She looks poor. Her face is lined and grey. Anthony guess she's in her early fifties though she could pass for a much older woman.

Amanda is a similar age, but slim and toned from Pilates and Yoga. Amanda models a tight-fitting dark blue Rab puffer jacket, black yoga pants, a Jack Wolfskin hat and gloves and the best walking boots she could afford. Amanda's long blonde hair is pulled back into a ponytail. The neighbour woman's hangs lank. The two women are worlds apart, thinks Anthony. He prefers Amanda.

'We're Amanda and Anthony,' Amanda introduces them. 'We're your new neighbours.'

The woman isn't unfriendly. 'At Elva?'

'Yes,' Amanda smiles.

Anthony is curious; he asked the Estate Agent, but she didn't know. This woman is local. She looks like she's lived in this valley all her life. She'll know. 'An interesting name: 'Elva'. What does it mean?'

The woman says, 'It used to be Elf How in my grandmother's time, but they shortened it. They didn't like it spelled out.'

'Elf How?'

'A "how" is the local word for a small hill. You know what an elf is.'

Anthony smiles. He's thinking Tolkien, but he guesses the elfs that live here are altogether older and darker. Still, it's a nice reference. It makes him feel like he is involved in a place that's ancient and rooted.

'Sorry, I didn't catch your name,' Amanda says.

'I didn't give it,' the woman says, but there's a hint of a smile on her face. She's not too bad.

'Oh,' Amanda blushes, not knowing what to do now, but the woman saves her. 'Peggy Fawcett, that's me.'

'Do you live here alone?' Amanda asks, and Anthony winces because he thinks she's being too personal.

'I do now,' Peggy says. 'My husband left me, and my two lads live away.'

Just then, there's a clucking noise, and Anthony looks round to see a small flock of black hens. He hasn't noticed them before.

'That's my family now,' Peggy says, and she's smiling.

As they walk away, Amanda says, 'Well, she wasn't too friendly. I thought northerners were supposed to be warm and chatty.'

Anthony says, 'They're country folk — conservative.'

Amanda snorts, 'And from the way she looked at that persimmon, I don't think she knew it was edible.'

'Maybe never seen one before,' Anthony says and realises it's likely true.

'At least she'll be able to drink the wine,' Amanda says as they're within sight of Elva House.

'Maybe,' says Anthony. He glances at the hills—not much wine was ever produced round here.

It's the weekend, not that weekends make any difference to their working lives. On Saturday, they drive up to Grasmere and Ambleside so that Amanda can put up her business cards advertising her services as a Reiki Master, offering healing. 'It'll take time to build the business, I know', she says. 'But I'm hopeful.'

Anthony works in social media marketing. He can operate from anywhere as long as there are good Internet connections, and thankfully, Cumbria benefited from European Money to extend broadband connections to remote areas like Long Sleddale. They managed to get it in before the Brexit vote.

Saturday was driving around. It rained, but it didn't matter because they were in the car. Sunday is a better day. Crisp and cold and icy. A good day to test out their new hiking gear. They head out with rucksacks, walking poles and picnics. They need their polarised sunglasses, it's so bright.

'Not too high a climb today,' Amanda says. She's fit from all her exercise classes, but there aren't many mountains to practice on in London, so all she lacks is confidence. Hand in hand, they trudge along the rocky path up the mountainside. It's steep in parts, so they drop hands, and Anthony's glad they have their walking poles.

Halfway up the slope, they stop, unstopper the flask and drink a lidfull of steaming tea while looking back over where they came from. The valley gleams in the sunlight.

'It's so beautiful,' Amanda says.

He studies her. 'No regrets?'

'None,' she beams. 'None at all.'

'Look how narrow it is!' Anthony says, pointing. From here, they can see down Sleddale. The valley bottom is narrow between steep slopes that go up about five hundred metres on either side. Amanda follows his finger down the long valley.

'Is that a hill-fort?' she asks, nodding to the valley end.

Anthony peers. It's hard to tell. There is a round eminence, quite considerable and ringed with trees at the valley's far end. 'Maybe,' he says. 'Looks defensible.'

'I saw a programme about the hill-forts. The Celts built a lot of them in the Iron Age.'

'Interesting.'

She continues, 'But some are older still. Or at least on older sites — Bronze or even Stone Age.'

Then it's time to continue the climb. They're not even halfway up the fell yet. It takes them more than an hour to reach the summit, but at last, they pull up onto the flatter top. It's a ridge that runs for miles. At times it's flattish, and here it becomes a narrow cockscomb of vertical rocks. It's wide enough to walk along.

'Careful,' Anthony says, 'It's icy up here. Watch your feet.'

The slopes on either side promise a tumble of hundreds of metres that would almost certainly be fatal. It's quite scary. He's prepared not to go if Amanda is frightened, but she appears now surprisingly confident. It must be the sunshine raising her spirits.

They pick their way along the ridge top, heading west. It isn't as hard as he'd feared. They stop for a sandwich on the ridge. Amanda indicates ahead, maybe fifty yards. 'That's the cairn. That must be the summit. We'll go there then look for a way down to the valley bottom.

They reach the cairn. Who knows how long these heaps of stone have been there. They could be modern inventions or placed there by the men who made stone hand-axes here three thousand years ago. Anthony has found a trail going down. It's steep but should be manageable.

Amanda blurts, 'Hey, look what I found.'

She brings it up to him. It's a figure roughly carved in local stone.

'Not much of a craftsman — whoever did this,' Anthony said. 'Looks like it was done by a kid.'

And it's true. There isn't much definition— crude legs, arms, a round belly and head with big lentil shaped eyes and mouth dug out of the grey stone. It's about six inches long.

'It's archaeology,' Amanda says. 'It could be ancient.'

'How would one know?' Anthony says. 'Could have been made last week.'

She shakes her head. 'No, Tony, it's much older than that. Look.' She thrusts the figure towards him, but he's not convinced.

'Put it back, Mand.'

She hugs it to her. 'Could be worth a fortune.'

'Probably not. Besides, it belongs here.'

She looks at him slyly. 'I'll take it to the museum in Kendal. Then, if it's not worth anything, I'll bring it back.'

He grimaces. 'We don't need the money, Amanda. I'd rather we left it here.'

She says pointedly, 'You don't need the money, Mr Successful, but I'm only building up. We moved from London where I had all my clients...'

'I thought you wanted to move here?'

'I did. I do. But let me keep little Harry.'

'Little Harry?' He laughs.

She smiles. She can always get around him. 'That's what I'm calling him.'

'Put it back, Mand. Please.'

'Okay.'

THE NEXT DAY, Amanda goes to get some eggs from Peggy Fawcett's black hens. When she comes back, Anthony is at his iMac, working on a campaign for a client in London.

'Get the eggs?' he asks over his shoulder.

'Yes, got a dozen. Dirt cheap. They'll be tasty too, eating all the shit she's got around her cottage. I think she throws her rubbish on the heap.'

He says, 'The midden. That's what they do.'

Amanda comes into the study with a cup of coffee: Guatemalan that she got from Booth's in Kendal. He takes it. She sits down. 'She's a funny woman,' she says, sipping the coffee.

'Oh yes,' he says, turning back to the screen.

'You know Little Harry?'

'The effigy from the cairn?'

'Yes. She says it's called Mabbin.'

'What? She recognised it?'

Amanda nods. 'Apparently, you're supposed to leave them be.'

Still, without turning, he says, 'What's this Mabbin supposed to be then?'

'Some kind of local sprite. She took it very seriously. She said nobody should ever move it.'

He turns to her and says quietly, 'Good job we didn't then.'

A WEEK LATER, they decide to take a walk as far as they can to the end of the valley. It's a flatter walk than their previous one, and they head for what they took to be the hill-fort at the far end. From afar, they see it rising above them with its ring of thorn trees like a broken crown. They're still a mile or so off, but it's distinct. It looks like a special place, whether built for defensive purposes or maybe ritual ones, they can't say.

The land rises, and they follow a stone path that sometimes gets lost in the grass. Finally, they come to a boggy area, and their boots squelch through the sedge. Then the weather threatens change, and clouds gather on the tops.

'I think it's going to rain', Amanda says, picking her way with her chromium walking poles. The brown mud is over her boots and has spattered her fancy leggings. She has a fake-fur headband to keep her warm. She takes off her sunglasses as the light gets worse and folds them into their case, which she puts in her rucksack.

Anthony looks up at the fell tops on either side. The cloud creeps further down by the minute. 'At least we're not going up there,' he says.

She gazes and nods, and he sees her shiver. 'Looks scary,' she says.

'We do have to climb a little bit,' he says. The hill fort, or whatever it is, is about two to three hundred feet in elevation in front of them. 'We don't have to go today,' he says.

'No, no,' Amanda says. 'We're nearly there now.'

So they continue to climb. It is much lower than the fell tops they did last week, but it's still a hike to get up to the fort from the valley bottom. The path is hard, though it looks like it is walked because they see some old orange peel by the side of the trail, and a little later, there's a cigarette butt.

They climb higher. Their breath is steaming in the damp air. The light has failed now, and it's getting dark even though it's only 3 p.m.

The clouds reach halfway down the mountains now, and they see the top of the hill-fort has scraps of mist above it.

'Not far now,' Anthony says. 'Then we can have our picnic.'

'I don't want a picnic,' Amanda says, 'Not there.'

'We don't have to go at all,' he says. 'We can turn round.'

'No, no, don't be silly. I want to get there, then we can turn round.'

They struggle on in silence. The path here is set between raised banks on either side.

'This must have been the entrance to the fort,' Amanda puffs as the path spirals around the hill, promising to take them around the back before it delivers them to the gate.

'They could stand above and throw spears at invaders,' he says.

She shudders. 'I feel like we're the invaders.'

'We have every right to be here,' he says.

'Do we?' she answers but keeps on walking.

THE SPIRAL PATH winds round the rocky green hill at the valley's end. They trudge up it until they find themselves above where they were between the high banks of the track, and the broken mouth of the hill-fort opens in front of them.

Rock piles stand on either side of what must have been the gateway, but they are tumbledown and ancient, covered by lichen and moss. The air here is almost silent; there are no sounds of mankind save their own ragged breathing. The high croaking of ravens haunts this place, and the soughing of the wind, and the soft drizzle of water dripping somewhere unseen.

'It's creepy here,' Amanda says.

'It's because it's remote,' Anthony answers. 'That and the closed-in weather,' and he points up to where the grey clouds have sunk down to less than a hundred feet above their heads.

In front of them, the middle of the hill-fort is raised up. Raised up so far that it catches wisps of mist. The centre waits and broods in front of them, obscuring the view.

'We can go back now,' Anthony says. 'We've made it.'

Amanda says, 'Let's get to the middle. Say we've been and turn round.'

'It's in the mist,' Anthony says.

'Yes, but it's not dangerous. We go up, touch the middle and turn round. We can't come all this way and not get to the middle.'

'Okay, if you want,' Anthony says, but his voice sounds uncertain.

Amanda strides forward abruptly, and he follows after her. She's walking fast, and he breaks into a run. Then she runs ahead, and as she climbs to the middle, the fog encompasses her.

Sudden panic catches at him, and he runs after her. He finds her standing in the middle of the hill-fort. It's a raised platform of rock and grass and around the centre stands a ring of standing stones. The stones are grey and of uneven height. Two or three of them have fallen.

'Someone's had a barbecue,' she says, grinning. Relief washes over him. Barbecues seem suddenly normal and comforting. What was that stupid panic about? The odd way she ran forward like she had something to do.

He looks at the giant heap of sodden ash and charcoal sticks.

'Just a fire,' he says.

She gestures. 'There are bones in it.' She pushes the wet ash with the toe of her boot.

He looks and sees the bones — long ones. He frowns. 'Sheep maybe?'

'It looks big for a sheep,' she says. 'Someone's cooked it.'

'Hog roast?' he volunteers. Maybe the remains of some midsummer party.

'I don't know.' Then she takes off her pack and rummages through it.

'Thought you didn't want a picnic here.'

'I don't. It's too foggy. It's cold.'

'Then what—'

But as he asks, he sees her take out the stone effigy from the mountain cairn. 'Little Harry,' she says.

'Mabbin. I thought I told you not to take it?'

She frowns. 'Sorry, I thought it might be worth something.'

'But you can't remove archaeological artefacts.'

'You said it was modern.'

'I said it could be modern.'

'Then it's not archaeology.'

He's about to argue further, but she says, 'Whatever you say, I'm putting it here.'

'But this isn't where it belongs. It belongs on the fell top.'

She indicates up where the fog is completely obscuring their view of the surrounding mountains. 'We can't go up there in that. And I didn't want this thing in the house. It started to give me the creeps.'

'But why put it here?'

She shrugs. 'It's kind of a sacred place. I didn't think they'd mind if I put it here. It's some kind of reverence, isn't it?'

He has nothing to stay. The breeze stirs the fog. It's almost as if there's somebody there with them. He looks around him.

She places Mabbin beside the remains of the fire. 'Let's go,' she says. She forces a smile, but he sees she's as unnerved as him. Something about this place makes them both feel unwelcome.

·　·　·

Back at Elva How, Anthony opens a bottle of wine. He's done with work for the day. They sit on their leather sofa in front of the log burning fire. The curtains are drawn. They could be anywhere. Outside, the wind is up and howls down the valley, getting into the chimney, fluttering the flames in the fire, moaning through the corners of the window and lifting the curtains like spectral fingers.

'Need to get that double glazed,' he says, sipping the wine.

'I hope you're not mad at me about Mabbin,' she says.

He frowns. 'No, of course, not. But you shouldn't—'

She puts her slender hand on his arm. 'But it's back now.'

He shakes his head. 'It's not back.'

'As good as back. If you want—tomorrow, or when the weather's better, we can drive as close as we can to the fort, get the statue and take it up the fell to put it back where we got it.'

He thinks of the weather outside and the clouds that sit heavy and low on the mountains. He doesn't say anything. Instead, he reaches for the remote when there's a knock at the door.

Amanda furrows her brow. 'Visitors? I don't think so.'

He shrugs. 'I'll go see.'

At the door, Peggy Fawcett stands. He steps back in surprise. Maybe she wants to borrow some food or something, but she stands without coming in, clutching herself against the wind. She says, 'You shouldn't have moved it.'

'Eh?' he says, but he knows.

'The stone man: Mabbin. You shouldn't have moved it. They saw you.'

Anthony furrows his brow. How could anyone see them? They were on a mountain top. There was no one around for miles.

'They came and asked me,' Peggy says. 'I couldn't lie to them. So I said she'd been here with it, asking, but I'd told her to put it back.'

'Who's 'they'?'

Peggy shakes her head. 'Never mind. But you've got to leave. I saw them moving.'

'Who?'

But Peggy continues. 'They only come at night. You need to go. Please. You're not bad people. You don't know our ways. You didn't mean anything by it. I told them that. But they don't listen. They don't listen to us.'

Anthony is riled by her. 'I don't know what you're talking about.'

She says, 'I've come to warn you. I didn't need to do this, but I thought you're not bad people. You didn't know.' She says sourly, 'They don't care you didn't know. You touched it. That's the thing.'

'Who are 'they'?' Anthony says again, but Peggy Fawcett has turned and vanished into the howling dark.

'Who was that?' Amanda says, wine glass to her lips. Her wine-wet lipstick has smeared the crystal like a bloody kiss.

'Our crazy neighbour.'

'What did she want?'

He sits and grunts.

'What?' Amanda says, more insistent. She looks worried.

He sighs, rubs his mouth.

'What, Tony?'

'That stupid statue thing. She says we shouldn't have moved it.'

'So what? We put it back.'

'Sort of. Anyway, she's gone now.'

'She came all that way to complain about us moving the Mabbin thing? Why didn't she say that when I first showed it to her?'

'No, she's not bothered. Or as bothered. She says mysteriously, 'they' saw us take it.'

'There was nobody there to see us.'

'Unless they were invisible,' Anthony says.

'More likely binoculars. But why would anyone be watching us?'

'Maybe they watch all strangers.'

'If they were watching us then, which I don't believe,' she says, 'they'll have been watching us today and seen us put it back.'

'You.'

She puts down her glass on the table.

'Me? So it's me only now, is it?' She sparks anger at him. He knows he deserved it. The word had slipped out. 'Sorry,' he says.

'So you should be.' She snorts, takes more wine. 'I don't believe Peggy Fawcett. She's cracked.'

They go to bed. It's not late, but it's so dark that it feels late. The wind drops. He looks out of the bedroom window to check the weather. The vanished wind allows the fog to gather. It's thick. There are no streetlights outside. The house lights hardly penetrate the mist. It doesn't matter. It's night.

Amanda is already in bed, her cheeks rosy from the wine. They'd had a second bottle. She has her black silk nightie on. That means she wants to make love. He feels the flush of desire rise in him. He climbs onto the bed. He kisses her, and she kisses him back.

Then a noise clunks from the back of the house. Amanda freezes, stops kissing. 'What's that?'

He pulls himself to his knees. 'Don't know. Sounded like something being knocked over.'

'Could be an animal. A fox maybe prowling around?'

'I don't know.' He is in two minds now, his ardour subsiding, but he turns back to her. Then the clunk comes again.

'Must be an animal,' she says.

'Not a fox,' he says. 'Something bigger.'

'A sheep come down from the fells?'

'I don't know,' he says and goes to the window. He's still wearing a t-shirt and underpants. He draws back the curtain that would show him the yard at the back of the house, except now it shows nothing but a shifting screen of fog.

'Did you lock the door?' she asks.

He nods. He'd said they wouldn't need to here, but it's an old London habit and hard to break.

'Well, no one can get in.' She pauses. 'Back door too?'

'Yes, yes.'

'Then come back to bed. I'm getting cold.'

But he can't settle. He goes to the front window. 'I think there's someone out there.'

She sits up, gathering the duvet to her knees and hugging it to her. 'How do you know? You can't see anything.'

'No. I just feel it.'

'Imagination.'

'But the sounds?'

'That's what's set the imagination off. A sheep has wandered down and knocked something over. That starts all sorts of thoughts off in the dark.'

He comes back to bed. 'You're right.'

He sits next to her. 'Sorry, I've gone off it.'

She strokes the back of his head. 'Don't worry. Lie down.'

He lies, and she switches off the light. It's totally black. Not city black. Not Bible black, worse than that—as black as the black before time began. He feels queasy, unsteady, lost—like nothing exists, nothing familiar to grasp onto. But he can feel the bed. He can hear Amanda breathing beside him. It's all real. It's all normal. He exhales. She stirs. She's not asleep either.

'Are you scared?' she asks. 'You sound scared.'

'Of what?'

'I don't know. The dark. This place.'

'No, of course not.' He wouldn't tell her if he was. He doesn't want to set her off. He knows what she's like. He's breathing quickly.

'What's that?' She sits bolt upright.

'What?' His heart is hammering.

'Something downstairs. The door. It sounded like it was opening.'

'It's locked.'

'Are you sure?'

'I think so. Yes. I think.' He pauses. 'Do you want me to go check?'

She reaches out and squeezes his hand. 'No. If you say it's locked. Just hold me. I'm spooked—not used to this country quiet.'

'Or the country dark.'

She whispers, 'No. It's so dark. We're not used to it being so dark.'

'No.'

He hears her breathing.

There's a scraping sound below.

'That was definitely downstairs,' she says.

'How can it be? It's a trick of the sound. The fog makes things sound different.'

'Okay.'

It's less than two minutes before another scrape—like something is being dragged.

Amanda moans. 'I'm scared now, Tony.'

'I'll go and check.'

'I don't want you to.'

'I'll be all right.'

She reaches out to squeeze his hand, but he's up already. The floor is cold under his bare feet. The temperature has dropped. He shivers. He can't see where his fleece dressing gown is. He reaches for his bedside lamp. The switch clicks, but the light doesn't go on. Everything in this place is unreliable.

He stands, reaches and feels for the wall switch in the dark. At first, he doesn't find it, but by sweeping his palm across the old, uneven wall, he touches the metal light switch. He flicks it down. That light doesn't go on either.

'Fuse must have gone,' he says.

'Where's the fuse box?' He hears the fear in her voice.

'Downstairs.'

'You'll fall.'

'I've got the light on my phone.'

He finds his phone on the bedside table and presses it on. Pale blue light floods the room, making it strange and cavernous. 'I'll go do the fuse.'

He steps over to the bedroom door, puts his left hand on the handle's cold metal, and turns it. He stands with the door ajar and listens. The scraping sound comes from downstairs, a scraping, dragging sound. Maybe they're being robbed? His computer? The sound system? But they wouldn't drag those.

Anthony strains to hear through the partly open door. It's hard to say, but there is more than one of them. Without doubt, they are downstairs. They must have broken in and killed the electricity. He switches off his phone screen. He doesn't want them to see the light. Maybe the burglars thought the house was empty.

But the car's outside. So they must know he and Amanda are in.

He takes a big inbreath. He's not built for fighting. 'Amanda, hide,' he says.

'What? she hisses.

'Hide. Please.'

He hears her move. He switches on the phone and steps down the stairs. Then he stops.

They're at the bottom. There are a lot of them. They have eyes, eyes that glitter in the light from his phone—lots of eyes and teeth. They're not men.

THERE IS movement in the valley. The wind rises. By midnight, the fog is all blown away.

She sees the smoke and the flames at the Hill Fort all the way down the valley. She sees the fire clearly from her upstairs window. She checks her watch. It's near dawn now but still dark. Dark apart from that fire. Peggy Fawcett pulls her curtains closed.

CHAPTER 4

THE HIGH HARRINGTON HORROR

I had a strange experience when I was twelve. I must say I've had nothing like it before or since, but this one episode has stayed with me so clearly that I remember it now as if it was yesterday rather than many years ago.

We had moved to High Harrington that summer and my mother was careful to remind me to tell my friends it was *High* Harrington, in case anyone thought we'd moved to *Low* Harrington, which, to her mind at least, was an altogether different place.

Near our new house on the brand-spanking estate was an old Victorian Mansion. It so happened that I was in the same class as the lad who lived in that house: Stephen Sharp. Now, Stephen was a friendly lad. He later became famous for composing experimental music, and the last I heard was that he was producing big bands out of a studio in an Amsterdam canal house. But at the time I am talking about, he was twelve and in my class at school.

His dad owned a nightclub in Whitehaven called *The Red House*, and they had plenty of money. They had enough to buy the dilapidated mansion in five acres of grounds — the paddock of which he'd sold off to build the estate where my house was. His dad hadn't bought the farm next door, which was a dirty old place, ankle-deep in slurry at all times of the year, but which produced excellent cream topped milk. In fact, in the summer, the top half of the glass pint bottle was yellow cream.

But this was Autumn. We were back at school, and for the first time, he'd invited me to the Mansion. He was obviously proud of the place because he offered to show me around.

The leaves were turning red and brown as I walked up the long drive to the Mansion, my mum's command to be back in time for tea ringing in my ears.

I diverted from the gravel path to kick around in the ankle-deep leaves searching for golden brown conkers. And finding unopened pods, I greedily cracked them to reveal the golden-brown nuts that later I would harden and string to play conkers at school.

And then, after a bit of dawdling — I always was a dawdler — I was there. Standing in front of the Mansion, I tipped back my head to take it all in. It had a big three-storey front with peeling black and white paint and leaves and other debris around the door.

A tall tower stood from the left-hand side, going much higher. It had mock crenellated tops, but the whole place had seen better times. I stepped on the worn sandstone steps and knocked on the dull black door. There was a bell-pull from earlier times, and I tugged it, but it didn't ring. I had to rely on my knuckles, which stung after each rap.

Stephen's mum answered. She was a dowdy-looking woman who seemed ancient to me though she was probably about forty. It was said (by my mother) that Mrs Sharp had a taste for sweeter sherry and younger men. Her husband knew about the first and probably about the second, but these are not important topics when you are twelve, so I paid them no mind.

Stephen came to the door at his mother's call. We were going to play and then have tea, but he wanted to show me the house before that. There was a courtyard to the back with the old stable to the right and a way through to the farm further down. There were overgrown kitchen gardens behind the house and, of course, the tower. The tower formed part of the main fabric of the house, but it had its own entrance from the courtyard.

Eventually, the tour put us at the tower door. 'This is the coolest part of the house,' Stephen said and pulled the creaky door open.

The tower smelled musty of damp and old wood. It was very cool in style but colder than outside, as if the damp had seeped into the walls creating a Victorian refrigerator effect. The walls needed painting, and our footsteps echoed as we mounted the ancient stairs. Off the various landings were doors; I tried the handles, but they were all locked.

'What's in those?' I asked.

Stephen shook his head. 'Dunno. Never been in.'

We continued to climb up the bare wooden stairs that groaned with each footstep.

Stephen muttered, 'An evil ship master lived here once. That's who built it. He built it so high that he could sit at the top and look through his telescope to see his ships in the harbour.'

We continued to mount the stairs. We still weren't at the top, and I was breathing heavily.

'Why was he evil?' I said.

'Cause, he sank one of his own ships, and all the crew drowned.'

I was amazed. 'Really? Why did he sink his own ship?'

'For money.'

'Insurance money?'

'Yeah. Insurance money. Fifty men drowned off the coast of Carolina. He arranged it.'

'Sounds a nasty man.'

'He was.'

The story of the evil ship master told, we stood on the top floor of the tower. From this fifth-floor landing, a dirty window looked out to the west, and I gazed all the way down to Low Harrington with Copras Hill and the harbour. There were no big sailing ships in the dock now. Some yachts bobbed as the rough waves pounded the sea wall, but Harrington's ocean-going past was now in the history books.

'So he used to sit up here?' I asked. Somehow the story of the evil ship master fascinated me.

'In that room there.' Stephen pointed to a closed door. Instinctively, I went to try the handle.

Before my hand touched the metal, Stephen shrieked, 'Stop!'.

I nearly jumped out of my skin. My hand froze in mid-air, halfway towards the doorknob, trembling slightly with the tension of wanting to know what was inside the room but at the same time terrified in case it was the bones of the evil ship master.

Stephen whispered, 'My Aunt Mary lives in there. She used to live in Bransty, but she's here now. She likes to see the sea out of the big window. That's why my dad put her in this room.'

'Oh.' I stood back, my hand dropping to my side. Not as dramatic a story as I had hoped.

Stephen lowered his voice further. 'She's weird. She's scared of electricity. She only uses candles. Dad had to switch off the electricity for the whole tower because she got it into her head the power running through the wires would start a fire.'

'Candles are more likely to start a fire,' I said.

Stephen agreed, and we both nodded wisely.

Aunt Mary sounded weird. I was glad I never met her. We stayed on the fifth-floor landing for a while, staring out of the window at the wind moving the treetops far below and shaking a piece of ivy that had fastened itself to the grimy windowpane.

As we descended, he giggled. 'Watch out for the ship master!'

I knew he was winding me up, but I stopped and looked about me nervously.

'Yeah,' Stephen said. 'You're right to be scared of him.'

'I'm not scared of him.'

'Yes, you are. But it's right you are. He sank a boat, but he did worse than that.'

'How?' I said.

'He killed a kid. He pushed them downstairs. A kid who came snooping in the tower. Ended up at the bottom. Dead as a doornail.'

THEN IT WAS HALLOWEEN. The clocks went back, and the nights grew suddenly dark. It was spooky. I liked it, and I liked getting invited to Stephen Sharp's Halloween Party at the Mansion. They held the party in the old stable, which they'd cleaned up a bit. No horses now, but the stalls were still in place. His mam had put a long trestle table in there, and there were plastic pails with apples bobbing in them for us to go dooking with our hands behind our back. There were apples on strings hanging up that we had to go after with only our mouths.

A table stood, groaning with goodies, among them toffee apples and Scotch Pancakes. Hollowed out turnips with wicked faces hung from strings around the stable. Their eyes and mouths flickered as the candles inside fluttered in the drafts from opening doors. I remembered how hard it was to hollow out the turnips and was glad I hadn't had to do it. The mouths with their crooked teeth and their weird slanted eyes gave me the shivers.

The place was lit by paraffin lanterns that swung in the draft coming from under the old stable door. The stable smelled of straw, smoky candle wicks, paraffin fumes and was full of the laughter of eight twelve-year-old boys.

After we'd eaten and got soaked dipping our heads going after apples, the next thing was Stephen's dad telling us ghost stories.

We sat open-mouthed as he told us about the rustling silk ghost of Siddick pit and about Bella Sheep Head on the Broughton Moor Road. He told us about the Knocking Monk of Carlisle and the Ghost Ship of Whitehaven, and we lapped it up, listening in awe and terror as he recited the stories and puffed on his Benson & Hedges Gold cigarettes.

He was a cool dad with long sideburns and a flowing brown moustache. His khaki shirt was open three buttons to reveal a gold St

Christopher Medallion. I wished he was my dad. My dad was an accountant and wore cardigans.

Just as Stephen's dad finished a story, a loud growl erupted from outside. Stephen jumped. Some of the lads shrieked. I froze. Stephen ran to the door to open it a crack with shaking hands. Soon I was at his shoulder, peering out into the courtyard. It was dark, and I could see nothing. Stephen pulled the stable door shut, his hand still trembling. 'It was a werewolf'! he screamed.

Then there was a stomp from above that shook the ceiling. We were terrified, cowering in the corners, expecting at any time that the werewolf would burst in the stable doors and come and gobble us up. Then I saw Stephen's dad was laughing.

Stephen snapped. 'Was that Uncle Joe? Making those noises?'

Stephen's dad was clutching himself and rolling in mirth.

Stephen yelled. 'Dad! How could you scare us like that!'

Stephen's dad said, 'It's Halloween, Stephen. If you didn't get a scare on Halloween, you'd think you'd been shortchanged.'

AFTER THE NERVOUS giggling died down, and we were all happy again, we decided we needed further excitement. What better place for Hide and Seek than the Mansion courtyard and surrounding area.

Some of the lads were doubtful. 'What about the werewolf?' One said, a dim-witted lad called Tommy from Kiln Green Avenue.

Stephen turned on him. 'There is no werewolf. It was my Uncle Joe.'

Another of our friends, Clifford, who lived on Scaw Road, said, 'But what about ghosts?'

Stephen looked at him scornfully. Finally, he said, 'Come on. Let's go outside to play Hide and Seek. I'll be 'it'. I'll count to twenty, then I'm coming ready or not.'

. . .

IN A WAVE OF EXCITEMENT, all us kids scattered into the dark. I fell behind a bush with Clifford, but he snarled, 'Git! Git your own spot!' So I stumbled off into the shadows looking for somewhere to hide.

Stephen counted loudly where he stood just inside the stable, head on his arm against the wall, probably peeking.

Everywhere I went, looking for a spot to hide, was already occupied, and some of those kids would be easy finds for Stephen.

I ran on. Then I heard him yell, 'Coming, ready or not!' and I was in a panic, scuttling over the courtyard, desperate not to be caught in the open. Any second, and he'd see me, and I'd be his first catch. I didn't want to get caught first.

The door to the tower stood in front of me. It was my only chance. I tried the handle. It was locked.

I heard Stephen's tread on the gravel behind.

Then I saw the key was in the door. How could I have missed that? I turned it and yanked at the door in my panic.

I stepped inside the damp tower and pulled the door quietly closed behind me. My heart thumped, and my breath wheezed as I stood in the dark. It was pitch black in the tower. I strained to hear Stephen's footsteps on the gravel outside. Then I heard a muffled yell of 'Clifford!' He'd seen that dope. There was a run and a scuffle, and he got him.

I listened hard. Someone was walking on the gravel outside. Stephen shouted, 'I know where you are. You might as well come out.' It was a bluff, though, and he didn't mean me, anyway.

Then his footsteps got louder: crunch, crunch, crunch.

He was right outside the Tower door. He might come in at any minute. I reeled backwards, putting my hand out to touch the wall. I heard Stephen at the door. I turned, quick as I could and felt my way up, my shoe bumping the first step and feeling my way up it. Once on the first step, I quickly went up three and leaned against the wall, trying to make myself as flat as I could to avoid detection. But I felt a thrill of excitement all the same.

Then the door below opened. I froze.

'Anybody in there?' Stephen didn't have a torch, and he didn't put on the light. I remembered he said his aunt was scared of electricity and only used candles. He couldn't put on the light even if he'd wanted to.

'I know you're in there!' he shouted. Another bluff. I almost laughed out loud, and I shook to keep the excitement inside.

Then he said, 'Pah. Should be locked anyway.' He closed the door, and then I heard the key turn.

He'd locked me in.

I felt my way slowly down the few steps to the bottom and got to the door. I tried the handle as gently as possible because I still didn't want to get caught. But the door was indeed locked. I thought about knocking and yelling, but I didn't. The game was still going on and if I shouted out, I'd be caught.

I stood for a while, scared, excited, and scared again.

It was the sudden cold, really. A sudden chill and a feeling of someone standing next to me in the dark. The temperature dropped ten degrees. Someone was moving next to me. The idea that it was the ship master seized me, and full of horror, I jumped backwards and went sprawling.

A dark shape moved towards me. I scrambled to my feet and fled backwards. As it came, or I imagined it came because I couldn't really see anything, I ran up the stairs, hand on the wall, toes bumping the steps, going as fast I could. I sensed it coming up after me. I heard rough breathing. I heard shuffling feet.

I got to the first landing. There was a window, but it looked west into the trees. Still, it was lighter here, and I could see the locked doors that lined the landing. What was in those rooms? Maybe the doors would open, and something would come out? I was shaking like a leaf.

I heard shuffling on the stairs. What was that? A cat? No cats were quiet. A dog? No, it didn't sound like a dog. Rats? They'd scurry more and scratch. Bats would flutter. It wasn't an animal. I knew what it was.

THE SOUND GOT CLOSER, a shuffling, dragging, heavy sound. I had to get out of there. In what light there was from the far window, I saw the start of the next dark flight of stairs, so I ran to that and was up them before the horrible thing turned the corner onto the landing.

I stopped halfway. It was very dark now away from the windowpane, and I could hardly see my hand in front of my face.

Maybe whatever it was would stop on the first landing and not come up after me. Maybe. I stood shaking.

Silence. I began to calm. I was just scaring myself.

Phew. I ran my fingers through my hair. Just imagination after all.

Then the dragging noise—the noise of old man's feet.

I heard it mount the bottom steps and turned and ran. I missed my footing in the dark and fell, banging my chest on the stairs. I was down. I was helpless. It could get me. It could grab my foot. I scrambled and stumbled and got onto my knees and then was standing, and running, jumping up the steps, feeling my way, reaching out my hands to stop me from falling again so it couldn't grab me.

It came up after me. Heavy feet creaked on old wooden stairs. It was behind me. I heard it breathing.

I knew it was the ship master. He sank a ship for money and drowned fifty men, and he didn't care they'd died, and he wouldn't care if he killed me.

I was on the second landing now. Pitiful light ghosted through the dirty second-floor window glass. Hardly enough to see. Not enough light to see to run safely. But more than enough to see the Ship Master's horrible face. He was on the stairs leading up. I hoped he would stop. I heard his slobbering. I listened to his breath. He was up on the landing. I turned and ran.

In my panic, I nearly tripped again but stopped myself with outstretched hands. I couldn't think straight because of my fear. I could hardly run. I was shaking so much.

The Ship Master was after me. He killed a kid. Pushed him down the stairs.

I ran up to the third landing, then the fourth, and he never stopped coming. He kept climbing with his breath and his heavy feet. He would keep on coming till he got me: breathing, slobbering, heavy, with his cold dead hands.

He was a ghost, a walking corpse, a ghoul, a ghast, a zombie. I was just a twelve-year-old kid. What could I do?

I ran up to the last landing. I could go no further. I pressed my back against the topmost window. The night outside would not help me, neither would the owls or the trees. There was just me and him. The wind murmured and sobbed. The darkness fretted. The window-pane shifted and muttered.

Here I was. Alone in this dark place, and here he came.

In the poor light from the window, I saw his shape. A shadow against shadows, the walking corpse of a murderer. I heard him groan. I listened to his slobber.

I jammed back against the window sill. 'Please, don't hurt me.'

But he came still. Not fast, but eager, greedy, murderous, malicious.

The Ship Master: a horrible, hateful monster of a man, in his hate and wickedness from beyond the grave, was going to push me from the window so I fell and broke on the ground far below.

His rotted hands reached out. His dirty fingernails inches from my face. The stink of his foul flesh making me gag.

A door opened. Candlelight spilled out. The landing was illuminated, and the Ship Master fell back, hands up to his eyes, protecting them from the glare of the flame.

'Get ye gone, foul spirit!' A voice yelled. It was a woman's voice. And I realised it must be Stephen's Aunt Mary who lived up here without electricity. In my panic, I'd forgotten about her. She was my guardian angel. I sobbed in relief.

Faced with the light of her candle and the strength of her voice, the Ship Master stood and turned and stumbled away down the stairs.

I said, 'Thank you.'

Aunt Mary shook her head. She was old and grey-haired and dressed in old-fashioned clothes. 'No, he's not gone. He's just hiding. He never leaves here. He just waits in the dark to catch frightened souls like you.'

I said, 'Will you help me find my way out?'

'Yes, I will, son.'

I said, 'Are you Stephen's Aunt Mary?'

'Yes, I am, son,' she said.

'Stephen told me about you.'

'Did he? That's nice. He always was a good little boy.'

She held up the candle to light the surroundings, and feeble as the flame was, I was somehow dazzled by it and couldn't make her out properly.

I said, 'I don't like it here. Please take me down.'

'Of course.'

'But the door's locked. They locked me in.'

'Don't worry, son. I've got a key.'

And so she showed me down the steps, ambling behind me. I had to wait sometimes for her to catch up because she was old and couldn't walk well, but her candle lighted my way down the stairs. Finally, at the tower's bottom, she unlocked the door with her key. It turned with a clunk. She smelled of violets.

'There you are, son,' she said.' You're safe now.'

I ran back into the stable, where they were all waiting for me.

'Here he is, finally,' said Timmy from Scaw Road.

'Where've you been?' grunted one of the others. There were seven of them there, including Stephen. I was the last to get back. They leered at me.

'You win then,' Stephen said. 'You win the Hide and Seek. You're last to be found.'

But I was stammering. 'I got locked in the Tower.'

'Then he doesn't win,' said Clifford. 'He cheated. We weren't supposed to go into the tower. It's too dangerous."

'You shouldn't have been in the tower.' Stephen's voice was full of reprimand and of something else.

'It was unlocked.'

'It shouldn't have been unlocked.'

I blurted, 'I saw the Ship Master.'

Stephen tilted his head. 'The ghost?'

My voice quavered.

'You're scared,' Clifford said with glee.

In the dim electric lightbulb of the Stable, I guess my face was spectre-white.

'You didn't see a ghost. That's crap,' Timmy spat.

'You're a liar,' one of the others laughed.

I turned angrily. 'No, I saw him. I ran all the way up the tower.'

They laughed at me. 'That's obviously not true,' Clifford said.

'Why?' I demanded.

'Because, if you were locked in, how did you get out?'

I said, 'That's easy. Stephen's Aunt Mary let me out. She scared the ghost away with her candle.'

Stephen looked at me strangely. 'Nah, that's not right, mate,' he said finally.

'It is, Stephen. Honest, it is.'

He shook his head. 'No, it can't be.'

I was incredulous. Why didn't he believe me? I said, 'I'm telling the truth. Why can't it be true?'

'Well,' he said. 'It can't be true because Aunt Mary died two weeks ago.'

So that Halloween, I didn't see just one ghost; I saw two.

CHAPTER 5

THE BUTCHER OF BOTCHERBY

It was the door that caught everyone's attention — a heavy black iron door with reinforced bolts and that on a butcher's shop in Botcherby. It was out of place and it appeared suddenly one day in August. Not that it was August any more. No— now, it was December, dreary December, the strings of Christmas lights doing little to bring any cheer to the picture.

The butcher's shop windows were boarded up as well as the door, not with an ordinary board but with steel anti-bandit screens — like there could be anything that valuable in a butcher's shop in Botcherby.

Ian Inky Stephenson arrived on the scene on 11th December. It was a Wednesday. Ian was a tattoo artist who'd snagged a job at *The Border Goth*, a run-down, low-profit tattoo studio in the heart of Botcherby run by an ageing wannabe comic-book artist who'd missed his chance, Milky McAllister.

Ian was skilled at what he did, and he could have made better wages elsewhere but ended up here. That might strike the casual observer as strange, but the truth was, Ian Inky Stephenson was on the run. He'd made some false friends and worse enemies down home in Forest Hill, South London, and Botcherby was as obscure a place as he could think of.

He'd glanced at a map of England, saw Carlisle and thought it sufficiently remote. And he didn't end up in Carlisle proper, but in the once rural village of Botcherby now tagged onto Carlisle's eastern flank between the River Petteril and the M6.

Ian came up to Carlisle on the National Express bus, got out at the bus station on Lonsdale Street and met a bloke in the Howard Arms who told him Botcherby was nice.

After a few pints, he got the bus east, alighted in Botcherby and scouted for accommodation until he saw a 'To Let' sign outside a butcher's shop with an iron door and steel windows. The rent was cheap, and it needed to be because the place was a dump, but it would do. Ian liked being upstairs above the shop, and the reinforced door downstairs made him feel safer.

A woman from the local Estate Agent who thought she was well posher than she was, showed him around. Inky knew she didn't like him straight off. People like her didn't like people like him. He had a neck tattoo and a face tattoo and hand tattoos, mainly reptiles but some spiders and one of Lord Ganesh, the Indian elephant god, on his inner right forearm.

The Estate Agent looked like she wanted to hold her nose and stop breathing all the time she showed him around. Once through the iron door, they stepped onto the bare boards of the entrance hall. A row of coat hooks with no coats and piles of ageing junk mail clogged up the doorway. A door to the butcher's shop proper was to the left on the ground level. It was iron too, locked, bolted, chained and reinforced with a black iron frame to stop it from getting forced off its hinges.

'The butcher's shop's in there, is it?' Inky pointed.

She pursed her lips. 'No, he no longer works as a butcher.'

'What do they call my landlord?'

'Mr Relph.'

'Is he retired?'

'Something like that. He can't speak,' she added. 'He had an accident and lost his tongue some years ago.'

'An accident?' Inky's mind searched through the possibilities of an accident that could cut out your tongue. 'Any other injuries?' he asked.

'I don't think so,' she said. He could tell she wanted to be out of there pronto. 'I don't honestly know. Should we look at the flat?'

Once again, she wrinkled her nose. In fact, there was a peculiar stink in there. Not overpowering, and he was sure he'd get used to it, but it was like old meat left lying around—a slightly off smell. He could put up with the vague stink, and he didn't plan to be there too long. He'd stay long enough for the heat to die down, then he'd be back to London and his real life.

The flat was bare, dirty and, more or less, empty. They advertised it as furnished, but there was only a sofa with no chairs, and the sofa sagged in the middle. There was only one room, and the end away from the street served as a kitchen with a small table, a cooking surface, an old, dangerous-looking gas cooker and a fridge that gave off an annoying buzz.

'What do you think?' The agent woman forced a smile. 'It's very reasonably priced to reflect— '

'—how shit it is?' Inky grinned.

She blushed. 'Well...'

'I'm only messing. I'll take it.' Truth was, compared with London rents, this was laughably cheap.

'One condition, though,' the agent woman said.

'Yes?'

'You must never, ever leave the front door unlocked. Mr Relph is very strict about that.'

'Okay.'

'There are lots of keys. A bar on the inside and a chain.'

'What's he got to hide?'

She ignored him. 'Those are Mr Relph's stipulations. He wrote them out personally in the contract.'

'That's okay. I'll still take it.'

Inky took to the work at the tattoo parlour in Botcherby. The studio wasn't busy at first, but word got around about his skill, and there was a discernible up tick in business. His boss Milky McAllister said, 'Really pleased with your work, Inky. You do some fantastic designs.'

Inky laughed over his cup of tea. 'Does that mean I get a raise?'

Milky frowned. 'I wouldn't go that far.' He cleared his throat. 'We'll see.'

Inky guessed McAllister didn't want to lose him. Looking out over the street, they could see Inky's digs from the tattoo shop window.

'Enjoying your flat?' Milky asked, lighting a fag. Inky noticed the fine tremor in Milky's hands. It looked like it was about time for his mid-morning whisky. He'd nip into the back office soon to top up. That was the routine. Better he did because a tattooist with a shaky hand's not a good thing.

'The flat's okay,' Inky said. 'Nice and quiet.'

'You see your landlord much?'

'Nah, never met him.' Inky thought he'd heard movement in the disused shop a couple of times, but he'd seen no one.

Milky muttered, 'He's weird — Old Relph.'

'He can't speak, I understand.'

'No, but he was weird before that. He's from Longtown.'

'I don't know where that is. Does that make him weird?'

'They're queer folk in Longtown. Nowt like Carlisle folk at all. They might as well be Jocks.'

From a London perspective, Inky thought that was probably true for Carlisle too, and probably all of Cumbria and Northumberland as well.

'Why do you say he's weird, though?'

'See how he's boarded up that place? He's nuts. He's a recluse.'

'What?' Inky was taken aback. 'He lives in there?'

'Oh aye, in the shop.'

'Really?'

'Yes. He didn't used to. But he moved in then got it boarded up at the end of the summer. Weird, I told you.'

TWO DAYS LATER, Inky finished work and went home. It was already dark and cold. Old chip papers blew down the street, and a mangy cat wandered around searching for something to kill. Inky turned the key in the lock, shoved it open and was met by a bald fat man, round sixty years old, about five foot eight wearing a striped butcher's apron over white overalls. Except they weren't white; they were dirty grey and stained with faded blood and smeared fat. In the washed-out light cast by the bare electric bulb hanging from its frayed thread in the hallway, Inky saw the man had watery blue eyes that stared and fat blubbery lips shiny with spittle. Relph's cheeks flushed crimson against his pale skin, looking like high blood pressure from eating too much red meat.

'Mr Relph?' Inky said.

The man nodded without smiling.

'I'm your tenant, Ian.'

Relph nodded again, his jowls wobbling, his lips wetter.

'I live upstairs,' Inky explained pointlessly. He was about to say how nice it was, but both knew that was a lie. There was a strained silence. 'I'll be going up, then.' Inky nodded. He started to push past Relph, who hadn't moved out of his way, his butcher's bulk blocking the hall, but Relph frowned. He pointed at the heavy iron door to the butcher's shop and shook his head. The message was clear: don't enter. From the set of his face, it was actually don't *ever* enter.

How could he enter, with all the chains and bolts and padlocks that were generally on the door? Inky shrugged. Relph moved, and Inky climbed the stairs to his own dingy flat.

That night, Inky drank his cans of Red Stripe, listened to Cradle of Filth through his over-ear cans and mused about the world and when it would be safe to go back to London. When that thought faded, he doodled some designs that had been running around in his mind and lit up a blunt to take the cares away. As he watched the whorls of smoke go blue and vanish in the air, he heard movement downstairs.

It sounded like the butcher was dragging furniture. Inky listened through the music, but it all went quiet down below, and he resumed his drawing. Cradle of Filth's *Mr Crowley* came on — one of his favourite tracks. After that, *Hellbound* by Pantera boomed out. He nodded his head in rhythm to the savage beat.

There was an almighty bang from downstairs. Inky took off his headphones and listened hard. What the hell was the nutter doing? It sounded like Relph was knocking the hell out of his furniture. Perhaps he had an anger problem? Inky frowned. Given all the meat cleavers and knives, he didn't fancy meeting a butcher with an anger problem. He bowed his head and tried to get on with his sketches.

The banging continued. Someone was beating on something. It sounded like a fight. Maybe somebody had broken in? Maybe there was something valuable in there, and the butcher locked it up so tight to keep it safe. Maybe somebody found out. What if the poor guy was getting burgled or mugged? Inky stood. The butcher had been okay with him in his own crazy way. He didn't much look like a street fighter either. He would need help if someone was having a go.

Inky rubbed his eyes. It was none of his business. He had enough problems himself. He shifted his weight, undecided whether to get another can, or light another spliff, or go and see what the matter was. It would be better to sit back down.

But there was more banging. Something serious was going on. Could it be the guy was having a fit or something? Some kind of medical emergency?

Inky sighed. Okay, he'd go listen. He went to his door and slipped off the chain, and opened it a crack. The noises were louder now.

From the open door, he glanced over to the bedside table. In that drawer was a blade. He'd carried it in London to protect himself but only ever pulled it once, and that resulted in the would-be mugger running away down Elephant and Castle Tube station.

Should he take the blade with him? Another sigh. That would escalate things. No, that wasn't necessary. This was nothing.

There was a crash.

This wasn't going to stop. He'd have to check it out. He couldn't leave someone to this without doing anything. What if Relph got murdered? He shook out his shoulders, flexed his hands, took off his chunky watch and went downstairs. He didn't take his knife.

At the bottom, Inky stood at the heavy iron door into the butcher's shop. Even through this formidable barrier, the sounds of conflict echoed. He heard heavy breathing, but no words, no shrieks or shouts.

Inky knocked on the door. It hurt his hand. The sound made was pitiful compared with the clamour from inside. No answer came. This time, Inky kicked the door instead of knocking it with his hand. It was louder, but there was still no answer. And then Inky thought, what if it was the butcher who'd got someone in there and was cutting them up with his cleavers?

That was a nuts idea, but unsettling. With a shudder, Inky went back upstairs to his flat. He locked the door from inside and put the chain across.

THE FOLLOWING DAY, Inky was astonished to see the door open when he went downstairs—not only the usually chained, bolted and barred front door but also the door to the butcher's shop inside was open as well.

A horrible stink issued from the open shop door, a sour smell, like ammonia, and it made his nostrils wrinkle. Inky peered into the gloomy shop interior. There wasn't a single item of furniture — only an old stained mattress with a filthy sleeping bag. That must be where Relph dossed down. It was hard to see the room properly because the steel window screens kept the daylight out, but the butcher wasn't home. Inky reached around for a light switch, tripped it, but nothing happened. He glanced up to the light fitting in the middle of the ceiling, but there were no bulbs. Relph must live here in the dark.

The state of the room was shocking. Around the walls were smears and stains. Some were blood. Quite a lot of blood. But there were also yellowy mucus stains—maybe liquid fat—smearing the walls. It gleamed in the faint light, greasy and thick and congealed.

Worst of all was the state of the floor. The floorboards were broken. There was an uneven hole six-foot square in the middle. Worrying about Relph coming back and catching him, Inky nevertheless went in and stood at the edge of the hole. He peered down. The hole was deep. It went down through the dirt and disappeared. Maybe it was some kind of meat cellar from when the butcher's shop was open. It certainly felt cold enough. Inky felt a draft of chill, ammoniac air rising up, and he reeled back, gasping.

As HE ENTERED the tattoo shop, Milky said, 'You're late.'

'Sorry. It's just...'

But Milky waved him down. 'Nah, never mind. Nobody in, anyway. Fancy a brew?'

Inky said he'd have a coffee. He was settling himself into work, wondering about Relph and his meat cellar when Milky said, 'Did you see *The Cumberland News*?'

Inky shook his head. 'No, I don't read it.'

'You're an internet man, are you? Well, it's on *Cumbria Crack* too.'

'What is?'

'The murder!'

Inky glanced out of the window where he could make out the gaping open door to Relph's butcher's shop. 'The murder?'

'Aye, a fella found in Melbourne Park, over yonder. Chopped up.'

'Chopped up?'

'Aye, dismembered.' Milky levelled a finger at him. 'I know what you're thinking.'

'Do you?'

Milky nodded sagely. 'And, I agree. I think he did it too.'

Inky wasn't sure he had been thinking that. But all that noise last night. 'Should we tell the police?'

Milky scowled. 'No way, I'm no grass.'

There were lots of police around all day. Inky nipped out to Gregg's for a vegan sausage roll, and they were going door to door. He saw that the butcher's door was locked again. Out of curiosity, he walked to Melbourne Park, but it was cordoned off with police tape that flapped in the breeze. Crows sat in the bare treetops looking down at the police CSI teams.

There were hordes of people there and TV cameras. People were grinning and taking selfies. He saw someone doing a Tik-Tok dance against the background of the grisly murder. He grunted his disapproval and turned around. Inky had never been a massively law-abiding man, but this disgusted him — using someone's murder as entertainment and material for your Instagram feed. It was repulsive.

Then his mobile rang. He recognised the number and anyway the name came up: *Carl*. He didn't want to speak to Carl.

He rejected the call. Before he got back to work, a text message pinged through.

'You better answer, Inky boy. We know where you are.'

Inky gulped hard. That was bad shit. They knew where he was? But they could be bluffing.

The phone rang again. This time with a heavy sigh, he answered. 'Carl?'

The South London voice said, 'Inky, me old mucker. Long time no see. Where've you been then?'

'Here and there.'

''Ere and there? I like it! You always was creative. Now, listen, Inky. I ain't calling you for fun. This is business. See, fing is, mate, you owes me a lot of sovs. A lot of p, get me? And then you disappears wivvout a word to your old mate, Carl. And so I finks, maybe my little mate Inky's gone and done a runner. And you know what?'

'No.'

'Sorry, mate, didn't 'ear ya. Watchya say?'

'I don't know, Carl.'

'You don't know what I finks? No, I bet you fuckin don't. See, fing is Inky—unless I sees you back in Old London town before tomorrow, I'm gonna come and pull your fingernails out? You get me? And fingernails is only the start.'

Inky said quietly, 'You don't know where I am, Carl.'

'I don't know where you are?' The man's rage exploded over the phone. 'Don't you never heard of phone tracing? Don't you know I can put you within a mobile phone cell mast range?'

'Only the police can do that.'

'Anybody can do that if they got the right connections, and believe me, Inky, I got the connections. I need to see you, wiv the moolah, tomorrow. Get me?'

'I get you, Carl.'

'See you, Euston Station, four o'clock. Don't be late. That'll give you plenty time to get down from Car fucking Lisle or whatever Scotch place you is in.'

The phone call ended. Inky stared, horrified, at his mobile phone. They could trace him through this! With a gasp of despair, he hurled the phone through the air, back into the park, where it landed out of sight.

He hurried back to work. That wasn't clever. It was still within two hundred yards of where he lived. He should have taken the phone and put it on a train to Cornwall or Aberdeen. He went back and searched and searched but couldn't find it. Somebody maybe nicked it. Some kid. Poor them.

.   .   .

HE WAS LATE BACK to work, but Milky didn't say anything.

That night, he tried to sleep. He tried cannabis and alcohol, then coffee and Black Metal music, but he couldn't take his mind off Carl. Carl was an evil man. Inky knew what he'd done to others who owed him money, and it wasn't pretty. Inky was going to have to move from Carlisle. Maybe try Glasgow. Maybe Ireland. However far he had to get away, he'd go.

It was three a.m., and a light rain beat against the window, yellow sodium street light fuzzed through rivulets of rain. Outside, the Botcherby streets were quiet and empty. Inky still hadn't slept.

He had brought home the copy of *The Cumberland News* that Milky had in the shop. But he hadn't read it until now. The murder was on the front page. When he read it, despite Milky's assertion that the victim was chopped up, it only said the body had parts missing, and what was left of it was covered in a congealing yellow fatty substance.

At four a.m., the noises from downstairs began again—the knocking and clattering. It was the same as last night—the same sounds that happened before that man was found murdered in the park: dismembered.

Inky's mind raced. It was hard to believe, but Relph was so weird with his watery blue eyes and his wet lips and his stained butcher's overall.

How the hell was it stained with blood and that disgusting greasy fat when he didn't even work as a butcher any more?

And what the hell was in that hole that led down from the middle of his room?

Inky grew scared.

He got up and checked the door to his flat was locked and chained. He pushed a hand through his hair. He needed to leave here. Carl was one thing, but now he had this crazy, dangerous man downstairs. He went back to sit on his bed and lit a roll-up cigarette.

Something was happening downstairs. It sounded like more than one person. Inky's heart hammered. His mouth went dry.

He got up and pressed his ear to the door. What was Relph doing? Chopping somebody up?

Inky swallowed hard. Without thinking it through, he went to the bedside table, opened the door and took out his knife. He gripped the handle as the long-pointed blade shone dully in the light. His hand was sweaty. He was going to have to sort this. It was true about Carl, and it was true about Relph. He wouldn't hang around to be a victim.

He went to the door and took off the chain. With his left hand, he turned the key and stood listening.

Nothing but the drumming of the rain on the window glass, the moaning of the wind pushing at the loose window frames.

He waited on the landing, and then there was a clattering and an unchaining, and the door to the butcher's shop opened.

Inky thought he would faint. He didn't know what to do. Relph was coming out.

In the spill of light from his bedroom door that barely reached the landing, Inky saw Relph standing there. He wore his stained butcher's apron and his butcher's overall. But he was covered in blood. Fresh blood, still wet.

It must be the victim's.

Relph turned and looked up the stairs, his watery blue eyes meeting Inky's.

Inky cowered back, the knife in his hand. 'Don't come up!' he yelled at the butcher. 'I'll stab you if you come near me.'

Relph had a bloody cleaver in his hand. It was covered in that congealing yellow fat that dripped thick and warm onto the floorboards.

But Relph didn't speak. He couldn't speak. He just stared with his blank blue eyes.

Relph had a strange expression. Inky couldn't read it. It could be hate, it could be fear, it could be pure insanity.

With a scream, the butcher ran up the stairs at him. Inky jumped back into his room. He had the knife in his right hand and pulled awkwardly to drag the door closed, but he wasn't quick enough.

Relph was there with his cleaver, bounding up the last stairs towards him — covered in blood, cleaver in hand dripping wet fat. Relph's eyes screamed insanity, his fat slobbery lips tried to say something, but they only made noises as his stump tongue twitched in his empty mouth.

'Get back!' Inky said, brandishing the knife, but the butcher was crazy or panicking. He was trying to tell Inky something, pointing down the stairs, but Inky, in his terror, lunged with his knife.

Inky's blade plunged into the butcher's chest. Relph's eyes blinked once then stayed open, startled, gazing dumbly at the knife sticking from his breast. A flower of blood blossomed through his overall, and he fell gurgling, slumping against the wall of the narrow landing outside Inky's flat. Relph was still trying to say something. He dropped his cleaver, and it clattered down the stairs. He pointed down, and Inky followed where he was pointing.

Heaving its way up the stairs was a horrid fat worm. It was huge — about twelve feet long, dragging itself along with vile undulations like a giant maggot. It shuffled and slurped and pulled, feeling its senseless way towards him, lifting its foul head to where it sensed fresh meat.

Inky screamed in horror. The butcher hadn't been barricading people out; he had been keeping this thing in. This is what had burrowed up through the butcher's floor, attracted by the scent of fresh meat.

Relph had closed down his shop to protect the world. It must have escaped last night and digested the man in the park. Even tonight, Relph had run up to warn Inky to get out.

He'd been so wrong. But it was all too late now.

The acrid ammonia smell grew as the maggot got closer and closer, raising its blind head to smell him. It came, shuffling and pulsing, dragging its mucus-smeared body up the stairs. Inky couldn't get out. He couldn't ring for help. He tried to close the door, but the maggot was already on him. Its weight pushed open the door and sent Inky sprawling. It opened its soft mouth, vomited enzymes and, after it had killed him, began slowly, laboriously to lay hundreds of slimy white eggs in Inky's prepared corpse like the good mother it was.

CHAPTER 6

FROM WHITBY TO WHITEHAVEN

MR SEBASTIAN DE LA FONTAINE, WHITBY, N. YORKS, TO MISS CARMILLA CAIRSTON, WHITEHAVEN, CUMBRIA: 17TH DECEMBER 2019

Ma Chere Carmilla,

Forgive me writing to you by hand. I am using that glass handled dipping pen you so admired when you visited. You know my penchant for tradition! Ah, Carmilla, it seems so long since we met, and it must truly be nearly two years! Two years, how time has flown, *tempus fugit* indeed, and how my life bleeds away in this (self-imposed) exile.

I *lurk* in my humble emporium here perched above the North Sea, and you remain isolate in your tower (as I imagine it) perched high above the White Haven (what a delicious name it is, though I have never visited. *Though I have never been invited*). Always, I imagine your yearning crepuscular beauty as you stare pensively out over the Irish Sea, imagining the coming of Mannanan Mac Lir! (Or even Bran the Blessed). While, on the altogether more continental coast, I await Dracula and his brides!

Oh, Carmilla! We are as two twins, separated by circumstances apart: England whole between us....

How, (at times, and at times *only*) I wish I could drive a motor vehicle (I fear coach and horses no longer run 'cross the Stain More.), and in my gleaming engine of silver and chrome, I would come coast-to-coast to attend on you, if you would have me! But alas, my infirmity (invisible, but still very *real*. Despite the gossips!) will not allow me.

Here business fluctuates. I do best during Goth Weekend, and only slightly worse during the Steampunk Festival. The Pirate Gathering however, does little to improve my coffers, though I have toyed at buying in trinkets to tempt our seadog friends. Perhaps a stuffed parrot or two, or maybe a crutch for would-be Long John Silvers would be an investment?

Yes, how, I miss you, my darling Carmilla. How I *pine* for you! I still have the photograph you gave me. Black and white of course, your dark beauty in chiaroscuro, your wine red (dark grey in the photograph obviously) lips, your snow-pale cheeks, your hair as black as the raven's wing. And your corset! But, oh my, I must retreat from that subject before I become quite overwrought!

On another matter, I don't know if you remember Tizer? The ruffian dealer in sweet smoke, other powders and items he wishes to fence? He entered my emporium the other day and, I, looking up, was disappointed to see his pocked face. But, for once (not just once to be *fair* to him, for man does not live by claret alone!) he had a proposition. He had found (I use that word loosely to include *finding* things in another man's house to which you have no right of legal entry) some letters. And they were Victorian, and very interesting. He, the fool, the idiot, the mongrel, had no idea of their worth. Truth, neither did I — *instantly*— but I had an inkling. I offered him £5 and he bargained me up to £18, but still, I feel in my bones they are worth more. A *lot* more.

And then when I have published, and profited, I shall visit. I shall traverse the neck of England in an iron horse, sadly no longer powered by steam, and I will travel from Whitby to Whitehaven to see you.

Yours aye, your devoted Sebastian.

Copies of the Letters procured by Sebastian de la Fontaine from his underworld contact "Tizer".

FROM DAVID DOUGLAS, EDINBURGH, TO EUAN SINCLAIR, LONDON: 5TH JUNE 1896

Dear Euan,

I hope this letter finds you well. I, myself, and mine, remain the same. Weather has been somewhat disappointing up at Costorphine this summer, but I remain in good spirits. Pass my regards to your dear ma, although recast my rough words in your usual courteous style. Also my regards to the brothers of our Order, AE, Waite, WBY, etc. Not so warmly to Mathers, and not at all to Crowley.

To cut to the chase, you may know Radcliffe who owns Roslin Castle? It transpires that while restoring the castle from its previous ruinous state, he came across a room that had been bricked up and within that was a collection of papers relating to the Estate. They were of marginal historical interest in the main. However, when I saw him last month at the University dinner, he told me of his discovery, I expressed my interest in seeing them.

They appear to refer to some magical operation and Radcliffe has it from some authority, that they were penned by Michael Scot, our own countryman. You may be aware of Scot? If not, he was accused of being a necromancer and magician in the 12th Century, but was certainly a scholar and mathematician who spent a large part of his life in Italy. There is a legend, that retiring from the study of magic, he shut himself up in Wolsty Castle, where the monks of Holm Cultram kept their library, on the south side of the Solway Firth.

There is a further legend that Scot wrote a book there whose words were so corrosive that no one dared to read them, and they hung the book on an iron nail in the middle of the library. Somehow, it got to Roslin from Wolsty. Something to do with the Templars? It always is...!

Anyhow, I have a chance at reading them, Radcliffe promises. Who else does he know who can read Medieval Latin in decayed Blackletter script? I shall let you know my discoveries.

DAVID DOUGLAS TO EUAN SINCLAIR, 20 JUNE 1896

By the by, Euan, I found a copy of Bernardino Baldi's *Life of The Mathematicians*, c. 1586. He writes:

Michele Scoto, that is Michael the Scot, was a Judicial Astrologer, in which profession he served the Emperor Frederick II. He wrote a most learned treatise by way of questions upon the Sphere of John de Sacrobosco which is still in common use. Some say he was a Magician, and tell how he used to fetch on occasion, by magic art, from the kitchen of great Princes whatever he needed for his table. He died from the blow of a stone falling on his head, having already foreseen that such would be the manner of his end.'

I can find no evidence that Baldi ever saw the book written by Scot that Radcliffe has now sent to me and which lies on my desk — as yet unread, awaiting a day or two when I have little else to do, so I can devote myself to the Latin.

DAVID DOUGLAS TO EUAN SINCLAIR. 30 JUNE 1896

Dear Euan,

I have been beavering away at the papers. Here's a summary: Michael Scot born 1160 or so, probably in the Scottish borders. Went to Roxburgh Grammar School, then Durham Cathedral School then over to Italy. He had various jobs in Italy, but most significant was his translation of Averroes and other Arabic alchemical works into Latin. Sicily had been under Arab rule until the Normans took it over just decades before Scot was there, and the Arabs had compiled a great deal of esoteric material from their conquest of Jerusalem, and of course the great libraries of Egypt. There was much secret lore to be learned and Scot took to it.

Scot was an alchemist and a mathematician, an astrologer and almost certainly a demonologist. He returned to the Scottish border area towards the end of his life and got a reputation as one who could perform wonders. Quite often with the aid of demons. For example there is this passage:

✠ *Experimentum Michaelis Scoti nigromantici.*

Ego sum ausus scribere Michael Scotus, hic magnus usus est magica operatione. In hoc libro, sunt arcana nunc est bibendum hominis anima, etsi oculos eius...

Si volueris per daemones haberi scientem, qui in forma magistri ad te veniet cum tibi placuerit..

Which I would translate:

Michael Scot's Experiment in Necromancy.

I, Michael Scot, have dared write how this great work is a magical operation. In this book are secrets of how to drink a man's soul through his eyes. If thou desirest to have knowledge through demons, who will in the form of masters come to thee as thou wilt...

The Latin is straightforward. The Blackletter script slightly less familiar to me than Half-Uncial, but no real trouble. I have come across some words that I am unfamiliar with. They are not Latin, not Greek, probably not Hebrew transliterated. Possibly, Arabic. Possibly Coptic? Maybe something older still!

He seems to use these obscure words to activate his magic ritu-als— words of power then and they may represent an older sacerdotal language, such as with theories about the Pictish on the ogham slabs in Scotland, or even Latin in an English-speaking society. Sacred, secret words indeed!

Never fear, I will unravel them! (I hope)

Yours aye,

David.

DAVID DOUGLAS TO EUAN SINCLAIR. 7TH JULY 1896.

...Damned book. Still stuck with those words. I've been tracing them out and I'm minded to send them to Forsyth at the British Library. He was always a whizz with the the Semitic stuff when we were at Oxford. However, I've been laid low with some damned lurgy. Headaches like you wouldn't believe. But worst of all they've affected my vision. I now have lacunae in both eyes - damned white blobs missing. I am sure I shall be fine forthwith. Until then, I remain, aye, your devoted friend, David.

EUAN SINCLAIR TO HIS BROTHER CAMERON SINCLAIR, BELLADRUM, INVERNESS-SHIRE, 25TH AUGUST 1896.

...Did you hear David Douglas died? You will remember him best from the summer of '66 when he stayed with us and we went out on the Black Isle? He was a fine man and a great scholar. Far better than myself, which I recognised even then. He bequeathed me some papers he'd got. He's translated them apart from these strange words he couldn't decipher. I took a look at them but haven't got a clue.

ERNEST FORSYTH, BRITISH LIBRARY TO EUAN SINCLAIR

Thanks for the loan of the manuscript and poor old David Douglas's translation of it. What times we had at Oxford! I was only thinking of him the other day then I heard he was dead!

I am spending a few weeks at Roslin for the summer and will take them with me to make a stab at them when I have some leisure time.

I didn't know much about Michael Scot's work until now, but being familiar with the field, I can say that he's turned up some rum stuff. I have never seen some of those demon summoning formulae before or such an emphasis on entry via the eyes. Very odd. Unique even.

At a cursory glance, I would say the words Douglas struggled with were a corrupted Ancient Egpytian, with errata from miscopying and my guess would be the transliteration was from hieroglyphs, to Greek, to Latin by people who didn't actually understand the words. Some kind of words of initiation in any case.

I shall let you know what I find. Presuming of course you care! Enjoy Crete!

Ernest.

EXCERPT FROM THE LOTHIAN STAR: SATURDAY 30 AUGUST 1896

Deaths: Ernest William Dougal Forsyth, son of William Alexander Forsyth of Roslin, MidLothian, died at Roslin Castle after a short illness. Flowers to Roslin Chapel.

SEBASTIAN DE LA FONTAINE TO MISS CARMILLA CAIRNSTON 23 DECEMBER 2019

My dearest Carmilla, I trust you received my last, and its enclosures, though you never write. I *wish* you would write. I have been looking over the unfortunate David Douglas's translation of the cursed Michael Scot's work on demonological matters, while sipping claret from a silver goblet.

Most of it is dull, damnably, dreadfully, devastatingly dull. Dull beyond the comprehension of an average man. However, there is some fun stuff on the summoning of demons! You would enjoy that, Carmilla, oh how you would. Would that I could tempt you to Whitby? As I mentioned before, I believe you can come on the train, yeah even all the way from Whitehaven to Whitby, and doing such would allow you eschew the bucolic pleasures of Penrith, the wilderness of Stainmore (though actually, we don't mind a *little* wilderness, do we? As long as we're well wrapped-up and fortified with sherry.) It would also allow you to travel quickly through the industrial hellhole that is Middlesborough, and rise swift to the empty moors and Whitby beyond.

In fact, though I abhor all the contraptions of the modern age, I own to finding Google (cursed be its name) moderately useful. In idle curiosity, I looked up David Douglas. He was a scholar of some fame in his time. It transpires his death was unexpected and they refer to some wasting disease accompanied by blindness.

Death seems to have followed the wretched manuscript as a devoted footman because Ernest Forsyth of Roslin was also struck down (and here we have a solution to the mystery of how it ended up bricked up in that room at Roslin Castle — Forsyth, or his anonymous followers hid it there!). Forsyth's death was caused by Glaucoma? Does that make sense? Something to do with his eyes in any degree.

How, I wish you would visit , Carmilla. How I miss your pale neck, your long fingers, all the things you whispered to me after dark. Those nights on absinthe and opium! Gothic heaven indeed my Bella Donna!

SEBASTIAN DE LA FONTAINE TO CARMILLA CAIRNSTON, 2 JANUARY 2020.

Well, Carmilla, I read that manuscript and now I wish I hadn't. It was the black words. Words that moved on the page as I attempted to read them. I copied out the script, though I had no idea what I wrote, but the words twisted and writhed like black beetles on the paper. Later, at night, when I slept, I heard them whispering to themselves. As I slept, I felt them crawl over my cheek and bother my eyelids, lifting them to gain entry. And then when in there the words dropped like burglars into my retina and from there swam the optic nerve entering into my occipital lobe where they made themselves at home and subverted my processing of vision.

I write this through a fog. They have cut out shapes in my vision like paper doilies or intricacies of lace. I feel them moving and breeding. I can now say the words, but I will not utter them. To do that would allow them mastery.

It seems to me that the words become lord of all that read them. The monks of Wolsty were wise to hang that book on an iron spike and forbid any from opening it!

The words worm inside my head. My vision fails even as I type this letter. I have an appointment with a doctor. I can only hope that this is some kind of stroke. I can only hope that the words do not drink me up.

Forgive me, Carmilla, I do not think we shall meet again.

EXTRACT FROM POST-MORTEM REPORT, PATHOLOGY DEPT, JAMES COOK HOSPITAL, MIDDLESBOROUGH ON RAYMOND SMITH, (KNOWN TO FRIENDS AS SEBASTIAN DE LA FONTAINE).

...Examination of sclera, retina, cornea and fovea showed infiltration by strands of neoplasm. Neoplasm biopsied for histological report revealed novel cellular structures, lacking nucleus which are reminiscent of fungal tissue, but which proceed in long strands down neuronal and axonal pathways to enter the occipital lobe via the optic nerves. In form, the black tumour cells resemble nothing more than letters.

From there the tumour structures extend extensively into the substantia nigra and under the neocortex where they have fully colonised the speech centres.

LETTER FROM CARMILLA CAIRNSTON TO MR M RELPH, ESQ SOLICITOR, WHITBY

Thank you enormously, Mr Relph for your help in arranging the postage for poor Raymond's papers. I received them yesterday.

LETTER FROM CARMILLA CAIRNSTON TO AUDREY CHAMBERS, LITERARY PROJECTS COORDINATOR, NORTHERN ARTS, NEWCASTLE UPON TYNE.

Thank you for your generous funding of my project. As you know it is intended to be a tribute to my late friend Sebastian de la Fontaine, who procured these letters. However, I also hope that it will say something of the power over the centuries of the written word to enthral and captivate. I think that it is all the more fitting that the manuscript from which these passages were copied were kept for many centuries at Wolsty Castle not far north from here on the shores of the Solway Firth. I will write the event report to submit with the final accounts of the project.

EXTRACT FROM THE WHITEHAVEN NEWS

Carmilla Cairnston, local historian, artist and white witch will be giving a talk on the Demonological Manuscripts of Michael Scot at the Beacon Museum, Whitehaven. Special funding from Northern Arts has enabled the projection of selected words of the Ancient Manuscript into the clouds above Whitehaven. It should be a spectacular show!

BBC CUMBRIA NEWS BULLETIN

Hundreds of people in Whitehaven have been rushed to West Cumberland Hospital with sudden attacks of blindness after witnessing an arts exhibition using modern new high-power projectors at the Beacon Museum. Experts are looking into whether certain light frequencies could have caused this effect, but are so far baffled.

Doctors say there is every chance that all those affected will make a full recovery.

TRANSCRIPTION OF THE WORDS OF POWER

/KM-ṃ-JrT-SŇ /Ňs-tRj-ṃ-MK /KM-ṃ-JrT-SŇ
Through the Eyes of Those That Read, I Shall Enter In

CHAPTER 7

DUBMILL POINT

I am a painter. Not a painter and decorator; I don't do houses, though I can, albeit in an amateurish way. No, I do art. I'm an artist. No, I don't think that makes me better than you. In fact, I probably don't earn as much as you nor even the milkman, but it keeps me going; it's my *ikigai*, sense of purpose, and raison d'etre.

I was on a break looking for inspiration, so I'd come to the remote northwest corner of England and the wide empty coast where Scotland was almost close enough to kiss over the water when the mist wasn't down, or it wasn't raining. And the Isle of Man sat like a peaked boat to the south, but Ireland was invisible over the horizon.

I'd taken a cottage, a small place rented out by a company on the internet. It had fishing nets on the walls, model yachts and curtains, bizarrely covered by the names of ports in Cornwall: sea-side style.

It was Autumn. September and misty but not cold. My cottage was in the village of Allonby, and each day, I'd go out walking on the beach, looking for scenes to paint, to fix in my memory for later.

It was a time of the full moon, and because of that, the tides were huge. They pulled in and out and when they flooded in, they threatened the narrow coast road and dressed it in sand, seaweed and crab shells. And when they drained out, they exposed miles of flat red sand dotted with rocks, which were draped with black mussel shells, and on the sand, jellyfish dropped here and there like fallen stars, and at the distant line of waves, seabirds strutting and feeding in the mud.

I could walk for miles and not see anyone. Maybe sometimes I'd glimpse dog walkers far away throwing frisbees for their pooches, but that was the extent of the company I had on that lonely beach.

Until the third day when I saw him.

I had wandered north up to Dubmill Point at the end of the bay where the curve of the land sweeps out again. And on this point is a sombre looking farmhouse that's probably been there for four hundred years. And every time I saw it, the windows were shuttered. I guess that was so the waves didn't hurl rocks through the glass on wild nights.

And it seemed that the owner of the farm wasn't just a farmer with his few sheep and fewer cows, but he was a fisherman too. I know because I saw him out there with his nets.

That day, I was way out by the edge of the waves, about a mile from shore and between me and the grassy dunes, lay acres of flat sand dimpled by wind, sculpted by wave and runnelled by tiny rivulets of water that drained the necklace of rock pools; homes of crabs and shrimps and anemones.

Gulls hung halfway between sea and heaven. The sun glimmered, filtered white by cloud, pale and ghostlike, but still bright enough to throw a sparkle on the water. I measured the scene in my mind, thinking of canvasses and paints and brushes. I'd do it in colour wash, I thought: Turnersque—something diaphanous.

I had taken off my shoes and walked on the cool sand, leaving prints behind like a marooned sailor adrift from the dry-land world.

I didn't notice him at first. He was calf-deep with poles and nets that stretched about twenty feet, strung out like the briny sand was a tennis court.

He stood, dressed in black Wellington boots, black trousers, a black coat and black-hair-gone-grey plastered across his forehead, and he stared at me. It was hard to read the stare–it certainly wasn't welcoming: surprised, hostile, astonished? I couldn't say.

Given there was only him and me for miles and no help coming out here on the empty sands, I decided to disarm any aggression with a cheery greeting.

'Hello!' I yelled, but the words fell flat, and the waves lapped around my feet, and he said not a word but only stared.

I made my smile even more prominent. 'Hello!' I said and waved. I thought if he didn't answer, I wouldn't push it. Instead, I would veer towards the land as if I had intended to walk that way anyway, rather than along the waves' edge which had been my real route.

The fisherman just looked then nodded. Slowly, he lifted a hand in acknowledgement. I was about thirty yards from him now.

'Not a bad day,' I yelled across the distance, coming closer with every step.

He watched me like he knew me. That was odd. Then he put his hand to his throat in a movement that betrayed anxiety. Him anxious of me: and me a stranger and a woman past the flower of her youth, not in much of a state to run or fight, even if I had to. Odder.

'Fishing?' I said, stating the obvious.

He licked his lips as if to moisten them. Then, he said, 'I thought....'

I laughed. 'I'm a visitor. Just out for a walk.'

'Of course,' he said. 'I see that now.'

'Did you mistake me for someone else?'

He looked out to sea, then back, now composed. His hand went to his net. 'Not much today. Depends on the time of year. Sometimes we get cod, plaice, dabs, you know.' He shrugged. 'Salmon too, but we have to release those now. Government, you know.'

'I've not seen nets like this. What do you do? String them out?'

'They call them haaf nets. They go back to the Vikings. There used to be gangs of us who did it. There's only me here now.'

'I'm Vicki Bond,' I said abruptly.

"George Twentyman, I am. From Dubmill.' He gestured behind him to the dark farmhouse.

'The farmer?'

'I don't have much stock now. Can't manage it on my own. The wife's dead.'

'I'm sorry.'

'The lad's away at agricultural college at Penrith.'

'Do you get lonely?' I asked.

He shook his head.

There were crabs and seaweed and a few small fish twined through his net. The fish gleamed in the pale sunlight. The crabs flexed their dying claws.

"So, you thought you recognised me?' I said.

Some strange expression seized his face. He glanced down at the wet sand around his black boots, then looked to sea again. 'On holiday?' he said.

'I'm a painter.'

'Ah, a painter,' he said like he didn't know what I was talking about. 'Dressed in black.'

I shrugged, self-conscious. Dressing in black was a habit I'd got into during my days following The Cure. My husband always said I should brighten up my image, but I kept it as a pose. I was an arty type, you see.

'Don't worry. It doesn't mean funerals,' I joked.

'Doesn't it?' he said.

A silence fell between us.

I paused, working up my courage, then said, 'Listen, would you mind awfully if I came back another time and did some sketches?'

'Sketches?'

'Of you. It's a great image. You out here all alone with your nets on this vast open beach. And because it's a dying tradition, it gives it resonance.'

'You want to paint me?'

I nodded.

For the first time, he laughed. "Really? Me?'

'Yes, please.' And as I said the words, I became more convinced that was what I was meant to do—what I'd been brought here for.

'I don't think I'd make much of a painting.'

'On the contrary. I think you will be perfect.'

He smiled, perhaps flattered. 'Will you come til't farm to do it?"

I shook my head. 'No, out here is best. It's so open. I'll come back with a sketch pad and a camera, if you don't mind.'

'Out here then,' he said. And as he said it, an unfathomable look came into his eyes as if he sensed the play of fate, and in my overblown artistic way, I imagined us surrendering to powers beyond my knowledge.

The next day, I went looking. Foolishly, I hadn't made a time with him. I just thought I'd see him there as if he were a fixture on the beach. The weather was worse today, and this time I took my Wellingtons and raincoat. The rain was spotting, a mizzle more than a downpour and even that cleared with the clouds moving. Scotland was invisible, just lines of waves retreating flat and faraway. I had a camera and a sketchbook and some charcoal pencils. The scene suited black and white, a chiaroscuro in vapour.

And he was there. With his nets he stood, gazing across the sands as if he expected someone. This time he saw me and waved from afar, but when I got close, despite the faint smile in his salt-tanned face, he looked haunted: that was the word. It popped into my mind and it was the correct one.

'So you're going to draw me?' he said.

I tapped my camera. 'I'll take a few photos, then do some sketches—just to capture the mood and the lines. All right if I call you George?'

'Aye, lass. What else would you call me? Mr Twentyman?'

I shrugged. 'If you'd prefer.'

'No, lass. George is fine.' He frowned. 'Which way did you come?'

I indicated vaguely with a stretched arm. I wasn't concentrating on where I'd come from; I was planning images and pictures that would capture the man and this empty, waterlogged world that was his, and it seemed his alone.

'You've got to be careful of the channels,' he said. 'They fill up behind you. You can be out on the sand like this, and when you turn to walk in, the sea's come in and you're cut off.'

I nodded. I had a mirrorless camera, a Canon M50 mark ii, smaller and lighter than a DSLR, but still good quality. I checked the light, took a few snaps. 'I'll bear that in mind,' I said.

'It's just you don't know the shore, the channels and the banks and the rocks. The rocks all have names.' He pointed to a big lump of granite sitting in a pool of water, draped in seaweed like a bad haircut, a gull perched on it. 'That's t' Inging Styan: the Hanging Stone. I navigate my way by them. But you don't know them.'

'Have you ever got lost out here?' I asked.

'Sometimes. You can lose your sense of direction when the sea mist comes in.'

'It sounds treacherous.'

'It can be. But, like I say, I know the shore.'

I grinned. 'I'll stick with you then.'

He stood awkwardly. 'What do you want me to do?'

'Maybe fix the nets?'

'Fix them? They're in good repair, though.'

'Then, erm, I don't know—examine them?'

He shrugged and went stiffly to look at the nets. He was not a natural model.

I took my photographs, placed my rucksack on the sand, got out the small sketchbook, and began drawing him in lines and strokes.

We'd been there maybe twenty minutes; I'd lost count of time when he jerked his head around and started back. He was staring seaward where the tide had gone even further out, revealing flat, shining expanses of sand before the retreating waves.

'What?' I said. He looked alarmed.

He jerked his head around. 'Can you see her?'

'Who?'

He levelled his arm and pointed. I saw his hand trembled. I followed his finger but saw only waves and wading birds picking at the water's edge.

'Erm. I can't see anyone.'

He shook his head. 'Just I thought I saw her.'

'Who?'

'The woman.'

I narrowed my eyes and looked again. There was nobody there. It started to rain, and the warbling sound of a curlew rose eerily from the water's edge.

'I'd better be getting back,' he blurted.

'Oh. Okay. Just....'

'Can you draw me another day? I need to milk the cows.'

He'd already told me that he had hardly any cows anymore, but he'd stepped back a way, leaving the net to stand in place and catch the next tide. He paused. He was definitely spooked by something, staring out to the turning tideline.

'That's fine, of course.'

'Come back with me if you'd like. To the house. I'll tell you there.'

And then he strode off, and I hurried after him.

He was right. After about five hundred yards, we came to a deep channel that was already filling with water.

'It's turned,' he said, indicating the swirling brown seawater. 'You can wade through this. But if it gets deeper.'

The water was just below the tops of my Wellington boots, but if we'd delayed, I would have got wet feet. That was probably why he'd decided to come back; he'd remembered the incoming tide.

When we arrived at his lonely farmhouse, he made me a cup of tea, cows forgotten about. The house was not comfortable. I could smell the damp in the walls. The shutters were open, but the light outside was poor and the light inside not much better. There was a fire laid ready in the ancient hearth—piled sticks of kindling wood surrounding by coals and crowned with twirls of newspaper that he'd rolled and twisted to serve as firelighters. He put a match to it and when the kettle whistled from the kitchen, went through and brought me a mug and the tin kettle with the flame-blackened bottom. He made the tea for me by spooning tea leaves with a tarnished silver desert spoon into the mug and adding boiling water straight, then he spilled a dash of milk from a glass bottle, maybe milked from his own cows. No teabags or teapot for Mr Twentyman. The tea was strong and curled my tongue. He offered me a ginger-snap from a packet, the plastic wrapper torn away at the top end. I took one, and he urged me to take another, so I did.

'Who did you think you saw?' I said, sitting there as the room warmed with the fire.

He went quiet and stared at the curling flames, then took a sip of tea. 'I first saw her when I was a lad. It was a low tide like this one. It was Easter. I was out with my father and grandfather. They knew pools where the lobsters were, and when the tide went out that far, you could find them. We were busy getting the lobsters and tying their claws so they didn't kill each other when I saw her out in the water. The tide was up to her middle. I thought she must be in trouble, so I ran into the waves.'

He rubbed his mouth. 'Grandad and fadder were busy and didn't see me at first. I was halfway to her when I saw her face. She was dressed in black, and the clothes hung on her, wet through. She had long black hair, but her face was like it'd been in the water a long time; perished and withered and wet with empty eye-holes where the fishes had been at them.'

'I fainted. My fadder brought me back. Grandad was quiet. They never asked what I'd seen.' He lifted his eyes to mine. "Never once in all the years after."

'I told my mam. It was in this room.' He indicated around him. 'I remember it like it was yesterday. She said it was the drowned woman. She'd always been there, but not everyone could see her. My mother's family were from Mawbray. She'd never seen her, but my father's family were from here, and they did.'

'It sounds horrible—nightmarish.' I didn't know whether I

believed in this drowned woman. But he certainly did. Even in his own front room with a cup of tea and the fire going, his face grew grey.

'You see,' he said. 'She comes as a warning.'

'A warning?'

'Aye, when I see her. I know someone is going to die. They always do.' He looked at me keenly.

I cleared my throat. He'd spooked me. I don't think he meant to frighten me, just that he was so convinced in what he was saying and that conviction of foreboding was infectious.

'I didn't see anyone,' I said.

He looked down. 'No. Only a few of us can see her.'

'How many times have you seen her?' I asked.

'Just three.'

'Ah,' I said, relieved.

'That first time,' he said. 'My grandfather was drowned two days after. He shouldn't have drowned. He'd known those channels and those banks since he was a lad. He was brought up on them.' He nodded. 'She took him.'

I shrugged. 'Well, you don't know. It could be a coincidence.'

'It wasn't a coincidence.'

'What about the second time?'

'I was a grown man then, living here with my wife. I saw her like I saw her today, standing in the water, her face all eaten by fishes.'

I waited for him to tell me what death or disaster followed that sighting.

He did. 'The Solway Spirit went down. She'd caught fire out there, and I saw the light of the flames. I went out, but the tide was high, and I saw her burn about a quarter-mile out. We called the coastguard. Some of them jumped off, but the water was cold, and the currents fast.'

I sat back. Even if he'd seen this drowned woman, it had only been twice before today, and the deaths that followed were surely coincidences, whatever he thought. This third time meant nothing. Certainly not for me. After all, I was a stranger here.

The more likely explanation was that George Twentyman was a lonely old man who spent his time on this lonely farm or on that empty beach, grieving his lost wife and his lost mother and father. Such a solitary fate would turn anyone's mind and get them believing in old tales.

'Thanks for the tea, George,' I said. 'And the gingersnaps.'

I stood. He stood too.

'Will you come back?' he said. 'To paint me?'

I smiled. 'Of course, I will. But not tomorrow. I have to do some shopping.'

He nodded and saw me to the door. As I walked over the narrow road to the path over the dunes that would take me back to Allonby, I turned round to see him standing at his door, watching me. He raised a hand to wave goodbye, and I waved back.

The next day, I went shopping in Workington. On a whim, I went into the public library where they had back copies of the local paper: The West Cumberland Times & Star. The librarian, a Mr Jones, who was Welsh by his accent, was very helpful. He found the record of the burning of the Solway Spirit. So that had really happened. As for the other incident—there was no trace of the death of George Twenty-man's grandfather, but then I didn't know when it had been or what the man's name was. There was certainly no tale of the drowned woman in black, even in the Local Legends Column from the 1970s

The next day I went looking for George on the beach, intent on finishing my sketch. But he wasn't there. Way off to the south, a couple was walking, but nothing much else but birds. The day was grey, not raining, but promising that mist that comes in when the land is warm and the sea cool. So far, the threads of mist hung offshore while the tide ebbed away, dragged by the unseen moon. But it would turn soon and come flooding back.

No George though.

I was disappointed. I thought of going home but then turned, and to my right, I saw his farmhouse at the point. I stood now halfway between sea and shore. I could have turned back, but I went looking for George.

I went up to his dismal front door and at first knocked tentatively. Then, figuring I hadn't knocked hard enough, after a minute, I knocked again. But there was still no reply. I paused, shrugged and turned and then I heard a radio playing inside—some middle of the road music that might come from a local radio station. So there was someone at home. The windows were shuttered up, so he must be sitting in the gloom. I rapped on the pane. 'George?'

He said, 'I'm not ready.' His voice sounded half-strangled. But what was he not ready for?

'It's Vicki,' I said. 'The painter.'

'Oh, Vicki,' he said. 'I'm so glad you're here.'

I didn't know what to say, but I heard movement and then noise at the door. I went back and saw he had it open a crack, but the door was on a chain. He stared at me. He had black rings under his eyes. His hair was wild, his mouth half-open.'Vicki,' he said. He undid the chain with trembling hands and shoved the door open.

I was astounded at the change in him.

'Come in, come in. I'm so glad you're safe.'

'Safe? Why wouldn't I be safe? I mean, Workington can be a bit rough, but even so....'

My joke fell flat.

He re-chained the door, bolted it and turned the big brass key in the lock. Only then did he seem to calm down.

'I didn't want her to come in,' he said.

'Who?'

'The woman.'

I studied his face. "Can I have a cup of tea, George?"

He said, 'Tea?'

'I'll make the tea. You go through.' I ushered him back into his house and followed him to the front room. It was shuttered up, and he had one electric lamp on. His threadbare armchair had an old blanket scrunched upon it, so it looked like he'd been there all night, not going to bed.

I went to the kitchen. The kettle was on the stove, which I lit with a match. I found a teapot, milk, and biscuits. When I went to the living room, George sat, head in hands, his eyes closed.

He didn't speak till after his first gulp of scalding tea.

'She was outside the house last night. The tide was full in. It comes over the road so I thought maybe she could come in the house, but she didn't. I'm so glad you're all right, Vicki.'

I tilted my head. "Why are you so worried about me?'

He sighed heavily. 'Well, I first saw you the day I saw her. I thought your coming was connected and that she was showing....' The hand that gripped the mug trembled.

I leaned forward and put my hand on his arm. 'George, I had an anxiety problem once. But I beat it. I know when it comes, it feels overwhelming, and your mind plays tricks on you. I used to check all the plugs and doors and windows, even though I knew they were safe, but I'd get overcome with the idea that there would be a fire. So, I know what it's like.'

He shook his head. 'She's not in my mind, Vicki. I need you to listen to me and leave. Go back down south where you're from.'

'Preston?'

'Somewhere away from here.'

It was my turn to sigh. 'So you think you saw her again.'

'I saw her in the waves. She was just outside the house.'

'But you had the shutters drawn, and it was dark.'

He stammered. 'I saw her.'

There was no point annoying him, so I tried a different tack. 'You know, George, with a fear like this, you have to face it. That's the only way you overcome it. Otherwise, it becomes your boss and stops you doing things.'

'This is not a fear.'

'You look pretty scared to me.'

He exhaled and covered his eyes with his left hand. 'I know her. I know what she wants.'

'I know you say she was outside the house.'

'She was.'

I raised a placating hand. 'But she's mainly associated with the beach.'

He nodded without meeting my gaze.

'So, I think we should go on the beach.'

This time he did look up but shook his head rapidly. 'No. We mustn't. You mustn't. You need to leave."

'George, I'm not frightened. I'll go to the beach with you. You'll see there's nothing to fear. And then you'll feel better.'

'It's you I'm worried about, not me.'

'But I've never seen her. So I'm not worried, honest.'

I drained my tea. 'Come on. No time like the present. Can I leave my camera and sketch pad here?'

He grunted, and I put them down. I got up, but he didn't. 'Come on. It's for the best.'

'No,' he said.

'Please, George. For me? Just humour me. I'll hold your hand if you want.' I regretted saying that instantly. I'd meant it as a joke, but he might take it as me belittling him. In the event, he didn't even register it.

I reached out. 'Come on.'

He took my hand and rose. I opened the shutter. 'And we'd better have some light in here.' The sun shone behind the house. It wasn't yet noon. The tide was further out now. The beach was huge.

'There's a sea fret,' he said.

I raised an eyebrow.

'A mist off the sea. It'll roll over the sand.'

'We'll be quick. Anyway, you know your way.'

'The tide's coming in.'

He was just finding excuses. I knew what it was like. I'd done the same when I had to face up to my anxieties. Nobody wants to do it, but it has to be done.

We crunched our way over the pebbles and shillies down onto the sand, past the tidelines of seaweed, sticks and plastic bottles that marked each in-breath and out-breath of this cold northern sea.

Then we came to the first channels of water and picked our way over the weedy stones until we arrived at an expanse of sand.

'We shouldn't be going out now,' he said.

'We'll be quick. Where do you see her most?'

'At the waves' edge.' He gestured.

The mist was gathering. I couldn't see the water because of it, but I knew where it was.

He turned to me. 'You don't believe I see her, do you?'

I shook my head.

'If you saw her, would you leave?'

I gave a dry laugh. 'Instantly, believe me. But...'

'But what?'

'I won't.'

He nodded. 'Then the only way to save you is for you to see her for yourself. Come on.'

He strode briskly out to sea. The sand was damp, and we got to another patch of rocks covered in black mussel shells. He knew his way and picked the driest path. He went on so quickly, I struggled to keep up, and at one point, he became a misty shadow — half lost in the gathering sea fog.

I yelled, 'George! Wait up.'

He stopped and turned, puzzled. He'd been lost in his mission and hadn't noticed me falling behind. He waited. I caught him up, and he turned and hurried further out.

The sea went out miles here. I was glad he was there because the billowing walls of mist made everywhere look the same. The sun was lost behind clouds, and it was hard to tell which way was which. So I followed on behind him.

'How far now?' I asked.

'Still a way.'

'Incredible how far the water goes out, nearly all the way to Scotland.'

"Autumn tides, see.'

Then he went quiet. I heard his footsteps and his breathing, and he was much faster than me, despite his age.

I hurried to keep his dark form in sight. The fog was thicker way out here.

Then we came to an area where the sea was already running back in. 'Careful,' he yelled back.

He stopped, and I caught up, panting slightly.

He said, "The sea only uncovers these sands here a few times a year, and there are some patches of mud.'

I looked down at my feet. He was right.

'So, be careful where you place your feet. Just walk where I walk.'

'What?' I said, alarmed. 'You mean it's quicksand?'

'Yes, aye. But you'll be safe. Just walk where I walk.'

We went on. I heard the waves before I saw them. It was as if I was lost in the clouds with the sloshing sea on all sides. It was really flooding back now.

'Is this safe?' I said to George's back.

'No. We can't linger here. But you must see her. If you see her you'll believe, and if you believe then you will go away."

My heart beat fast, and I was afraid, but I was the one who insisted he face his fears. The irony was that I was not facing mine very well.

'She's not here,' I said. 'Let's go back.'

He put up a hand. "Wait.'

'We're not going to see her, George. She doesn't exist.'

'That's what you think. Listen.'

So I listened. I heard the waves and the gulls, but nothing else. 'What?'

'Can't you hear?'

'No.'

But as I listened hard, I heard. I heard the sound of someone in the water, someone wading through the waves.

'She's there. Come on.'

Even amidst all the water, my mouth was dry. I had heard someone thrashing through the waves. There had to be a rational explanation. It would be another fisherman. But still, I trembled.

'Come on.' And George dashed off into the fog. I saw him fade and wanted to run after him, but I was in a state. I hesitated and called, 'George, wait!'

But I couldn't see him anymore.

The mist boiled around me, cold and vaporous. The waves were near. The tide flooded in, slowly, slowly, just above my toes now.

I looked around, eyes wide: where had George gone?

'George?'

I heard his voice calling, 'Come to me.'

But I didn't know where he was. The mist baffled the sound. I couldn't work out what direction anything was. I plunged into the fog, running now, my boots slopping through the water, and then I came to a channel where within seconds, it was knee-deep. The cold water soaked to my skin. Terror gripped me.

I remembered what he'd said about the quicksand. I spun round, looked up to see the sun. The sun would be south and almost overhead as it was mid-day. I needed to go east. But the light was refracted through the fog, and I saw no bright disk that would guide me in the mist so I turned and stumbled into the waves again.

I cried out, "George? Where are you?'

Again he called in reply. He seemed near, but here the near sounded far away and the distant very close. The tide had come in quicker than I thought. There was water everywhere. I splashed forward and came to a sandbank. At least it was dry here. But which way was safety?

I would try to find which way was east and head in that direction. That way, I would hit the beach. Even if the sea had come round behind me, it couldn't be too deep yet. I would wade if I had to. I could wade through water up to my chest. Even if there were currents, they couldn't be strong enough to carry me away. Surely they couldn't.

Then I remembered the prevailing wind was from the southwest. That meant I could work out which way was east. I licked my finger and held it up. But it dried on all sides equally. There was no wind today, not even a breeze to blow the mist away.

'George,' I yelled, 'I can't find you. So I'm going back to the beach.'

This time he didn't reply.

I turned and walked. There was water everywhere. The tide was sheeting over the sand. I would have to wade long before I got to the shingle. Just because there was water in front didn't mean I was going out to sea. The channels cut round behind. He'd said that. I needed to go into the water to get out of the water.

The seawater got deeper. I kept my nerve and kept on going. The swell overtopped my rubber boots and filled them. That made it like I was walking with weights on my feet, so I bent down and wrenched the boots off, sobbing. I hurled the boots away, heard them splash out of sight and overbalanced. I landed on my back and, spluttering in panic, jumped up again. My black clothes were blacker still now, drenched with seawater and clinging to my body.

I stood and ran, plunging through the waves until they were too deep and it was like pushing through a wall. I was shivering and crying, sodden black clothes hanging on me, my dark hair running with seawater plastered to my face.

I had a vision of a woman wearing soaked black clothes, with a face eaten away by the fishes. I heard a woman in panic thrashing about in the waves, trying to save herself. She was only a hundred yards from dry land, but a hundred yards too far.

Ghosts are from the past. But, it seems, ghosts are from the future too.

George Twentyman was truly haunted. He was haunted all the days of his life by a drowned woman. Yes, George Twentyman was haunted. He was haunted by me.

CHAPTER 8
EACHY OF BASSENTHWAITE

I was already out of the door when the shopkeeper called back, 'You've forgotten your milk.'

In my haste to get back in, I knocked into a woman coming out, making her drop her loaf of bread on the pavement. She stooped, scooped it up and smiled. She was wearing a clerical collar. She was a woman, but I understand most Anglican vicars are women now, and I'm cool with that. After all, times change and I'm happy to change with them. As for her, she clearly didn't hold a grudge about me knocking the bread out of her hand.

The shopkeeper brought the milk to the door, and I took it.

'Fisherman, eh?' The vicar nodded at the rod in my hand and the gear hanging from my rucksack.

'Yeah.'

'Camping?' She smiled at the sleeping bag and tent I was carrying.

'You're very perceptive." I smiled. She laughed. She seemed pleasant enough. Nodding, I turned to go, milk bottle in hand. I aimed for the footpath through the fields and woods to my camping spot by the lake.

'I'm Mary Priest, by the way,' the vicar yelled after me.

Halfway to the footpath sign, I looked over my shoulder and laughed. 'Good name.'

'Almost as if it was my destined job," She said that. I once knew a copper called Robin Banks and a GP called Dr De'Ath. These things happen. Nominative determinism they call it.

I turned again to my route.

She shouted, "If you're around on Sunday, you're welcome at church.'

I raised a hand, half-turning so as not to be rude and smiling. 'Thank you. Maybe? Who knows?'

Sunday was tomorrow. I would be in the area, but I didn't plan to go to church; I would be too busy fishing.

I left the single street, then over the main road, which wasn't that main, stepped over a stile into the field, and left the village with its Victorian church spire behind me.

I strolled through a wood. The birds sang all around and the path was crowded in on both sides by foliage, made luxuriant by the recent rain and last week's sunshine. I dodged nettles and foxgloves, dock leaves and the spiky arms of hawthorn that grew wildly over the road, and then I stopped.

A man stood in front of me, right in the middle of the path. He was a grimy man in filthy clothes, and his hair hung in unkempt dreadlocks. His face was smeared with grease and dirt, and he wore Wellington boots, and in his hand, he had a plastic bottle of cheap cider. From the label, I saw it was the strong kind.

'All right?' I asked.

He nodded. 'Yeah.'

He didn't budge, just kept staring.

"Can I get past?' I asked.

'Sure.'

But still he didn't move. I had the glass milk bottle in my hand, and I might have to hit him with it. Or put the bottle down and punch him. I sighed. I didn't want to do anything like that.

'Listen, mate. I need to get past. No beef, no sweat, no trouble—just past.'

'Sure. You can get past.'

He still didn't move. I groaned. 'But I can't really, can I? You're blocking the way.'

'I can step into the wood.'

That would work. 'Right," I said. I waited until he did. But he didn't.

I sighed some more and walked forward. I stopped about three feet short of him because he stunk.

'Step aside then, or I swear I will deck you.'

I must admit I have decked men in my time.

I was in the Army for years, then when I was honourably discharged, worked security on the doors down Botchergate. But the truth is I don't like hitting people. When I hit a man, I've failed. But I still hit them if necessary and have to live with that sense of failure.

'I'm Raymond,' he said. And this time, he stepped aside into the trees. 'I like you,' he said.

'I'm glad.' When I was level with him, keeping a wary eye, I got a whiff of petrol as he took a gulp from the plastic bottle and wiped his lips with the back of his hand.

I shouldn't have asked, but I said, 'What the hell are you drinking, mate?'

'Raymond.'

'Yeah, Raymond. But what's in that bottle?'

'Petrol.'

I narrowed my eyes. 'You drink petrol?'

'Yeah.'

'Why?'

'Gets me drunk more than cider.'

'But petrol will kill you.'

'I'm still alive, though. I'm forty-two.'

His body was still alive, but I wasn't sure his brain was. I shook my head. 'You take care, mate.'

'Raymond.'

'Okay, you take care, Raymond.'

'What's your name?' he called after my back.

'Don't worry about that, Raymond. Bye-bye.'

I FOLLOWED the path through the fields and beside a dry stone wall until it came to a gate. From there, it was a short walk through an old oak wood and by the ancient stone church that stands at the water's edge on its own. I was camping on the lakeshore to the right of the church by the wood. It was a peaceful place with a view over the lake to the Derwent Fells beyond. Bassenthwaite Lake is the quietest of the lakes; you don't see many people on it. The land here belonged to a mate of my old commanding officer. He got me permission to be there. It's who you know, you see? I needed peace, and he knew it. This place helped me forget.

I pitched my two-man tent. I'm not the slender young lad I was, and I need a two-man these days. Tent up, I moved my chair close to the stove and got a brew going.

It was warm: June, as warm as it gets up here anyway. It would be chilly by eight o'clock, but still daylight way up to eleven so I could sit out in my coat and enjoy the dying day.

First, I set up my rod and sat by the water.

Fishing happily, I fell to thinking about nothing much: just how I like it—empty mind, and when the thoughts came up like little fishes, I watched them swim around and let them go on their way. I don't attach to thoughts and feelings. Mostly. And when I do, I try to unattach myself from memories and regrets as quickly as I can.

About eight, with the sun settled beyond the mountains to the west, I was in a pleasant mental state when something moved in the woodland to my right. I snapped my head around, old habits coming back, heart hammering, focusing on locating the threat.

It had gone. It must be a deer. Of course it was. I relaxed and laughed at myself.

But then I saw it again.

This time the shape emerged from the trees. It was my dread-locked friend Raymond.

I sighed. I did not need this.

He came halfway across the field towards my tent, but I put up a hand. 'No!'

He stopped. 'I thought you might want to talk.'

I shook my head. "I don't. I'm happy on my own.'

'Oh. But I need to tell you something.'

'No, you don't.'

'Just—"

'I'm not interested, mate.'

'Raymond.'

'Raymond, leave me alone. No offence. I need to be alone, okay?'

He paused. Then he said, 'But I need to warn you.'

'Warn me?'

'About the lake.'

'Don't worry, I'm not going swimming.'

'No, it's not that.'

I sighed. "What is it then?'

'It's about Eachy.'

'Eachy?' I began. Then I shook my head. 'No, Raymond. Bye-bye. Don't come back.'

I was a tall man. I probably looked mean, shaved head, muscular shoulders and arms. Mad as he was, he saw that. He turned and shuffled back to the woods. He called back, "I hope Eachy doesn't eat you.'

I groaned. This was my little happy place. Whoever Eachy was, I wasn't scared of him.

I DIDN'T SEE Raymond again that evening, so I presumed he'd left. I settled down in my camping chair by the lakeside while night took possession of the world. The land grew still, and the lake fell quiet.

The moon showed her face above the bulk of Skiddaw behind me. Moths fluttered, and three-month lambs bleated. Then I got a bite.

The pull on the rod roused me from my meditations. I gripped it and tested the strength of what had bitten. It was a tug, the tiniest pull. I shifted my hands on the rod.

For a minute, I thought I'd lost it, whatever it was. Then it tugged again. It was most likely a perch or a roach or even an eel. If I was lucky, maybe a salmon, if unlucky, a stick snagged on the line. I played the line, testing it, reeling it in. The moon didn't give much light to see by, but as I reeled it in, I saw something break surface about ten yards out, just rippling the still water.

It pulled back hard. I had a 20lb monofilament line, so it shouldn't break with most fish I would hook here. But I knew from the way it fought me, it wasn't a stick.

The thing broke surface again. I almost dropped the rod. Then I thought it must be an eel. It didn't look like a fish. It was long and sinuous. It must be an eel, but if it was, it was a big eel, a big heavy monstrous eel.

And then the line went slack. The first second I thought it had got free, the second second, I realised that the thing in the water was streaking to land, like the flick of an arm. Was it was a squid or an octopus? But what the hell was a squid or an octopus doing in an English lake?

I dropped the rod and jumped back. The shiny, long tentacle broke out of the water and came slithering across the stones and up the bank to the short grass where I stood, hand to my face. I shouted out, but it kept coming. It was a snake. I got one glimpse and then my nerve broke and I fled back across the field. I didn't stop running for a hundred yards, then I stood, hands on thighs, breathing hard.

What the hell was that thing? I'd never seen anything like it. I shook my head. It must have been a length of rubber pipe I'd hooked and pulled towards me, mistaking it for a snake. But it had moved so quickly.

But of course, it wasn't a snake; there were no water snakes in

Bassenthwaite Lake. It was because of the poor light, and I'd been half-dreaming when it caught on the line. It all followed from that.

I walked back to the shore and stopped. There was something in the grass by my tent. Something was snuffling around my tent. It was no rubber pipe because it moved as if it was exploring. And it wasn't a snake either. In the pale moonlight, I saw that it extended out of the water, across the shore, up the lip of grass and to the tent. And to my horror to its left, I saw another of them, also coming out of the water, but this time shuffling around in the grass, left of the tent and then another rubbery limb to the right.

All in all, there were four of the long tentacle things, and they moved around coiling like mealworms. And then, one by one, they slipped back into the water, and after the ripples subsided, the water grew quiet.

I had no idea what the hell I'd just seen. It shook me. My first thought was to go home, but I'd come on the bus, and it was now about half eleven at night. Then I thought I could go look in the village. The Sun Inn might have rooms. But I couldn't let my anxiety get the better of me. I'd had years of treatment to keep a lid on that, years of therapy and bottles of pills. All that was behind me. I was better than that. I wouldn't let fear ruin my life again.

As a compromise, I took my tent and in the dark, stumbling and cursing, using the LED tent light to see by, I put it up again in the churchyard among the old worn gravestones. The churchyard had an iron gate, and I made sure that it was closed. Then I settled in my sleeping bag. I felt strangely safer among the human dead than beside the lake and whatever it contained.

I fell asleep not long after dawn and woke three hours later with the sun hot on the plastic of the tent. Someone was moving outside. My heart beat fast, but I determined to face up to what was out there. I unzipped the double door and stuck my head and shoulders out. It was the woman vicar, Mary Priest.

'Oh, I'm sorry,' I said. 'I camped here because...' then I realised there was no possible way I could tell her why I'd moved the tent without looking like a wimp or a lunatic.

'I don't mind you camping here, though some of the parishioners might. It's Sunday,' she said. 'We only have a service at the church by the lake here every couple of months, but you're lucky—there's one today.'

What could I do? She'd been decent with me. I clambered out of the tent and joined the handful of elderly parishioners in that ancient church by the lake. I half-remembered some of the hymns from school, but I didn't take Holy Communion; I thought that would be hypocritical as I was never confirmed, and I'm not really a believer.

After the service, Mary came to find me by my tent. She said, 'I don't mind you being here, but as I said, some of the traditionalists don't like people camping on consecrated ground.'

'No, of course. I've got permission to camp in the field.'

She frowned. 'So, why...' then she grinned. 'Ah, don't tell me you're scared of Eachy, a tall strong man like you.'

'Eachy?'

'Lives in the lake.'

I felt my expression stiffen. I didn't want to show any surprise or fear. Raymond had mentioned Eachy too.

'What is it?'

'A monster.' She shrugged. 'I don't believe in it, but plenty do.'

'There's no such thing as monsters,' I blurted.

She smiled indulgently "Of course not. Well then.' She paused. She fished in her purse. 'I forgot I had this.' Then she handed me a small silver coin.

I stared at it in the palm of my hand. 'What's this for?'

'Turn it over.'

On the side I was looking at was the image of a crescent moon. I flipped it over and saw a tentacled squid thing. The coin was old and smooth.

She said, "Lots of the locals believe in Eachy. An old lady gave me that coin years ago. It's old, a talisman of protection, apparently.'

'But if Eachy isn't real, then I don't need a talisman.'

'Exactly.'

But still, the talisman nestled in my hand. She didn't move to take it back.

'How long are you staying?' she asked.

'I was planning on staying tonight, then going home tomorrow.'

She winked. 'Then you'd better keep the talisman. Put it back in the church before you go. Just slip it on the lectern under the Hymn Book.

I studied the talisman in my hand. The silver glinted in the sun. She walked off and waved as she went. 'I've got another service to give at Bewaldeth so I need to be off. Perhaps see you around?" She winked. "But move the tent.'

I watched Mary Priest walk off to where her car would be parked at the end of the track.

I took the hint. I moved the tent. I half thought about leaving as I took it down, but that would be giving in to cowardice, and besides, it was a beautiful day. I set the tent up again close to where I'd been the previous night before I ran away. A painted lady butterfly sunned itself on my tent. That must be a good sign.

My next visitor was Raymond. I smelled him before I saw him. Given Mary Priest's kindness to me, I repented of my previous attitude, so I said, 'Hello, Raymond.'

'Hello, mate,' he said. He was looking at me sideways on.

'What's up?' I said.

'I saw you talking to the vicar.'

'Did you? That was this morning.'

'I was watching.'

I said, 'You shouldn't spy on folk, Raymond. It's bad manners.'

He blinked. "Yeah, but she's evil.'

'I thought she was a vicar.'

"Yeah, a vicar. But she doesn't believe in God. She believes in Eachy.'

She'd struck me as a decent sort. This was more evidence that Raymond's mind wasn't in balance.

'Come on, Raymond. You don't actually believe in Eachy, do you?"

And as I said it, I remembered what had come out of the lake last night. In the June sunlight, it seemed unlikely that I'd seen what I thought I'd seen.

Raymond said, "She believes in Eachy. I bet she gave you something.'

"Gave me something?" That set me back. 'What do you mean?'

'She gave you a la'al coin, didn't she?'

'What?' How could he know that? And he looked suddenly concerned. 'But don't be fooled. I bet she told you it would keep Eachy away, but it won't. It will bring him. They've always worshipped Eachy here. They think he's a god, and they feed him. They don't love no other gods, not as much as they love Eachy.'

I rubbed my eyes. 'Can we stop talking about this now, please, Raymond?'

He stuck out his hand. "Give me the coin thing, or Eachy will come for you.'

My hand went to the talisman which I had in my pocket. I felt it between my fingers. There's no way I'd give a valuable antique to a crazy drunk like Raymond. He'd either try to spend it or throw it in the lake.

'She didn't give me anything.' I lied, and from the way he studied me, he knew I was lying. I even blushed.

He wheedled. "Please, mate. Give me that thing. Give me it, or Eachy will get you.'

I sighed heavily, exasperated. 'There is no Eachy, Raymond. Sorry, mate, but you drink petrol. So any Eachy you've seen is conjured by the petrol fumes.'

'Please, mister. I just want to help you and keep you safe. Give me the coin.' He looked almost pained, and I almost believed him, or at least I believed he believed himself, but I wasn't even close to giving him the coin.

Raymond stood there, holding out his grimy left hand. In his right, he held a nearly empty plastic bottle whose liquid sloshed as he shifted from foot to foot.

'I'm getting bored with this, Raymond. I don't mind you sitting here quiet, but I'm not going to talk to you about this. I came here for a few days peace and quiet, and I haven't had any yet.'

'Please,' he said.

'No. And if you are going to be like that, you'll have to leave.'

'Please, give me it."

At this, I half got up from my camping chair and growled. He fled like a scared bunny, and I felt terrible about that, but he was doing my head in.

About half an hour later, I went up to the Sun Inn and had a roast beef Sunday lunch and two pints of Jennings 'Snecklifter' ale. That smoothed things out, and I came back to do a bit of fishing. I caught a couple of perch and threw them back, but the sun was warm, and because I'd had a bad night the previous night, I dozed.

When I woke in the late afternoon, I brewed myself some tea on the mini gas stove. Tomorrow, I'd go home, but now finally, I had the peace I'd come for. It was still warm. My hand strayed to my pocket, and I pulled out the silver talisman. I turned it over and over between my fingers and watched as the squid emblem caught the light. Someone obviously believed in Eachy enough to make this talisman to keep him away, or even to attract him, to draw him out of the water like bait. But that conjured all sorts of images I didn't want in my head.

About an hour later, I was pottering about, and I chanced to look up the track, through the sparse oak wood, past the bleating sheep, and I saw someone at the far end of the field. I recognised the figure as that of Mary Priest, the vicar. I thought maybe she was coming to check if I was out of the churchyard. I lifted my hand to wave, but she didn't wave back. She was standing there watching, and then as I peered, I saw she had a pair of binoculars fixed on me. I know she didn't want me in her churchyard, but this was a step too far. I put down my hand. They were all weird here. It was a beautiful place, but she and Raymond had freaked me out. They both said, one laughing, the other serious, that they wanted to keep me safe from this Eachy thing. They were both crazy, and I wanted to have nothing more to do with either of them, or with Eachy.

I didn't need anything to protect me from an imaginary monster, so I decided to return the silver talisman to the church. I stepped inside the churchyard and walked down the path beside yellow buttercups, pink campion and wild roses that grew among the ancient tombstones. There was a sign on the door saying, 'Please close this door to prevent birds flying in and becoming trapped in the church".

I pushed the door and entered the hush. In the quiet of the evening, it was cool in there and smelled of Bibles and old stone and piety. I took the talisman from my pocket, stepped right up to the pulpit and placed it there by the hymn book. I hesitated a minute, then put the hymn book on top of the talisman so it was out of sight.

Back out of the church, it was a delightful evening, I went to the lake's edge and cast my line. Then I sat and waited.

And I fell asleep. I woke to the chill of the night. I sat in my camping chair, head lolling, and as I wiped my mouth and looked blearily around, I saw the moon halfway across the sky, playing hide and seek with the bright dots of Venus and Mars, washing the lake in silver. My line still reached into the water but was undisturbed. I shivered and stood, my legs stiff, my back aching.

The water rippled a hundred yards out. It was happening again. I stared out and saw one tentacle break out of the surface, then another, then another, until they were like a coiling nest of worms, seething over the dark surface of the lake. They moved fast, snaking across the water. I turned and ran. I headed for the churchyard, but the slithering limbs were already on the grass behind me. I risked a glance at the water as a huge bulk lifted itself out.

Panicking, I span round. I lost sense of where the churchyard was. Then the rubbery wet things snatched at me. One of the tentacles went for my ankle, but I jumped away from it, landing on another. I shrieked, repulsed at its squashiness and the slime that oozed from it. I stepped as if I was dancing on red-hot coals, trying to avoid the slithering limbs until one coiled around my calf and gripped me. I grabbed at it, trying to prise it off with my fingers and where I pulled it away it left burning sucker marks, oozing with blood, on my flesh.

I sprinted off, leaving the thing behind me, but when I looked over my shoulder, I saw the great bulk of Eachy—a fat, swollen thing silhouetted against the moon. Clusters of eyes on stalks protruded from its skull and they blinked and searched. Eachy's toothless mouth opened, strings of slime drooling from one mollusc-like jaw to the other.

In my terror, I tripped, going full length on grass wet with evening dew.

My stumble drew its attention, and Eachy's eye clusters flicked round. With a soft mouthy squelchy sound, Eacchy came sliding and slithering, multiple tentacles feeling their way across the grass, each quicker moving than a running man.

I struggled to get up; I got to my knees and ran further away from the lake. I would head inland. That must be the way to safety. But the tentacles moved quicker than I could run. They would catch me and pull me back to Eachy. Then I saw a figure in front of me. I stopped dead.

A voice hissed, "Mate!'

'Raymond?'

'Yeah.' He pointed to where Eachy's vast slimy bulk slithered across the field towards me. 'Eachy!' he said.

'How far can it come from the lake?' I gasped.

'As far as he likes." He reached out a hand. "Come with me, mate. I'll help you.'

I was ashamed of myself for mistrusting him. Just because of the way he looked, I had doubted him. And you can't judge a book by its cover.

'Please, Raymond. Is there a safe place?'

'Yes, in the wood by the lake. I've got a den.'

From the right, I saw the flick of a torch beam. It darted around in the wood.

'Come on,' Raymond said. 'It's that woman vicar. She wants to feed you to Eachy. She worships him.'

It was beyond belief, but after mistrusting Raymond, I now had faith. I'd been so short-sighted, so bigoted against his appearance, but in truth he was my saviour.

Raymond ran, and I ran after him. We went, not further inland but to the wood by the lake's edge.

Our change in direction seemed to confuse Eachy, and I wondered how well the thing could see. Then it rolled after us again.

Half a field away, Mary Priest emerged through the gate, torch in hand. She shone the beam at us, blinding me. "Come here!" she yelled. 'Come back.'

Raymond gasped. "Don't listen to her, mate. Come on.'

I trusted Raymond now. So I ran after him, and we came to the edge of the wood.

Eachy slithered and rolled across the grass like a rumbling truck. He was close now and before him came the snapping tentacles, some thin as whips, others fat like giant flat worms. One flicked at me as if tasting my breath, and then Eachy roared. The sound split the night and boomed from the lake and over the wood, reaching as far as the mountain bulk and echoing back in mockery.

Mary Priest was still yelling, but I was running so fast I felt my lungs would burst and my heart pounded so loud, and my breathing was so ragged that I couldn't hear a word she said.

Raymond stood in front of me at the wood's edge.

'Come on. Quick. Eachy's just behind."
I gasped. 'How is this safe?'
'Strong trees, close together.'
'What about the tentacles?'
'Don't worry about them. Come on.'
So I followed Raymond, the man I had scorned and now the man I trusted with my life. We were hardly in the woods, just a few trees deep when we came to a clearing.
'Here?'
'Here.'
The trees weren't so close together. I thought they had to be close together to keep Eachy out.
Raymond stood at the far edge of the small glade. 'Come to me.'
I frowned, puzzled, but that thing was close. It dragged itself to the wood's boundary.
Mary Priest was shouting, but she didn't seem to know where we'd gone.
I had to trust Raymond. He hadn't betrayed me so far.
I stepped towards him, and a rope snapped around my ankle. It yanked me in the air and I shot up like a rabbit in a trap, my leg cracking and pain shooting through me. I was snared. It was a rope trap, counterweighted with a boulder. Now I hung, head down, dangling by my broken leg, all my things falling from my pockets.
Outside the vicar yelled. It seemed she really had been trying to save me, but she had now no idea where I was.
And then the first tentacles burst into the clearing and wrapped around me, then the next and the next, their suckers lifting out lumps of flesh as they digested.
'Why?' I croaked.
'Well,' Raymond said. 'Eachy lets me have what he doesn't eat.' He lifted his plastic bottle and sloshed it around. 'I mean, a man can't live on petrol alone.'

CHAPTER 9
BELLA SHEEP HEAD

Bella was a babe. A babe who drifted into my life in the dreamy days of summer in the year I turned seventeen. That was also the year I learned to drive and I bought a banger with the money I'd saved up from doing jobs for my dad. It was a clapped-out old thing with a hole in the exhaust, but it ran. So I ran it around all the leafy back roads and the shady side roads and dusty main roads all that summer long. And it was because of that old banger of a car that I met Bella.

Bella lived locally, I believed—somewhere outside Broughton Moor on one of the farms. I figured that out when I was just getting to know her and hungry to learn every little thing about her.

Bella hadn't been to school with the rest of us, but in those days, a lot of the farmers' kids were erratic with their schooling, what with tatie-picking week and haymaking and lambing, they were rarely there.

That evening I met her, we were at the Miner's Arms, me and Henry and Red. I was driving, of course, and they were supping Matthew Brown's Light, which was about two per cent alcohol. I had

111

a pint of shandy made with Matty's Light and Underwood's lemon-ade, which meant there was hardly any alcohol in it at all.

So, about seven-thirty, in came Bella and stood at the door, glancing around as if she was looking for someone. It was a hot summer's evening. Henry, who fancied himself as a ladies' man shouted out, 'Ooo—lass. What's a stunner like you doing in a dive like this?'

Bella, though I didn't know her name then, simply smiled and said, 'I was looking for my friend.'

Red, who, despite the name, didn't have ginger hair, said, 'Who's your friend?"

Bella smiled and dodged the question. Henry grinned. 'Sit down, and I'll buy you a lager and lime."

I never expected her to agree. Why would a good-looking young woman come and sit down with a trio of ruffians like us with our denim jackets, bell-bottom jeans, and the scratty sideburns we were trying to grow? But she did sit down.

And she was stunning, stultifying, stupefying, seductive as a summer night. She smelled of sweet green grass, of white musk rose and yellow honeysuckle. She smelled like she was the countryside itself. Her hair hung long and dark and shone with health. She had brown eyes and strong eyebrows, and the ghost of a smile always haunted her mouth. That night, she wore a blue dress with yellow flowers printed on it and around her slender wrist, skin tanned light brown by the June sunshine; hung a bangle of crystals that glinted clear and green and red, each one a different shade. When she sat, she smiled at me. And I looked away.

Henry bought Bella a half pint of Slalom Lager with a touch of lime cordial, and Red started talking about the cricket. Not to be outdone, Henry told her about the steelworks where he was an apprentice, and I said nothing. I had nothing to say in her presence, she robbed me of rational thought. But from time to time I stole shy glances at her to find that every time I looked at her, she met my eyes, like I was the one she really wanted to talk to.

We never found out who Bella's friend was—the one she'd come to the Miners' Arms searching for. I had drunk one pint of shandy, and because I was driving, I was on orange juice and soda for the rest of the night. The lads and me planned to go on to Great Broughton to the Punch Bowl Inn, but I hesitated to leave because leaving here would mean leaving Bella, and because I'd never seen her before, I feared I'd never see her again.

In the end, the lads got restless. Red looked at his watch. 'We're meeting Howard at the Punch Bowl in fifteen minutes.'

Bella leaned over to me. "You've got a car?"

I nodded.

"You couldn't give me a lift home, could you?'

'Oooo!' Red and Henry chorused.

I flushed. My cheeks burned. 'Sure. Where do you live though?"

She said, 'Top of Dusty Lonning — on the way to Ellenborough.'

Red shook his head. 'Wrong way, love.'

It was the wrong way. Because Bella had given no encouragement to their tales of cricket or the steelworks apprentices shenanigans, they were now keen to move on. She had given me no encouragement either, but I wasn't wanting to leave. I wanted to get to know her better. I gave an awkward shrug. 'No problem, it'll only take five minutes to drive up there.'

'We've got to get to Great Broughton!" Henry said.

Red agreed. "Aye, come on. Sorry, lass. You'll have to walk.' He pointed to the window. 'It's a nice night.'

I cleared my throat. 'Listen, I'm driving. I say we give the lass a lift. We'll be with Howard soon enough.'

Bella touched my hand. 'Thank you,' she said.

The midsummer sun was still high in the sky as we drove down the narrow country lane, speeding past barley fields and cows and woods on either side, hearing the jackdaws clicking from the tree-tops, rooks cawing and blackbirds giving lyrical melodies into the evening air.

I pulled the car up at the bottom of Dusty Lonning, crunching onto gravel. The lane was a long unmade track with grass growing in the middle that led up the hill and away out of sight between high banks of hawthorn and blackthorn and elder bushes. 'Want me to drive you up to your farm?' I asked Bella.

Henry groaned. Red rolled his eyes. Bella said, 'No, Tom. You've been very kind bringing me this far. I can walk."

She was sitting in the front, and she leaned over and kissed me on the cheek. Her lips were soft and delicate, and she smelled of the living earth, of nature at its most bountiful, light and sweet and floral.

I blushed even harder as she walked away down Dusty Lonning, head half turned, hand raised in farewell.

'You're in there,' Henry said, climbing out of the back and sitting in the passenger seat.

'But you'll never see her again,' Red said. 'Get your foot down. We're late as it is.'

But I did see her again. I had been to Maryport to get some tiles my dad ordered, and I was on my way back, a quarter of a mile short of Sunny Slack, when I saw Bella strolling down the road to my left. She was slim and lithe and lovely, and the day was warm and the sunny weather had been unbroken for weeks. I slowed down and wound down the passenger window. Bella turned and grinned. 'Hello, you. I was just thinking about you and wondering whether we'd run into one another again.'

Thinking about me? I had a feeling like bluebells and sunshine and the sun glittering on waves rise up inside my chest. I couldn't help smiling. The smile smiled out of me, grinning, beaming, foolishly unable to control my joy.

I stammered, 'I've never seen you before. But you live round here. How come I don't know you?'

She shrugged. 'My family keeps itself to itself.'

'Where are you off now?' I asked.

'I was heading into Cockermouth to see my friend.'

'The same mysterious friend?" I asked.

She beamed, but didn't answer. I suddenly worried it might be a boy.

'I can give you a lift if you want,' I blurted.

'Oh, thank you, Tom.' Without hesitation, she pulled open the passenger door and got in beside me. I felt the warmth of her sitting there. I smelled her. She was just like heaven.

As we drove to Cockermouth, I said, 'Funny bumping into you like that.'

She shook her head. 'Not really. I think if two people are fated to meet, they will meet again.'

Fated? I gripped the steering wheel so I didn't faint and crash the car. Fated? Me and Bella? Now it felt like cream soda bubbling up in me, going down my arms. I was sun-blind and dizzy and joyful. Fated.

I pulled over by the Mayo Statue in the middle of town, but Bella didn't get out immediately. Instead, she sat as if waiting for something. After we sat for five silent minutes while I worked up my courage to ask her out, she stirred. She turned the handle, pushed open the door, got one shapely leg out, and I blurted, 'Bella, do you want to go out sometime?'

"Go out? What, me and you? On a date?"

I nodded, blushing. She could say no. If she did, I would die, but I'd get over it. It might take a while before I did, but I would. It would merely be my battered pride, my self respect crushed, hammered down, my self-esteem smashed into oblivion. I'd look a fool. Everyone would know she'd turned me down. I would be subject to mockery. The lads would say, 'He should have known he'd have no chance with her,' and the lasses would sneer and say, 'Tom Faulder? Please! He's vile. No lass would ever go out with him.'

'Sure,' she said.

'What?' I was blinking. I knew it looked unattractive. I was flushed red as a beetroot. That was probably unattractive too. But it was hot. I was sweating.

Bella laughed at me, and I didn't mind because it was the kind of laugh that meant she liked me. She stood glorious, beautiful, enchanting with her skin and teeth and eyes and hair. She was alive.

'Where do you want to go?" she said.

I hadn't thought that far ahead. But then I remembered places my parents went to. 'Moota?' I said. 'For chicken in a basket?'

'With Black Forest Gateau for pudding?' She was grinning.

'Of course, if you want.'

'You're on.'

We went to Moota that Saturday, and after that, me and Bella were an item. I was the envy of my friends, though I didn't see them as much. Sometimes she and I went to Moota, but mainly to the Wimpy in Workington and other times, we simply sat on the shore at Allonby and watched the sea and held hands.

Like most seventeen-year-old boys, I had an interest in more than holding hands. She'd let me kiss her, and we snogged for hours in my car. She'd let me put my hand round her shoulders, but if my hands wandered south, that was a no-no. She was a good girl, she said.

My mates would ask me about my progress, but I wouldn't tell them for two reasons. Firstly, this was between Bella and me, and our love was sacred and not for their ears; and secondly, I didn't want them to think I was a failure with girls.

The other thing that niggled me was that Bella never let me take her all the way home. She'd let me drop her at the bottom of Dusty Lonning but never let me drive up to the farm.

One evening when I drove her home, it was hammering rain.

'Come on, Bella. You can't walk in this.'

'I've got my umbrella.'

'Let me drive you up.'

She shook her head. 'No, that lonning's rough. It'll ruin your axles. I'll walk.'

I frowned hard. 'Are you ashamed of me?'

She blinked innocently. 'What do you mean?'

'You never let me take you home. You've never let me meet your family. Are you ashamed of being my girlfriend?'

She laughed and stroked my cheek. 'No, of course not, Tommy. You are so silly. You're lovely but a bit oversensitive.'

'Let me drive you home now.'

'No.' Her tone was firm. Her mind was made up.

'I'd like to meet your family,' I said.

There was the faintest flicker in her eyes. 'You will,' she said.'But not yet.'

'When?'

'When the Moon is right.'

'Eh? The moon? What's that got to do with it?'

She leaned in, kissed me and stepped out into the rain.

THE FOLLOWING WEDNESDAY, my uncle Phil popped round after we finished tea. He was doing some work on the roof with my dad, and I was in the parlour, reading the Advanced Dungeons & Dragons *Monster Manual*. Bella didn't know I liked D&D, and I planned to keep that little secret from her.

Uncle Phil said, "I hear you are running around with that Bella Sheep Head."

I sat up and scowled. 'What? Why do you call her that? She's beautiful.'

Phil said, 'Lives up Dusty Lonning?'

I nodded.

He grimaced. 'All them Sheep Heads are trouble.'

I always try to be respectful to my elders, but he was pushing it. I snapped,'You don't know anything about Bella.'

'Aye, but I know about the rest of them. Have you been to their farm yet?'

I shook my head.

'Aye, well, mind you don't.'

'Why not?'

He grimaced. 'There was a lad my age who went out with a lass from up Dusty Lonning. John Shipp, he was. He was in my class. And he was besotted with a lass from up there. They called her Bella too.'

I said, 'Must be her mother or her aunt.'

'Mebbe,' he said. 'Well, John Shipp disappeared. Never found. Vanished. They say once in a generation a lad goes missing up at Dusty Lonning.'

'Well, that won't happen me. She won't let me go up to the farm."

Uncle Phil nodded. "Just as well. I was a good friend of John Shipp. They never did find out where he went, and as for his girl-friend, Bella. She wasn't seen out and about again either."

THE WEEKS WENT ON. Then one night, Bella said, 'You can come to my house tomorrow if you want."

I raised my eyebrows "Tomorrow?' It was short notice as I was supposed to be going out with the lads, but Bella came first in my affections; she always did.

'Can you make it?' she smiled, teasing me. She knew I would.

'Sure. Of course. Yes.' I knew I was a tad too eager, but that's how I always was around Bella.

She said, "My family are out. Except for my mam. But she will be in her room.'

My eyes widened. We'd have the place more or less to ourselves. We wouldn't be in a cramped car. We'd be in a room with a sofa. A sofa.

'Do you have your own bedroom?' I blurted.

She winked. 'No, I share it with my sisters, but my sisters are out until later too."

I thought my heart would jump out of my chest.

She blew me a kiss. 'See you tomorrow, lover boy.'

I spruced myself up that night, squirting on the *Hai Karate* and wearing my best jeans and cowboy boots. I had on my denim jacket with the Hawkwind 'Warriors On The Edge of Time' patch on that my mam had sewn on. Underneath I wore a white t-shirt so I thought I looked a bit like The Fonz in *Happy Days*. On my way out, I bumped into Uncle Phil, chatting to my dad.

"Look who's got a date!' My dad grinned.

Phil scowled. 'You still courting that Bella lass?'

I nodded. 'I'm going to her farm for the first time.'

He frowned deeper.

My dad looked puzzled. 'What? The lad's done well. Have you seen her? She's a bonny la'al thing, that." That was my dad.

In measured tones, Uncle Phil said to him, 'You remember my pal, John Shipp?'

"Aye, that went missing.'

'Well, he was going with a Bella from Dusty Lonning.'

My dad scratched his forehead. 'The same family? I didn't realise she was from Dusty Lonning.' He was looking at me. "Sheep Heads?"

I shrugged. 'Why's it important?'

My dad tilted his head. 'C'mon, Phil. That was years ago. John Shipp's got nowt to do with our Tom.'

Phil pointed a bony finger. "Aye, but it was a moon like this.'

Though the sun was in the sky, the moon had also risen and hung like a pumice stone. Tonight it was tinged red.

'The blood moon,' Phil said.

'You believe owt,' my dad said. 'Come on. T' roofing's done. let's gah til't the Miners for a pint.'

Phil leaned into the bag that held his tools. 'Here,' he said. 'If you're going there, take this.' He gave me a screwdriver.

I weighed it in my hand. "A screwdriver? What do I want this for?'

"To defend yersel. Tek it.'

AND I LEFT THEM MUTTERING. I put the screwdriver on the back seat of the car. It was a warm night so I took off my denim jacket and slung it over the back seat, covering the screwdriver. Why would I need to defend myself? He was a nice bloke, Uncle Phil, but he could be an idiot sometimes.

Bella was waiting for me at the bottom of Dusty Lonning. She wore a white dress patterned with red and blue flowers and brown leather sandals. Her hair was down, and she had put on lipstick and blue eyeshadow. She looked like a dream.

'Hello, Tommy,' she said.

"Hello, Bella. You look nice."

"Thank you."

I didn't know why she'd met me at the bottom of the lane. I'd thought I would drive to the farm. But, instead, she got in the car. 'Take it easy on the lonning, Tom. It's full of holes.'

And it was true. The lane's surface was so pitted and potholed that it was pretty much unfit for vehicles. I shook my head. They had to get tractors and suchlike down this track? So why didn't they keep it in better repair?

As we drove up the lane, the sun sank, and the blood moon rose, growing brighter and redder and higher.

The farm came in sight as a run-down, ramshackle place. There are neat farms and dirty farms. This was a dirty one. There were a few pigsties here and there. It had become unusual for local farmers to keep pigs. Horses looked over a stable half-door, big shire horses. I heard cows lowing and the bleating of sheep from the nearby fields. I couldn't see any motorised machinery—nothing modern at all. It was like a farm from two hundred years ago. The roof wasn't even slated. It was thatched with rough bracken and heather.

Bella grimaced. 'Sorry about the state of the place. That's why I never wanted you to come.'

I parked out front. There was no sign of life from inside the farmhouse. 'Can I leave the car here?'

She nodded.

'You've got no tractors?"

'No, mam doesn't hold with machines. She prefers animals.'

'What does your dad say?'

Bella shrugged. 'My dad doesn't say owt. He does what mam tells him.'

The farmhouse was old and chill, and gloomy too. Bella lit an oil lamp that sat on a bracket in the wall.

'No electricity?' I said.

'No. My mam doesn't like electricity. Electrickery, she calls it. She prefers fire and wood.'

I shuddered standing in that dim hallway. Even though I was with Bella, and it was her house, I was uneasy. I imagined rough farmer brothers, unhappy that I was meddling with their sister's honour. I stepped back out of the house into the dimming evening light.

From inside the door, Bella smiled. "What's the matter, Tom? Are you scared of me now?'

'No.'

'Why are you trembling?'

'I'm not.'

'And your arms are all gooseflesh like you're frightened.'

'I'm cold.'

'Cold?' She pointed. 'With a big old moon in the sky like that to keep you warm?'

'It doesn't give off any heat,' I said. 'Only light.'

'Light enough to see you by,' she said.

Of course, I wasn't cold, and she was right. I was frightened, but I didn't want to admit that. I guess something instinctive took over born of my fear because I said, 'I need to get something from the car.'

I stepped over and out of her sight, reached under my denim jacket and dragged out the screwdriver. I slipped it in my right cowboy boot.

I hesitated at the door still, and Bella reached over, took my hand, and dragged me in.

'There's no one here," she said. 'We can have a little fun.'

I stammered. 'You said your mother was in.'

'Oh yes, but mam's room's at the back. So she won't bother us.'

'What do they call your mother?' I asked.

'Bella, like me. Why do you ask?'

I cleared my throat. 'Did you ever hear of a man called John Shipp?'

Bella took me through to their front room. There was a horsehair sofa and some chairs. No television, no wireless, no books even—just some tarnished horse brasses on the walls and faded prints of country scenes.

She sat on the sofa, but I remained standing.

She patted the sofa beside her. "Sit."

I was torn between the desire to have her in my arms, to run my hands over her beautiful body, to feel her respond to me; torn between that and pure fear. Fear of I knew not what, but fear nevertheless.

My teeth chattered.

'John Shipp?' she said.

In my unease, I'd forgotten I'd asked the question. Now I said, 'Yes, my uncle knew him. He went missing.'

'My dad's called John Shipp,' Bella said. 'Or at least he was.'

"He was?" I put my hand to my throat. 'What do you mean he was?'

Bella was smiling. She said, 'When men marry into my family, they take the woman's surname. It's just a tradition now."

A strange slobbering broke out somewhere further back in the house.

I jumped in my seat. 'What was that?'

'What?'

'That noise.'

The noise slobbered on, it sucked and it heaved. I jerked my head round but saw nothing.

Bella said, "Oh, don't worry, it's only my mam.'

'Making a noise like that? Shouldn't you go to see her? She didn't sound well.'

Bella shook her head. 'She'll wait.'

I was still sitting on the sofa. Bella went to look out of the window, peering up into the sky turned now dark blue where the gleaming moon shone like a bright red shirt button.

I realised I didn't know Bella's surname.

Bella began to unbutton her summer dress.

'What are you doing?' My mouth was dry, but even as I spoke the words, I watched her and lust battled with fear, and lust won.

Bella said, 'I thought you wanted to have your fun with me.'

"Why now? You would never even let me touch you before."

'Ah,' said Bella, 'But the moon's right now.'

'The moon?'

'The blood moon. You only get a blood moon as bright as this once every twenty years. The sky has rhythms, Tom, like the sea has rhythms. And the earth itself has its rhythms of life and death and reproduction. And Tom—" She gazed right at me with her dark brown eyes. Her skin dyed red by the light of the Blood Moon that spilled in through the dirty warped glass of the sitting room window. "—I have rhythms too.'

A thought inserted itself in my stream of emotion. I said, 'Was it twenty years ago that John Shipp married your mother?'

She laughed. 'He didn't marry her as such. At least not in a church. But yes. I'm nineteen now.'

'But they said John Ship went missing, that he was never seen again.'

"Oh, he can be seen. Do you want to see him, Tom?' she said. Her dress was open at the front, and she was naked underneath.

My hand trembled, my breathing was shallow and fast. I put my hand to my mouth. See John Shipp? What did she mean?

The slobbering noise came again. Now it had a low undertone to it, echoing after the first noise. It sounded like a monstrous thing was stirring. I stood. 'I should be going.'

Bella stepped in front of me. "Going? But we have hardly started.'

'No, I think I need to go.'

I side-stepped her and was at the sitting room door when the slobbering noise came again, this time accompanied by a dragging sound as if something immense was pulling itself along, heaving its bulk towards us. I stepped back into the room. Bella stood, her dress hanging off her shoulder.

'What the hell was that?' I said.

She laughed a tinkling little sound. 'I told you. It's mam.'

'What the hell is the matter with her—making noises like that?"

'She's feeling a bit fruity.'

'What?'

Bella reached out and took my hand. She grasped it tight. 'Let's go and see my dad. Don't worry, we can go out the side door, so we don't run into mam if you're scared of her.'

Bella didn't bother to button her dress up. Instead, she pulled me along, and I followed like a lamb. Bella led me out of the farmhouse side door into the farmyard. Low buildings lay ahead, shadows upon shadows, secrets hiding from the red moon.

Bella took me to the farm buildings, squeezing my hand tight.

In the moonlight, I could see the field to the left. It was full of sheep. At least they seemed like sheep; they bleated like sheep. But there was something odd about them—something wrong about the way they stood in the shadows. I stared. I tried to make out why they were so disturbing.

Some of them half stood as if on two legs. Others lay humped up with heads that seemed plain wrong for sheep.

'He's in here.' Bella pointed to a rough-looking building like a giant pigsty.

I blinked. "Your dad's in there?'

She nodded. She stepped forward and pulled open the door. 'Hello, Dad."

An old man, worn-out looking, with a long beard, naked, hung on a set of rusty manacles. Even in the moonlight, I could see his eyes were dull and senseless. He made snuffling noises, and grunts that might once have been words escaped him, muttered now by a man who had forgotten what words even meant.

'Oh, my god!' I said, jumping. John Shipp pulled against his chains, but he was weak and ill and he moaned and fell quiet

'Yes,' Bella said. 'There's no life left in him. We need new blood to keep up the breeding stock. We need to keep our flock healthy.'

A terrible insight dawned on me. "You mean me?'

'Well, why not? You're young and strong and nice. You'll make lots of healthy lambs.'

'But what? With you?'

Bella shook her head. 'My sisters and I aren't lambs. Some of us come out almost pure human. Mam uses we pretty ones to go fishing for new seed. We get you here and leave you to her. She's the breeder."

"Oh, my God," I said.

Bella shrugged. "I would have warmed you up for her if you'd wanted. It might even have been a bit of fun for you before what comes next. I even started to take off my dress to get you in the mood for her. But you were too scared, so I thought I'd bring you straight here.'

'What?'

Bella yanked open the door of the pigsty next to her father's prison. I stepped back, but she seized me and with inhuman strength, shoved me into the pigsty. With the force of her push, I went sprawling on the dirt. There were chains there, but she didn't chain me. She slammed the door shut, and I heard a key turn in the old lock.

'Don't worry,' Bella said. 'Mam won't keep you waiting long. From the noises she was making, she'll be here soon.'

'Bella!' I yelled. 'Don't leave me!'

She gave a mock wave. "Don't worry, Tommy. I'll be back in the morning with your food. We need to keep your strength up. I hope we can keep you as long as we kept dad.'

And then she was gone.

That awful slobbering sound started again. Something had come out of the house. Something was dragging itself across the farmyard. Something was coming to me. I quaked in dread. Then I remembered the screwdriver that I had in my boot. I pulled it out. In the poor light I tried to unscrew the lock plate from this side, but couldn't get the screwdriver into the screws at first. My hand trembled and all the time that noise filled my ears and turned my stomach. I panicked but got a bite with the screwdriver, but no matter how hard I turned, I couldn't budge them. The screws wouldn't turn because they were rusted in place.

The noise came closer, the awful dragging noise, the dreadful slobbering noise, the vile heaving noise, and with them the low moan of wild excitement, the inhuman muttering and gibbering.

Soon the door would be flung open. Soon I'd see that thing coming for me. Soon I'd feel its hot breath on me. Soon Bella Sheep Head would come, and I couldn't escape

Then I thought: I can undo the hinges. I switched my attention from the lock to the shoddy hinges of the old door. I pushed and rived and turned, and eventually, one screw budged. It took only seconds but felt like hours.

The thing dragged and heaved itself outside. Its vast misshapen bulk blocked out the light from the red moon.

I got three screws out, and the fourth fell away. So now for the bottom hinge.

Bella Sheep Head was at the door.

I kicked the wood. I kicked and kicked, and the wood collapsed and broke asunder.

There in the light of the Blood Moon, the twenty-year moon that signified it was time to get a new husband, I saw the thing in the farmyard. It was huge and bloated and fat. Its fleece hung off it in rags. Its huge sheep-head with slotted eyes stared at me. It had the legs and arms of a human woman, albeit gross and hanging with sheep's wool, but its head was that of a sheep. It couldn't walk; it was too corpulent for that. But it came after me nevertheless, pulling and heaving, driven by its awful lust.

I screamed and ran.

I got to the hedge and pushed my way through the thorns while Bella Sheep Head dragged herself after me. I ran through the field amongst the flock. Then, in the moonlight, I saw the monstrous hybrid creatures, partly sheep partly human. Some had human heads, blinking mildly up from their nighttime grazing, others had human legs or bottom halves, some were nearly all sheep apart from human ears and eyes, but all were awful, horrific monstrosities.

In the washed out light of the blood moon, I fled.

I GOT uncle Phil to recover my car when it was full daylight. But for me, I never went down Dusty Lonning again.

I went to the police station in Cockermouth. The sergeant was a local man. When I asked him if they would prosecute Bella and her family for kidnap, false imprisonment, bestiality even, the sergeant looked at me slowly. Then he said, "I don't think so, son. It's just country ways.'

CHAPTER 10

THE MOLE CATCHER OF BARBON

"I never see the moles on wires." John Myerscough who farmed at Treasonfield near Barbon said to Joe Whittaker, the mole-catcher.

"That's because I don't put them on the wires."

"All the others do."

Joe Whittaker shook his head. "Be that as it may, I never do."

"Then how do you scare them away?"

Joe snorted. "You think moles on fences scare other moles away? Don't be daft. They're blind and they live underground. They can't even see their dead family on the fences."

The sack rested on Joe Whittaker's broad shoulders rustled.

Myerscough planted his hands on his hips. "But you've got some secret. You've done me proud. No moles left on my land now."

Joe Whittaker tapped his nose. "That's my secret. The secret of my trade, if you like."

"Do you want a cup of tea?" Myerscough said.

Joe laughed. "So you can worm my secrets out of me? You'll need more than a cup of tea for that."

"I don't need your secrets. I haven't got time to be clearing moles.

Your rates are reasonable. If I need any moles, caught, I'll just ring you."

Joe was about to walk away when Myercough said, "There's new folk moved into the big house at Mansergh. That lawn's riddled with mole hills. I'd give them a knock."

"Are they local?" Joe asked. If he knew them, he'd be halfway to getting the job because the quality of his mole-catching was famed from Kirby Lonsdale up as far as Kirby Stephen.

Myerscough scratched his head. "No. They're from away."

"Away, eh? Where: south?"

Myerscough shrugged. "Aye, likely. Maybe America."

"America?"

"Or New Zealand. I forget which. I always mix them up."

"Do they speak English in New Zealand?"

"Oh, aye. But not like us." Then he nodded. "Oh, yes. I remembered: Cheshire."

"Cheshire? That far?"

"Yes."

"Pretty far south then. I've never been that far."

"No. Why would you?"

Joe said, "They speak English in Cheshire, don't they?"

"Oh, yes. Don't worry. But anyway. You should give them a knock."

Joe rubbed his chin. His youngest was still at medical school and his wife wasn't working on account of the injury. Money was tight. Maybe he should have a wander over to Mansergh. Maybe later.

When he was clear of Treasonfield and a look over his shoulder told him John Myerscough had retired and was no longer standing at the gate, Joe Whittaker relaxed. A few hundred yards further down the empty country lane, the barley fields waving in the slight breeze, the summer sun still not set but rooks cawing in the tops of the oaks and ashes and elms, Joe Whittaker eased the hessian sack from his shoulder and stopped.

Something moved in the sack. He settled it gently on the ground and loosened the rope at the sack's neck. More than one thing moved in the sack. Joe opened it further and laid it on the ground at the lane's edge. Lush grass sprinkled with buttercups and stitchwort, kidney vetch and white campion grew high.

"You can come out now," he said.

One mole then another scuttled out of the sack, paused a while then ran away into the grass, black velvet fur, big white digging paws and blinking blind eyes. Three, four, then five, escaped into the grass and away. More than five, maybe ten went and Joe Whittaker the mole catcher called after them.

"And don't go back to Treasonfield. Old Myerscough'll have you if you do."

You see, Joe Whittaker was a mole-whisperer. He told the moles of the danger they were in, and offered them a way out: in his sack. He spoke to them. Whatever they understood—his words, or his tone of voice or the non-threatening body language, Joe Whittaker called the moles like a latter-day pied piper of the little gentlemen in black velvet waistcoats, and they came to his call.

He never killed a one of them. Others thought he must, but he merely took them somewhere safer to live. The landowners were happy, the moles were happy and Joe Whittaker could live with his conscience and go back to the cottage with roses around the door where he lived with his wife, Sheila.

And there he went that night. The sun was still up in the long summer evening in the north and Sheila gave him a kiss on his cheek and told him she'd made chilli. You'd expect Joe Whittaker to be a traditionalist and like his meat and two veg, preferably boiled beef with boiled carrots and boiled cabbage, but Joe Whittaker liked it spicy. He ate his food so hot that Shiela when she ate with him had to have a glass of milk to hand to counter the burn.

"How's the money?" Sheila asked.

"Tight," Joe said, rolling his chilli beef into a soft burrito and taking the bottle of chipotle sauce.

"Just the hoover's broke."

"Aye."

"And the washing machine's on its last legs."

"I know. Don't worry. I'll sort it. There's some new folk moved into Mansergh, the big house."

"Who are they?"

"They're not local—from away."

"Away? Where?"

"Cheshire."

"I've never been to Cheshire."

Joe shrugged. "I can't see the need. We've got all we want in Barbon."

Joe finished his burrito and then went to the pub where he had three pints of Robinson's Old Ginger Tom and sang folk songs with the youngsters—such gems as *Green Grow The Rushes–O!*, *The Lish Young Buy A Broom* and *The Appleby Election Hornpipe*. Joe didn't quite understand it but there were some of the lads who sampled his vocals and layered hauntological meanderings in an ambient, electronica fusion and put it out on Bandcamp. They bought him a pint every now and again to say thank you.

Joe wandered home, found Sheila asleep, snuggled in beside her and slept well on Old Tom, though Sheila told him in the morning, that he'd snored.

He didn't believe her. She often said things like that. She'd probably just dreamt it.

That morning he was up, and with time to spare, walked through the fine midsummer fields and woods until he came to Mansergh and there regarded The Big House. It had been empty since the Winchesters had died off. There had been trouble letting it because of rumours that it was haunted. Of course that was stuff and nonsense. The house was surrounded by a screen of yews and holly trees. It must be dark and damp in that house, he thought, standing now by the old stone gate with its chipped stone lions and rusty chain. He did notice that there was a shiny new padlock, but it was open. From here, he could also see the lawn looked like the moles had run riot, with their little hills all over the place in lines back and forward where they had dug their tunnels, hunting earthworms.

Joe didn't mind moles digging holes, but he worried for them. If the new owners were agin them, they might put poison down or traps that would snap the li'le gentlemen in half as they tunnelled blithely along. He couldn't be having that. Besides, he would expect some cash for his efforts at rehoming the mowdiwarp clan.

Sucking his teeth, Joe pushed at the gate and stepped in. The gravel path when he walked on it to the front of the house was full of weeds. The door, when he got there, needed painting. The brass knocker when he lifted it to knock, could do with some Brasso to shine it up. Sheila would never leave their knocker (shaped like a mole) so dull.

The knocker came down with a thud, thud, thud. And he waited.

Joe Whittaker was not a nervous man. In the course of his working life, he'd seen things that would make other men quail and shudder, but never him. But there was something about the pregnant silence that hung on this place that disquieted him.

He shook his head to clear away such fancies and smiled at himself for his foolishness. But still, he shifted his weight and bit his lip.

He brought the dull brass knocker down again three times. After a minute, he was minded to leave and half turned on his heel then he heard the sound of slow, heavy footsteps inside. As he'd turned to leave, he'd had sight again of the mess of mole hills, mini Alps across the mossy lawn and thought again of how people didn't love moles as he did: not even Barbon folk so heaven alone knew what someone from Cheshire would do with the li'le fellas.

So Joe Whittaker stopped there when he should have started off and that was his undoing.

There was a clanking of chains and a turning of locks and eventually the weatherworn front door opened and a man was revealed. He was a big man in roundness if not in height, with brown hair plastered in a cowlick over his greasy forehead. He had bright button eyes like a teddy bear, brown as the glass of a beer bottle. His lips were thick and blubbery and he licked them with his froggy tongue before he spoke: "Yes?"

Joe wondered if all the folk from Cheshire looked like this. He hoped not, for if so it was a place he'd never visit. But perhaps this man was particularly ill-favoured even for Cheshire men with his stomach engaged in a wrestling match with his leathern belt and his white shirt out like a marquee in full-wind and his hands stuffed in the pockets of his tweed jacket.

"Yes?" he said again, licking his lips once more as if in the intervening second they may have dried up.

Joe pointed. "Just, the moles."

"The moles?"

"Aye, moles, mowdiwarps, you know."

That seemed to register with the man. "What of them?"

"Just that you have a lot." He pointed to the ruined lawn.

The man shrugged. "Then we'll poison them. No matter."

Joe winced. "Oh, sir, you shouldn't do that. They are only doing what the Good Lord gave them to do."

"The Good Lord, eh? Are you a religious man?"

Joe remembered the last time he was in church which had been for the Christening of his grand-niece Darcy and the time before that which had been on Christmas Eve after a few pints of Old Ginger Tom. "I'm more spiritual than religious."

The man sniggered. "Oh, that. That won't offer you much protection." Then he said, "What's your offer?"

"For the moles?"

"Or your soul."

"What? My soul?" Joe thought that was a queer thing to say. His soul was his own business. He gave a nervous cough. "I'll get rid of all the moles and guarantee no more for a year for…" He sized the man up. He looked well-heeled. "Twenty-five pounds."

"Twenty-five pounds is a rare price. My master will give you twenty."

Joe stuck to his guns. He had costs. "No, sir. Twenty-five pounds and not a penny less. Ask anyone, I'm the best mole-catcher for miles."

The man studied him. "Very well. My master will give you twenty-five pounds. But on two conditions."

Joe cocked his head. "And they are?"

"That you complete the work today, and that you guarantee we will be free of the vermin for a year and a day, not just a year."

Neither of those seemed to pose a particular problem, so Joe agreed. Then he said, "But why a year and a day?"

The man gave a slobbery smile. "Because my master's bargains are always for a year and a day."

"And what is the name of your master, if I may ask?"

"My master is Alex Sanders."

"Oh?"

"The King of the Witches. You may have heard of him?"

Joe hadn't. It seemed a queer job being king of the witches. He didn't even know the witches had a king. He'd have thought it more likely they'd have a queen, if he'd ever thought about it at all.

"So you can do this in a day?" the man asked.

"Aye, yis, aye." Joe nodded. "I'll need cash. I used to have one of them card readers for contactless payments, but it was unreliable."

"Cash is fine. But only after the job is done. Come after dark for your money."

"After dark?" That would be late as it was June.

"After dark."

Joe shrugged. "Very well."

• • •

JOE WENT HOME to get his sacks and his special ingredients. Without giving too much away he drew the moles with a special powder whose recipe had been given to him by his father who had got it in his turn from his mother who was a Wise Woman from out Gawthrop. Every spring, Joe would sit in his shed and prepare batches of the Mole Powder which contained essence of marigold and tincture of daffodil and some other special ingredients which it wouldn't be prudent to give in detail other than to allude that they contained dried Liberty Cap mushrooms with slivers of Sativa leaves. Whatever they contained, the moles loved them and it made them docile.

So around eleven a.m., with the sun high and bright, Joe Whittaker entered that dark garden and worked behind the screening yew and holly trees and walked the moss ruined lawn and summoned his little friends.

It's hard to say what moles know. It's harder even to say whether moles talk to each other and whether the tribe of Barbon Moles knew of and chittered about Joe Whittaker the kindly mole-catcher, but it would nice to think they thought fondly of him and knew when he came to call his intention was to save them from a dreadful fate.

But come they did, half drowsy on his tincture, and he smuggled them into his hessian sacks. The sleepy moles nestled into one another until he shouldered the sack, went out of the gate between the chipped guardian lions and ushered his drowsy charges into the buttercup meadow near the River Lune.

When he got back after his first trip, something caught his eye. The Big House had a tall Victorian Tower and Joe was sure that someone watched him from behind the ivied windows. Despite the warmth of the day, and without knowing why, Joe Whittaker shivered.

Joe worked hard all day, and by dusk his work was done. No more moles were to be found on the grounds of the big house and he had told the moles, whether they understood or not, though he liked to think they did, not to return for a year and a day. He was quite specific about that, for he was a man of his word.

Joe began to crave a pint of Ginger Tom and a sing-song in the pub and so he checked the western sky to judge whether the sun was really down and when he thought it was, he walked up the beweeded way to the heavy front door and lifted the brass knocker to call the man so he could get his pay and be away to the inn.

The knocker thudded dully on the wood. Joe glanced around him and saw not a light in any window. The tower from which he thought he'd been watched was out of sight from where he stood now, so he couldn't see if anyone still lurked there.

No one came. That irked Joe. He'd done a good day's work and now wanted his fair day's pay. He hoped they weren't the sort to go back on an agreement, though he had heard that folk from away were like that.

He grumbled to himself and knocked again. This time, the door creaked slowly open as if someone had pulled it on a string. He'd been sure it was shut fast but he hadn't heard the mechanism open. Perhaps the wind had caught it.

Joe Whittaker stood there as the door swung open to its full extent, revealed the shadowy gloom of the house within. A cool breeze blew and brought up gooseflesh on his arms that had were not long since warm and dried the film of honest sweat on his brow. But the strange thing was that the breeze came from inside the house. He stood and peered but saw no one. He leaned on the door jam and turned his head to listen but heard no one either.

He sighed heavily. He needed his money, but there was something forbidding about the house. He put his hand to his mouth and bellowed, "Hello! It's Joe the Mole Catcher."

But his only reply was the sound of wood settling and creaking deep within the belly of the house.

Joe's mouth was dry. He looked behind him at the path that led to the gate and the gate that led to the lane and the lane that led eventually to the Barbon Inn and his own little house where Sheila would be sitting, waiting for him to come home.

"Hello!" he tried again, but all he had in reply was his own voice echoing in the empty corridors and soon fading away. Joe decided he wanted his money. He'd been in the garden all day and no one had left, he was sure of that, so the slimy man must still be in the house. He was sure now they wanted to cheat him and not pay him for his work. Part of him thought about bringing back the moles but then the man and his master would poison them. He would never expose his little friends to that.

He could leave. He could try the next day. But Joe was a firm and resolute man. He was quick to smile and slow to anger. But he wouldn't be made a fool of, so he stepped inside the house.

The place was desolate. The many rooms were mostly empty. Some sticks of furniture stood here and there, what looked like a piano covered by a dust sheet but no curtains on the windows so that what remained of the daylight seeped in. Just enough to stop him tripping up over himself.

He called as he went. It was so quiet. And then when he was halfway down the corridor from the entrance hall, the front door closed on its own.

He spun round. It was now much darker. He could still see a little so he found a wall switch and flicked it and to his wonder, light came on. It wasn't much of a light — one sixty-watt bulb in a light fitting that should have five bulbs, but enough to see that the corridor came to a hall where a large stairway went up and a smaller stairway went down.

He shouted out again, but this time there was a reply. A voice he recognised as belonging the the fat man in the tweed jacket called back.

"Just down here."

It came from the stairs leading down.

"Down there?"

"Yes. I have your money here. Come down."

Joe scratched his head. This was most odd. "Can't you come up?"

"No, you'll see why. It's perfectly safe."

Joe didn't like this. But if he didn't go down he would look and feel cowardly and foolish. He put his foot on the top of the stair and his hand on the bannister. "Where are you?"

"Just down here in the cellar." The man called back.

"What are you doing in the cellar?"

"Come down and you'll see."

Seeing nothing else for it, Joe Whittaker descended. Step, by creaking step, he went down, until the poor light of a dim bulb dangling from the ceiling by a dirty wire showed the man in the tweed jacket. He stood at the end of a series of rooms. It looked like a set of Victorian cellars, one after another but the doors between them were all open. The man sat on a plain wooden chair and in his hand he held bank notes. He waved them like bait.

Joe hesitated. "There's no need to make a do of this. I did the work. I deserve to be paid. No fuss required."

The man sat. He appeared to be sweating. The light was poor and there was a strange atmosphere down here – heavy as if house was waiting for something.

"What are you waiting for?" the man said. "Come and get your wages."

But still Joe hesitated. He felt dizzy. He felt something coming up on him unawares, out of sight. He felt something still there, watching, scuttling, waiting. "You come to me," he said finally.

The man laughed. "Oh, no, Joe. If you want your pay. Here it is."

Joe sighed, shrugged, stepped forward. He moved through the first cellar. The tweed jacket man sat watching, grinning, waving the cash. "Just another cellar to go through."

Some sixth sense rang alarm bells, but Joe wasn't a superstitious man. He ignored it. "Here," Tweed jacket said. "You can almost smell it."

Joe thought he'd grab the cash and beat a hasty retreat. Something about this place made him very frightened.

Before Joe got two steps into the middle cellar, the man pressed something and steel grilles slammed down before and behind Joe. He span round and saw he was trapped.

"What? Let me go!" Joe yelled.

But the man just laughed. "My master will see you soon. When midnight rings out on the old clock, he will descend the stairs and come and visit you. And in his hand he will have a knife and that knife will be so sharp it would cut off your finger and you would feel nothing until you saw the severed stump."

"What do you want with me?" Joe said. "I'm only the mole catcher."

"But you're a man with a beating heart and my master has need of beating hearts for his work."

"What work would he have that needed a beating heart?"

"The work of calling spirits to do his bidding. They get hungry and a human heart is a little treat that sweetens them and makes them more eager to do their part."

"But—"

"Enough talk. We won't meet again. And you won't be needing this." With a flick of his hand he stuffed Joe's pay into the silk-lined pocket of his tweed jacket. Then he rose, stretched his legs, scratched his arm and left by another staircase, leaving Joe alone in the cellar.

Joe checked his watch. It was nearly ten p.m.

The light was poor but in the corner, by the wall he saw the smear of dried blood. Someone had bled in this cellar before tonight, and they had bled copiously, enough to die from.

Joe paced. He grabbed the iron grilles on both doorways and shook them until they could be shook no more, but still they didn't budge. He heaved and he lifted but there was no way he could escape. He checked his watch: ten thirty p.m.

He tried the cage again. He didn't doubt the evil intent of these people. He'd seen the blood. The occult had driven them insane. He didn't doubt they would harm him.

And then it was eleven o' clock.

More pacing until it was eleven thirty

Joe Whittaker's time was running out and for the first time in his life, he got on his knees and prayed. He didn't want to die. He had a life to lead. He had Sheila. He had his daughters. He thought how he saved the moles and wished someone would save him.

And then he heard the grandfather clock distantly chime the quarter hour. He had fifteen minutes to live. Sweat dripped from his brow. He was still on his knees, facing the grille that showed the stairs down which his killer would come.

Five minutes before twelve, he heard the sound of someone above.

Someone was walking on the corridor above his head.

Three minutes before twelve, he heard the sound of feet on the stairs.

Two minutes before twelve, he saw the legs of the man who had come to cut out his heart.

A minute before twelve, the man with the knife entered the cellar

At twelve midnight, he saw the flash of the knife, he saw the gleam of madness in the eyes of his assassin, he heard the sound of his breath.

So this was the King of the Witches.

Joe Whittaker prayed. If there was a King of the Witches then there might be a King of the Moles.

The tweed man was behind his master. He pressed a button and the steel grille rattled up

The king of the witches stood, a wicked knife in his hand. It was of the sharpest steel, a kitchen knife designed for filleting. The King of the Witches stepped towards Joe, knife outstretched, madness in his glinting eyes, drool on his insane lips. His excitement evident on his deranged face.

And Joe prayed harder.

And behind him came a rumbling.

The King of the Witches looked past Joe as if something was happening. Joe turned round to see the floor heave up, the plain tiles cast aside as something burrowed up from below. The King of the Witches stopped and stared and behind Joe, a huge mole emerged from the hole, its whiskers twitching, its blind eyes blinking, its huge paws pushing aside the soil.

The King of the Witches screamed and the Man in Tweed screamed behind him and both of them ran at Joe.

But Joe felt the Mole King call him, and he turned and followed the great mole as it delved into the earth. The passage was big enough to crawl through and he hurried after the Mole King. Behind them, the King of the Witches entered the tunnel, but the Mole King was not alone. A hundred small moles also toiled in the earth, and they dug and they heaved and they collapsed the tunnel behind Joe and they buried the King of the Witches and his wicked Man in Tweed.

Joe continued after the Mole King and emerged in the garden in front of the Big House. He stood there gasping in the moonlight. The great mole bowed and then left him, digging its way into the earth and Joe thought he heard the mole say, "Thank you for what you have done for my folk."

Joe Whittaker staggered his way back to Barbon and almost collapsed as he came through the door of his cottage. Sheila stood there alarmed. "Joe Whittaker!" She said. "Look at the state of you. You're all clarted up! You look like you've rolled in a midden."

Joe Whittaker was hardly able to stand. With one hand on the door frame, he said, "Well, Sheila. It's a long story, but if you'd like me to tell you, I will. But first, could you bring me a bottle of Old Ginger Tom from the kitchen, and pour it into my favourite tankard, if you don't mind."

And Sheila Whittaker did just that. And Joe told her the story but Sheila didn't believe a word.

The next Saturday, Joe went to Kendal and in one of them craft shops they have there he saw a little silver brooch that was fashioned in the shape of a mole. It was a funny little thing and had sat in that shop for a long time as no one much fancied a mole brooch, but Joe bought it and took it home to Sheila.

"What is it?" she asked as he handed her the little package wrapped in tissue paper

"Open it and see."

Open it she did and she picked up the silver mole and pinned it to her cardigan. "A mole!" she said. "How appropriate!"

"Aye, lass," Joe replied. "More than you'll ever know. More than you will ever know."

CHAPTER 11

THE TRICKING OF LORD THOMAS

L ord Thomas went hunting. On his fine bay horse on that fine Autumn day, he rode from the great priory at Lanercost in the Vale of Irthing, on and down through Geltsdale, riding all the day long until he had reached as far as Castle Carrock and then, having lost the rest of his party, and his fine bay horse was weary and sweating, he came to a halt under the fell known as Tarnmonath.

He rested there and ate while he watched the eagles soar over the ridge to the south. And as he ate, he heard a man coming close.

Lord Thomas turned, hand ready on his sword, but then stood easy for it was only an elderly wanderer dressed in the habit of a brown friar. This one could be no threat to such a strong young man as Thomas Neville, youngest son of the Lord Warden of the West March, so Thomas's grip relaxed on the hilt of his fine sword, and he offered the stranger a greeting.

'Hail, father. Good day to you, doing God's work, praying as you walk in this wild country." Thomas talked, intending to put that man at his ease so he would not be afeard of the fine young lord with the long silver sword in its scabbard decorated with gold wire and shining stones. But the man only watched him, his long face peering from beneath the folds of his hood, his thin arms—strangely pale—visible within the cuffs of his simple, homespun habit.

Despite the feeble look of the man, Thomas's horse shied away and threw up its head. Thomas gripped its bridle and whispered comfort to it. The horse settled. There was something about this stranger, and Thomas thought of the tales of the elves and fairies who were said to walk this land in disguise. But Lord Thomas was a worldly man, and he didn't believe in such creatures.

Calming his horse's wildness and holding it tight, though it snorted and rolled its eyes still, Thomas offered the man bread, cheese and meat, and even a sup of Frankish wine.

The man shook his head. 'I want not bread nor cheese, nor yet wine from thee, Thomas Neville.'

Lord Thomas smiled. "You know me?' He was flattered by the stranger knowing his name, for he was a proud man, though that pride had nothing evil in it, only the joy of a young man, arising from his state in life and his high born blood.

The man said, "Truly I know thee, Thomas Neville, and I know what thou wilt, the most secret desires of thine heart. Perhaps I know it even more clearly than thou, thyself.'

'And what do I wish, father?' Lord Thomas grinned. 'Tell me my dearest desires, for you make me curious.'

'You wish to be greater in rank than your father, John Neville, Earl of Westmorland, even though he be Lord Warden of the West March of England, and as well as this, you wish to be greater in rank than your brother Ralph Neville who will be earl after him.'

Lord Thomas blushed. He had thought his ambitions were known only to himself though perhaps guessed at by his wife, Maud. He dearly loved both his father and his brother, but with them living, he would never succeed to high rank, being only the younger son. Because he loved them, he would never harm them, and so it seemed to him that his ambitions would come to nought, and so instead of seeking advancement, he spent his time in hunting and jousting and wishing for war, for on the field of battle he might show his mettle.

But this man had known what he had never told a living soul, and he said hastily, 'But what rank that I could attain would be greater than that of my father or my elder brother?'

'You know well what you want, Thomas.'

'Do I?'

The stranger laughed, and his eyes were dark and they unnerved Thomas with the sharpness of their stare. 'Yes, you do, Lord Thomas Neville. Because Lord Thomas Neville wishes to be king of England.'

Thomas glanced away back at the eagle that soared high above the mountain. But he said nothing, for the stranger had guessed true.

The man continued. 'And I alone can give this rank to thee.'

Lord Thomas snorted. 'And who art thou then but a poorly clad stranger, wandering the wilds of Cumberland as if he had no roof to shelter him. Who art thou who could give me the throne of England?" He added hurriedly, "Even if I wished it.'

The wanderer said, "If I give thee the crown of England, there will be a price to be paid.'

And Lord Thomas could not answer. His brow knitted, and his lips pursed as if to speak but he merely watched the brown-clad man as the stranger began to walk away down the path.

Thomas called after him. 'What about the crown of Scotland?" He said it in jest, but in truth it was only half jest.

Over his shoulder, the stranger called back. 'That too can be thine. But that too will cost thee a price dear to thy heart.'

Without halt or a backward glance, the stranger continued north along the fell path, and was going out of sight.

Just then, Lord Thomas's two men at arms caught up with him. 'Lord, you should not have gone off at such a tilt. We lost you until now.'

This was John Marr who spoke. Thomas shook his head and gestured. 'The only danger I came across was that poor old friar.'

Another of the men at arms spoke, a dark-haired Cumbrian man called Mungo, 'That is no friar, my Lord.'

Thomas shook his head. 'No? I took him as such.'

John Marr looked down from his saddle. 'No, Lord, not a friar, nor even a Christian soul."

Lord Thomas frowned. 'Who then is it?'

'That is Michael Scot, a sorcerer.'

BARELY A WEEK LATER, outside Naworth Castle, Lady Maud pulled at her husband's gloved hand as he sat by her mounted on his fine bay stallion. 'Do you have to go?' She asked.

The September breeze was chill, the year was turning, and winter would soon follow a brief autumn in the north country.

Lord Thomas Neville shifted uneasily in his saddle. The men at arms with him watched blankly, ready to follow his every word whether that led them to life or to death.

Though the grey stone of Naworth Castle stood sombrely behind them to the south, Lord Neville's eyes always strayed to the north.

'I will be back as soon as I can, my love,' Thomas said.

'But how long will that be — weeks? Months?" Her face fell. "Don't say months, my love."

Thomas shrugged. 'As long as it takes me to find what I need.'

Maud brought the sleeve of her gown to her face. She whispered, 'But do you truly need it?'

His mouth straightened as if this was a subject they had discussed before, rehearsing the same arguments both of them for and against. Emboldened by Michael Scot's words, he had decided to unburden himself and share his desire for great rank with his wife.

'I will be king,' he said.

'I am happy for you to remain a baron.'

'The second son! I won't settle for that. I will never be earl while my brother lives, and I wish him long life. Natural means will never make me king, so I must seek out the less natural.'

His horse grew restless, perhaps sensing his mood, so Thomas said, 'The day is wasting. We have miles to travel, and we had best be gone.'

At his words, the two men at arms with their long spears and small shields stirred on their shaggy border ponies.

Lady Maud's eyes shone with tears. 'Come back soon,' she said. 'Your daughter and I will be waiting.'

Lord Thomas bent to kiss Maud. 'Give my love to Isabel.' And then the three men rode off, heading out from Naworth, north beside the beck called Pol Teyrnan until they crossed the River Irthing at Lanercost.

LORD THOMAS and his companions journeyed north to Bewcastle and then over the wild moors as far as Hawick, and further to Jedburgh and Roxburgh and everywhere they went they asked the whereabouts of Michael Scot's tower, and everywhere they asked those they asked grew dark-faced, and some crossed themselves, and all left without speaking until it seemed Lord Thomas would never find the man who had promised him a crown.

The weather broke with flurries of snow across the vast, empty hills, and Lord Thomas and his two companions drew their cloaks around them, and their horses trudged on through sedge and heather over the bad, broken ground.

'My Lord, we should seek shelter for the night," Dark-haired Mungo said, pointing to the lowering clouds and the darkening horizon.

'Aye, sir, he's right,' said John Marr, sitting tall in his saddle, straining to see in the gathering gloom. 'What is that yonder? A building?'

Lord Thomas looked and saw a tower set up against the dark crest of a drear hill. "Without doubt, the lord of that place will give us shelter for the night.'

But the tower stood farther off than they thought, and as they rode, the mist rolled down from the higher ground as the clouds came to earth and bathed it in their melancholy grey.

'It's hard to see, Lord,' John Marr said.

Lord Thomas turned his head. 'Where is Mungo?'

Mungo was no longer with them. It seemed they had been separated in the murk, and they called out, but their voices were quietened by the rolling air and hushed by the acres of marsh and pools of dark water from which the bullrushes grew. And after some searching, they did not find Mungo but trusted he would make himself safe, for he was a resourceful man and no stranger to these wildernesses of the debated border.

'Which way was the lone tower?' Called Lord Thomas, and John Marr pointed. 'That way, I think. But I'm no longer sure.'

As they rode farther, the fog thickened, and the night fell, and they could see nothing, not even each other, and when Lord Thomas next turned, he found himself alone. Thomas stopped and cupped his hands to his mouth and called, but the only reply was the echo of his own voice from the empty wind ringing in the hollow mist.

And having no other choice, for there was no shelter near him there, and in that cold place a night without shelter was not something he relished, he took his reins in hand, gently urged his stallion with his heels, and rode on.

Of a sudden, the lone tower loomed up in front of him out of the darkness. And close-to he saw a broken building of lichen-clad limestone whose stones had fallen and whose windows were owl-haunted and blocked by grass and ivy.

He would not find the warmth and welcome of a lord's manor here. But some walls were better than none so he dismounted and led his horse through the door into the ruined hall so the stallion too would benefit from the shelter of its walls. Damp stood the walls, but they still held out some of the weather.

Lord Thomas had with him flint and iron, and he made sparks by striking them against wood shavings and dried leaves until there was a small blaze, and around that, he built a cage of the twigs that had fallen from crow's nests in that lonely place. His horse stamped in the corner, and he fed the fire with bigger sticks and he dried chunks of log fetched from a stand of trees outside, laying them around the uncertain blaze until that wood was dry enough to burn, and then he sat and smelled the smoke and hoped the light of the flame would be a beacon to his lost companions.

But they did not come. And then he rose and stood at the door and cupped his hands to his mouth and cried out, 'John! John! Oh, John Marr!' and 'Mungo! oh, Mungo Wallace! Where are ye both?' But no reply came, and he hoped they had got safe and at least found one another.

Thomas huddled in his cloak in the corner of the room, and as desolate a spot as this was, he dozed, and after dozing, slept deep, and while sleeping so deep, he dreamed. And as he dreamed, he was no longer in a broken tower in the moors of the Debatable Land but sat in a chair in a sumptuous room, tapestried with scenes of hunting and fair ladies, lords hawking and boats with coloured sails. And the floor was wood and strewn with fresh straw. And the tower had windows with diamonds of thick glass, and outside it was night. And furniture there was of oak and boards of yew, and a fire blazed in the great hearth.

And there was another chair and in this other chair sat a man with piercing eyes and Lord Thomas knew that man as Michael Scot and Michael Scot smiled, steepled his long fingers and said, 'Welcome to my home, Lord Thomas Neville. You have sought me long, and now your search is rewarded.'

'This is your home?' Lord Thomas said, locked in the dream but sitting as one awake. 'This broken tower?'

Michael Scot gestured. 'Look around thee, Lord Thomas Neville. Is it not a fine tower furnished from Italy and France?'

Thomas said, "But the tower I entered was broken and choked with weeds and damp and nothing but the abode of owls and mice.'

'That is the glamour I lay on it so that none should find me unless I wish them to.'

'So you wished me to find you?' Lord Thomas said.

Michael Scot nodded. 'Indeed, for we have a bargain to strike.'

'A bargain?'

Michael Scot gave a low laugh. 'Do not play the coy lad, Thomas. We both know what you want and why you came."

Thomas tilted his head, uneasy. "Are you sure you know my heart so well?"

'Aye, I do. You wish to be King of Scotland, and after that King of England too.'

Thomas bowed his head, and Scot continued. 'And I can give you these both.'

'And in return, you ask what?'

'I ask only for the dearest thing in your life. I think that is fair payment for my granting your ambitions.'

And as Scot named the dearest thing in Lord Thomas's life, his mind leapt to his daughter Isabel, and her picture sprang unbidden to his mind's eye.

As if the sorcerer could read Thomas's mind, though indeed he could not, Scot said, 'You have a daughter, do you not?'

Thomas nodded.

'How old is she?'

"Isabel is six years old.'

'And very dear to your heart? The most dear thing perhaps?"

Thomas sat silently in the oaken chair as the fire crackled and the wind moved outside the glass windows. And in his mind a picture of his wife, Maud, played, as beautiful as the sun rising on a spring morning.

Scot sat forward, 'But you have a wife also, the Lady Maud? Perhaps you love her more than your daughter?'

'I love them both equally,'

Scot licked his lips. 'Then perhaps both? For you wish to have two crowns, so I do not think that two souls is too dear a payment.'

Lord Thomas shook his head. 'I will settle for one crown, after all. Give me the crown of England alone.'

'One soul then? I am content.' Scot leaned forward and took out a gleaming silver needle. 'One drop of your blood is all I require to seal the bargain.'

Lord Thomas stared at Scot. He thought of withdrawing, but before he could speak, Scot darted forward and stuck him with the pin, and a bright bead of blood rose up like a garnet on his pale, freckled skin.

'I will make thee king of England, Lord Thomas, but thou wilt pay me with the soul and flesh of thy best beloved.'

'But how am I to decide which it is?" Lord Thomas said.

'That is a simple thing. You do not have to choose, for the one who loves you best will rush to you fastest, and so when you arrive home, the first living person that you see will fall dead by my magic, and as they die, I will drink in their soul, and they will rise no more between this place and the next.'

'And how will you make me King of England?'

"Once you have paid the price, I will teach you the words of the spell that Merlin gave to Uther Pendragon so that he took up the likeness of Lord Gorlois of Cornwall so that he could sleep with Gorlois's wife and she none the wiser. The same spell that Arawn King of Hell wrapped around Pwyll Prince of Dyfed so that he could rule in his stead for a year and a day in the underworld, and neither Arawn's wife nor his courtiers any the wiser. So, you shall go in the guise of King Henry of England and take his place. Do with him as you wish, kill him if you want, but with my magic, none shall miss him, mistaking you for him at every turn.'

'So I shall be as King Henry?' Thomas thought of the position.

The old sorcerer looked hungrily at him, and Thomas watched as the hood-eyed man licked the drop of blood from the pin end and sucked it down and smacked his lips after.

Scot said, "The bargain is sealed. I will teach you the words of the spell, and in return, you will give me the soul of the first living thing you see as you return home to Naworth.'

And Lord Thomas fell into a deep slumber. And in his sleep, he heard the echoing voice of Michael Scot whispering the words of the promised spell of changing, whispering them so quiet he caught only a hint and he would not be given them in full until he had paid Scot what he loved best in all the world. And he saw the face of his wife Maud and the face of his daughter Isabel and both were in tears.

When he awoke, his neck was stiff, and his back was sore from the hard floor, and the fire had died out, and his fine bay horse was hungry. The mist had gone, and he led the stallion out onto the open moors where a fine day had dawned. And he looked south, mounted his horse and headed back to Naworth Castle.

When he got to Bewcastle, he found John Marr and Mungo Wallace, who had waited for him and were glad to see their lord.

'What ails you, Lord Thomas? You look grey."

'Find me a priest.'

And so they found the priest who was in charge of the lonely church at Bewcastle, and Lord Thomas dictated a message to be written on thick paper with black ink.

The priest frowned as he took down the message. 'Are you sure this is all, my lord? It seems such a trifle to send a message as this.'

Lord Thomas smiled and gave the priest a silver shilling. He took the note, sealed it with hot wax and handed it to Mungo Wallace and bid him to ride hard to Naworth Castle and give the message to Lady Maud.

'Aye, sir. I shall.'

Lord Thomas said, 'You must get there before we do.'

Mungo Wallace frowned. 'If you say so, my Lord.'

'And if Lady Maud questions what I have written on the note, you must tell her to do exactly what I have said and not deviate from it.'

Frowning, Mungo Wallace left the church, mounted his horse and rode hard from Bewcastle south towards Naworth.

'Come, John Marr. Let us follow after him at our own leisurely pace.'

And so they dawdled and took their way almost at their leisure over the fell roads, first to Lanercost and then to Birdoswald and then to Naworth.

And it was evening when they arrived at Naworth, and Lord Thomas drew up his horse and said to John Marr. 'Go ahead and ensure that Mungo Wallace has arrived and delivered my note and that Lady Maud has understood it and is willing to do what I say.'

And Lord Thomas sat and waited, and in due course, John Marr returned. He nodded and said, 'Lady Maud has the note, and though she asked me why you would want to do such a thing, she agreed to do it.'

'Good.'

'And what now, my Lord?'

'We wait further.'

And so they waited until there was a noise as if a wind woke behind them, and a hot breeze and a turmoil in the air as if the devil himself had arrived, and Lord Thomas turned and saw Michael Scot dressed in brown. The sorcerer whispered, 'Why do you linger, Lord Thomas? Greatness awaits you. Greatness after you pay the price. Pay the price, and I will give you the words of the spell of change, and you shall have all you wish.'

John Marr gripped his reins as he saw the sorcerer and looked at his lord for guidance.

Lord Thomas said to John Marr, "Let us go forward.'

And Lord Thomas rode his fine bay stallion slowly — as slow as creeping death itself.

And Michael Scot said, "Do not think thou canst get out of this. I have taken thy blood, and thou canst not renege on that or I will take thee instead.'

Thomas ignored the sorcerer.

And as they came in sight of Naworth Castle, Lord Thomas spurred his horse and there propped up on the middle of the bridge that led to the castle, was a fine mirror.

'What nonsense is this!' Michael Scot yelled and followed Lord Thomas haltingly. There was no one outside the castle, not a child, not a servant, not a dog, nor a horse. But instead, the fine silver mirror brought from France stood on the bridge.

And the first living thing Lord Thomas saw as he came into the grounds of Naworth Castle was the form of Michael Scot captured in the mirror's silver face.

'What trickery is this?' Michael Scot yelled.

'You only said the first living thing I saw as I crossed into my castle would be what you took. You did not stipulate that I should not see it through a window or through glass or in the silver of a mirror. And you have sworn to take the first living thing I see, and the first living thing that I see is thee, Michael Scot."

And the sorcerer was consumed in smoke and blood and his soul dissolved by his own dark magic.

Lord Thomas stood by the blackened ring in the grass and the smoking brown rags that were all that remained of Michael Scot, the sorcerer.

'But why did he take his own soul?' John Marr asked his Lord.

'Because a bargain sealed in blood can never be broken, as he well knew. Not by all the devils in hell nor all the angels in heaven, but only by the power of the good Lord himself, and Michael Scot was far indeed from such grace as that.'

CHAPTER 12

A BRIEF STOP IN BARROW IN FURNESS

Winter is a time of interrupted journeys, and this is deep winter, just before Christmas with the snow coming down. You're on a train trying to get home from London. As far as you can tell, you're in Lancashire.

The train shudders to a halt. The guard walks up and down, chanting, 'All change. All change.'

Bleary-eyed, you blink. 'I thought this was direct for Carlisle.'

'Sorry, sir. There's a defective train blocking the way north. This is Preston. You'll have to change here and go round via Barrow.'

You groan. 'Via Barrow on the coast line? That'll take forever.'

The guard shrugs, uninterested in your plight. He's heard the sad stories of discomfited travellers a million times; their sorrow washes off him now like rain off a new Macintosh coat. He walks on.

This is outrageous! Typical, but outrageous. They can't treat their paying customers like this. What if you sat here? They'd have to do something then. They'd have to make arrangements. They couldn't make you add—what three hours to your journey? Grange and Barrow and Millom and Ravenglass, and Whitehaven and Maryport and Wigton and then Carlisle. It will be after midnight when you get home.

No, you decide you'll sit until they offer a better alternative.

You sit. People get their bags and put on their coats. You sit some more. Everyone else is gone. Some folks walk down the cold platform. Railway staff chat outside the train, and one sees you through the window. From the platform, he waves you off—big gestures like a football referee issuing a red card. You fold your arms and become resolute. You're not going anywhere.

In a minute, he gets on, walks down the carriage and stands there weighing you up before he speaks. 'This train's going into the sidings for the night. You'd better get off.'

'No.'

He sighs.

You say, 'I paid my fare. I got my ticket. You have a duty to honour the contract and get me home.'

The guard tips back his hat and rubs his seamed forehead. 'We have a duty to get you home. But we don't say when. So if you want to get home tonight, you'd better look sharp. The Barrow train is about to leave from Platform 5.'

You study his tired face. He's serious. It's not his fault their trains are defective and blocking the line north. You push the heel of your hand into your eyes, breath heavily, retrieve your bag from the luggage rack above and heave it over your shoulder. As you walk towards the door, the guard says, 'I hope you get home. Merry Christmas, by the way.'

You nod. 'Merry Christmas to you too.'

You've missed the Barrow train he meant, but there's another in an hour. It's freezing, so you retreat to the waiting room, where you have a gingerbread latte and an oat and raisin cookie.

You doze off in the faux leather seat by the waiting room fire beside the tinsel and bauble-decked Christmas tree, and you are woken by the cafe waitress shaking you. 'You for the Barrow train?'

You are so tired. You blink. 'How did you know?'

'Not many trains at this time of night, so I guessed. Anyway, it's about to leave. It's the last one tonight, so if you want to get home, you'd better run.'

You board the train that stands bright yet forlorn at the platform. Finding your seat you sit, the fluorescent lights make your headache worse. You see that the carriage is only a third full. A man sits opposite, reading the North West Evening Mail. After only three minutes or so, the train begins its journey west.

The black miles pass, juddering and jolting among the mountains, and you enter Cumbria. The bright inside makes the windows impossible to see through. The glare and the hour hammer your head. It's getting late.

Then the train jolts to a stop. Outside, snow flurries fall in the darkness, sticking to the windows. You're between towns, and all that's outside is the bottomless dark of a December night. You pity the animals and the people that are out on a night like this.

Catching your eye, the man opposite smiles. He's about forty, ordinary looking, but friendly. He says, 'It's a slow one, isn't it?'

You give a hollow laugh. 'You could say that. How far are you going?'

'Barrow. What about you?'

'A bit further. To Carlisle. What's the next stop?'

'Barrow. But Barrow's the last stop too. This train won't be going to Carlisle.'

You start. Involuntarily, you clench your fists. 'What? I need to get home.'

The man shakes his head sadly. 'The train before this was the last one that goes all the way. This doesn't.'

You groan and throw your head back. This can't be happening. You aren't going to be home tonight.

The man says, 'It'll be past ten by the time we get to Barrow.'

You check your watch. 'How did it get so late?'

He smiles. 'Time does that on dark winter nights. It moves quicker than you think but slower than you imagine.'

Then the train starts again and chugs painfully on through the night. Minutes pass, then an announcement over the tannoy. 'This is your driver speaking. This train will terminate in Barrow.'

Your fellow passenger grimaces. 'Not so good for you.'

Of course, he's all right. He lives in Barrow. The train starts and limps its way into the station.

There's not much of a station here now. You glimpse a row of terraced houses over a chain-linked wire fence and a mostly empty car park. Such cars as there are there look like strange animals burrowed under the snow. The train stops. Then you stand. You'll need to hurry to get any hotel bed that might still be free in Barrow at twenty past ten on a cold night in late December.

The man opposite has decided to be your guide and protector because he waits as you stand. 'What are you going to do?' he says.

You shrug as you step onto the platform, and the cold hits you like you've opened a fridge door, so you turn up the collar of your coat against the snow. You walk along to the exit and the smiling station staff. It's all right for them to smile; they have a home to go to.

Your guide is still with you.

'I've just got to make a few phone calls,' you say, and he waits while you speak to your nearest and dearest and tell them you won't be back tonight. 'Can't be helped. Sorry. Love you. I'll be okay, don't worry. See you tomorrow. You bet. Sleep tight. Kiss kiss.'

And then you ring the Premier Inn, which is a no go. Travel Lodge: No rooms. There is no Marriott in Barrow. Things are looking bleak.

'There's a B&B,' your friend says, pointing. He's indicating the row of terraced houses you saw from the train. It's hard to make it out through the snow that blusters through the haloes of orange street lights, but there is a sign. You'd have preferred somewhere anonymous like a Premier Inn, which are all the same in every town you go to. This family-run B&B will have character. You could have done without character tonight.

'I'll walk into town, see if there's somewhere there.' you say. He nods and walks with you. He's very kind. Not pushy, not creepy, just thoughtful.

But by the end of fifty yards, the idea of walking around Barrow town centre tonight looking for a hotel that might have a room seems desperate. You glance down the terrace of houses. There's that B&B your companion indicated. You'll have to try that.

'Listen, I'm going to go back to that first place you pointed out.'

He nods. 'I've heard it's good. Clean like. I'll walk back with you if you like.'

You shake your head. 'No, I can't put you out.'

'You sure? I don't mind.'

'No, no. It's late and cold. I couldn't possibly ask you.'

Your guide says, 'I'll leave you then. I'm sure you'll find somewhere, even if not there.'

You wave and watch his back disappear into the darkness—what a nice guy! But you're preoccupied with your own concerns. So you walk down the row. There's a shop that's closed up. The snow-streaked sign says:

'M. Dawson and Son: Pork Butchers.'

But there's a door next to it that says, Ma Dawson's B&B. It sounds dire, but what choice do you have at this time of night, in Barrow in Furness?

The bell's broken, so you rap on the door. You wait, but no one answers, so you knock again. Still nothing, and you're about to leave when the door opens, and a pale yellow light spills out. A woman stands there, in her sixties. She looks a bit down-trodden. 'Can I help you?' she asks in a broad Barrow accent.

You clear your throat. 'I'm looking for a bed for the night. Do you have any?'

The woman regards you with dark eyes. Her mouth is slightly open, and you notice her teeth are brown and uncared for.

She doesn't immediately respond, so you blurt, 'I know it's late, but the train wouldn't go any further, and I'm really stuck.' You give what you hope is a winning smile.

She says in measured tones, 'It so happens that we do have a room. Come in.'

So you step in. The house is hardly warmer than the outside, but at least it's dry. The woman stares at you. 'I'll show you the room.'

You follow her as she mounts the narrow stairs. The carpet looks like it dates from the 1960s. The walls were painted white once but are now yellow. The sixty-watt bulb without a lamp-shade doesn't help. At least the woman isn't a chatterbox. All you want to do is sleep, then get up early and catch the train north.

The room is dismal. There's no carpet, bare floorboards with an old cheap wooden wardrobe, a single bed with nylon sheets and a ratty curtain half shut. When you lift the curtain, the window stares out onto a back alley, a view improved by the fresh coating of snow.

But you're tired. You undress, tiptoe across the cold wooden floorboards to switch off the light and get into the hard bed. You put your coat on top of the thin duvet after five minutes, reaching for it in the dark. Slants of light come in through the inadequate curtain. This is going to be a long night. You wonder if you'll ever sleep.

But you do. For a while anyway.

A slithering, scuttling noise wakes you. Alert instantly, you don't sit up; instead, you lie there trying to sense what's in the room with you. Did you lock the door? You're not sure you did.

But then it's quiet. You relax. It's only the sounds of this old house. Or rats. God forbid it's rats. You listen hard. Nothing again. Maybe it's your imagination.

Then it comes scuttling and slithering, like something with clattery claws and a soft afterbelly that drags behind it. Your heart hammers and the hairs stand on your arms. The sound stops. A long silence unfolds itself. You calm down. This is stupid. But you still need to get up, switch on the light, and show yourself there's nothing there.

But you don't. You realise you're too scared to get up.

Instead, you listen. You listen very hard, and when nothing happens for three minutes, you are convinced it was just imagination. It's all down to the strange room and the upset of the interrupted journey.

But it's not just that. It's not just that at all.

A dragging sound. A clicking sound. A sound of breathing.

There's definitely something in the room with you. And it's between you and the light switch.

Maybe if you lie still, it'll go away?

Gripping the sheet tightly in nerveless fingers, you pretend to be asleep. But whatever is there knows you're not sleeping.

With one burst of courage, you sit up, ready to confront this intruder, your right hand balls into a fist. You're ready to fight.

The partial curtain lets in light. And the light is enough to see what stands there in the room with you.

You scream, but no one's coming to your aid. Your only source of help could be your landlady. She's the only soul who knows you are here. But your landlady is not going to come to help.

In the slatted light from the alley, your landlady squats naked, and she shuffles, with long toenails clattering on the floor like a dog. She moves like a monkey using feet and elbows, her calloused heels scraping along the wood. Then like a big-bellied spider, all legs and claws, she sprints and jumps into bed with you.

You push at her and push, but she bites and licks and bites and chews and eats. And when she eats, she swallows and licks up gobbets of flesh that hang on her pointy chin, with thin hands stuffing raw meat into her mouth, with sharp fingernails scrabbling and gouging her tasty treat.

And you flop and lie and watch and die.

· · ·

THE FOLLOWING DAY, the man who sat opposite you gets on the 09:30 a.m. train from Barrow. He's obviously well known to the guard who stops to chat.

'No, it's fine, Mr Dawson. I don't need to see your season ticket again; I know it's valid!'

Mr Dawson nods and smiles his gentle smile.

'You're a butcher, aren't you? I didn't know butchers travelled so much.'

'I go looking for meat up and down the country,' Mr Dawson says, still smiling.

The guard pushes back his cap and scratches his head. 'I suppose you'll always be looking for people who can supply you meat at good prices.'

'Carcasses, yes. That's it.'

'Is that where you're off this morning?' the guard asks.

Mr Dawson shakes his head. 'No, this trip is strictly pleasure. Mother dealt with business—last night.'

CHAPTER 13

THE SCREAMING SKULLS
OF CALGARTH

I had business with the Lowthers, or rather my employer had. For you see, I worked for Binns and Hall, Solicitors in Lancaster, and there was the matter of customs and excise due on some liquor held in a bonded warehouse in Whitehaven, Cumberland.

The warehouse belonged to Sir James Lowther, 1st Earl of Lonsdale, but my business was to be not with his great and corrupt mightiness but with his humble legal agent John Wordsworth.

It was for such things as these that saw me journeying at the back end of 1788 as the old year drew wearily to its close, and the weather set in. I had come up by stagecoach from Lancaster to Kendal.

Though the more sensible route might have been to go from Kendal to Penrith and thence to Carlisle on the turnpikes, I had relatives near Wynandermere—or Windermere as they corruptly have it these days. I say relatives when I mean *a* relative: one, a distant cousin of my mother's called Myles Philipson. He held a modest hall at Calgarth, as my mother's family had been well-to-do in those parts once over.

Mother married a solicitor from Lancaster and rarely returned to her ancestral lands, finding them too wild and uncouth. For my part, I had met cousin Myles only once before and then not for a long time. I judged that he would be in his late forties by now. I went to Calgarth not so much to see this stranger, kinsman though he was, but from curiosity to see the circumstances my mother had been raised in and to bask in the glory of being a member of a long-established family in those parts.

I wrote to inform cousin Myles of my trip and my earnest wish to come to Calgarth Hall. He did not reply to my letter for many weeks until I began to think he had either not received my letter or was not minded to show me hospitality. Then, in mid-November, a few days before I departed, he simply wrote:

Come if you wish, cousin, but do not wish for too much. Times have been hard on me, and this will be reflected in my hospitality.

THE COUNTY of Westmorland is wild, and from Kendal, it got wilder as we travelled north, channelled on narrow, muddy roads, funnelled between dark, moody forests, and overlooked by steep moody fells. The mountains grew more rugged, and the cloud crowded on them heavy making them more sinister in aspect.

As we turned bends in the road, sudden views of lakes and forests appeared —bleak, desolate and naked of any civilised habitation, and my heart quailed to think of what creatures lurked in those godforsaken acres.

I arrived at Calgarth with around three hours of daylight to spare, and the coachman left me by the side of that rude road between the thick woods and set off at haste with his few passengers and his mail for Ambleside and Grasmere and then over the pass to Keswick.

No one had come to meet me, so I trudged down the stony, puddled track until I came in sight of Calgarth Hall.

I exhaled. It was not a grand place at all, though once it had been. Now it stood half in ruins, draped in ivy with its roofless rooms a haunt of bats and owls.

A man emerged from an outhouse and stood in sullen challenge at the gate. He was a rough-looking man with dirty, hard hands and a brown beard. His dialect was thick but not so different from Lancashire that I couldn't understand it.

'What brings ye to Calgarth, stranger?'

I drew myself up, assumed the legitimate rank of Mr philipson's kinsman and said, 'I am here to see my cousin, Myles philipson.'

At the name, though it may have been a mere coincidence, the man spat and studied me with dark eyes. Finally, he jerked his chin. 'You'll find him in the big house.'

The 'big house' was the main body of Calgarth Hall. Some of it at least looked habitable, with glass in the windows, wooden shutters drawn tight in most of them and a door that looked sturdy enough, though old. A mongrel dog sat by the step regarding me with little interest.

'Will you show me the way?' I asked courteously enough.

The man laughed. 'I'm sure you can find it yourself.' Then he turned and went about his work, clicking his tongue at the dog which got up and slunk after him.

Of course, I could find it myself, but that wasn't the point. Presumably, this labourer worked for cousin Myles, and if so, he was guilty of great discourtesy to any stranger, not least to a kinsman of his master.

But these were remote country parts, and the denizens could not be expected to practice town manners.

I strode to the great door and knocked. The door swung open under my blow and hung ajar there while I stood outside. No one came to answer the knock, so I raised my voice and called, 'Cousin Myles. It is I, William Timperley of Lancaster.'

I stood, foolish-like, wondering what to do next when the labourer returned with his dog. 'Not answering you, is he?'

He came to stand by me, the odour of his body making my nostrils wrinkle, and bellowed, 'Mr philipson, your visitor is here.'

At this, the sound of heavy boots was heard descending the stairs then crossing a wooden floor, and the door was grabbed and heaved open. With a snarl, the newcomer said, 'What dost thou want, Barnabas? Hast thou not enough work to fill thy time?'

Barnabas laughed. 'Aye, plenty of work, Mr philipson, but I thought you'd want to greet your kinsman from Lancaster, and you didn't seem to hear his feeble voice or heed his feeble knock.'

Looking down, Myles snapped, 'Get thee gone about thy errands, Barnabas Bouch.'

'As you like, sir.' This Barnabas turned, the cur dog at his heel and clumped his way across the courtyard in heavy boots to the farm buildings beyond, disappearing down a path fringed by nettles and curling-dead ferns.

Now we stood alone, my cousin studied me. 'So, you came, Timperley.'

I smiled. 'William, please, cousin.'

He shook his head. 'I doubted you would. I couldn't see why you would have any interest in this god-forsaken place.' He gave a dry laugh. 'Unless you hoped to inherit. And then, God knows, you're welcome to it.'

As he held me on the threshold, it began to rain softly.

'May I come in, cousin?' I said, looking up and blinking the soft raindrops from my lashes.

He nodded. 'Come,' he said. 'It's a poor enough place, but it used to be poorer.'

I stepped in, taking off my hat and dropping my valise on the bare boards.

Myles gestured at the windows and the door and at the floor and furniture that seemed of reasonable quality. 'This is all new for one thing.'

Then Cousin Myles yelled at the top of his voice, and from somewhere, a mousey-haired woman appeared, trembling as if she were terrified.

'Bessie, this is my cousin, Mr Timperley. He's come from Lancaster.'

'Lancaster?' she said, regarding me as if I were an exotic beast, and he'd said I'd come from Samarkand or Timbuctoo.

'Show him to a room,' Myles commanded without meeting her eye.

She blinked rapidly. 'Which room, Mr philipson?'

He shrugged. 'Whichever is in the best repair.' Then he laughed. 'Preferably one with a roof.'

'Very well, Mr philipson.' She turned, and after a second, with no further verbal instruction from Myles, I scurried after her to the far door.

As we were about to leave that front room, cousin Myles yelled, 'Not the middle room, Bessie.'

As if he'd suggested she were a fool, with disdain, Bessie answered, 'No, of course not Mr philipson. I'd not thought to put him in that room.'

'Good,' Cousin Myles said and then to me. 'We will eat together tonight and drink, and you can tell me what goes on in the civilised world.'

I RESTED a few hours and later washed with jug and ewer in the top bedroom, I descended.

I dined with Myles in the Hall's main room, where a colossal hearth blazed, piled high with logs. A long oak table stood in the centre of the room, set for dinner and piled with wooden platters, silver dishes and brass candlesticks. These flickering candles illuminated our meal, and I was unnerved by the flickering shadows they summoned from the dark corners and the imagined visitors they conjured from the tarnished mirror.

I shivered as I sat there. It seemed to me that we were not alone in that room but that the spirits of our ancestors had chosen to dine with us. We ate beef and potatoes and drank brown ale. I do not know what the ghosts ate, and trying to turn my disquiet into humour, I chuckled to myself at my fancies.

Though the meal was simple, I had to admit it was good. The beer seemed to loosen Myles's dourness. After he had drunk deep, he gestured around, choosing to play guide for the first time. 'This was the medieval Hall. It was built by Robert the Devil, as they called him, many centuries ago. Our family owned it after him.'

He raised his pewter tankard to his mouth, drained it then slammed it on the wood. This was the signal for Bessie, and she hurried in from the passage outside.

'Bring another jug of ale, Bess,' he said.

I put my hand over my tankard. 'I have enough still, thanks, Bessie.'

Cousin Myles gestured with his bony hand towards my tankard. 'My cousin here will have more beer too, Bessie. Whatever, he thinks, he won't sleep without it.'

While I waited for Bessie to return, I asked about our family's history in the Hall. My mother was always vague about her kin. She was a modern woman and had no interest in such old-fashioned things.

Bessie came back with a foaming jug and filled both our tankards. Until he'd gulped his ale, Myles was silent. He then sat back, sucked his lip and said, 'My father—your mother's uncle—was a gambler. He wagered our Hall on a horse at Appleby. And he lost. Not that it was worth much.' He snorted. 'If you think it's tumble-down now, it was worse then.'

I glanced around the room. 'You've effected some repairs?'

'I have done what I could—what I could afford to.'

A silence fell. I sipped my beer. 'But you suggested your father, my great-uncle, lost the hall in a wager?'

'He did.'

'Then how is it that are you back here?'

Myles's face twisted. 'This house and this land have been ours for centuries. It was a disgrace that my father lost it. It was an affront to me that it fell into the hands of strangers, and it should be an affront to you as well.'

As he spoke, some strange pride grew in me, even though I'd never been to the place before and my own mother showed no interest in it. Myles spoke with intense fervour, instilling in me a sense of blood and soil and heritage.

He continued. 'My father lost the Hall and died soon after. My mother brought me up, her only son, in a mean house down on the estate, and I became a tenant and servant where I should have been master.' He met my eyes. 'Did you hear the way Barnabas spoke to me?'

I nodded. 'With some disrespect, I thought.'

'Exactly. Because when we were growing up, we were not different in rank, though our blood is nobler than his, and we go back to the ancient families of Westmorland, while he and his were always commoners. Even so, we lived as neighbours, though by rights, I was lord of this place, not a servant here.'

I still didn't see it. 'But you got the hall back?'

'I did.'

'That was very industrious of you.'

He laughed. 'Not by industry as such. I tell you this as a kinsman. Blood is thicker than water, cousin William, after all, and I can tell by your eyes and the colour on your cheek that you feel as I do: that our family belongs here. And after my time, I have decided the Hall shall come to you.'

I sat back. I blinked. 'Really?' We had only just met.

He shrugged. 'I have no wife and no children. No woman will look at me, and no father would ever let his daughter marry one such as me in any case.'

Suddenly he looked terribly weary. He slumped back in his seat, tankard to his mouth.

'So, will you tell me the tale of how you got the hall back?'

'Not tonight, Cousin. As the nights get darker, my strength fades and my courage with it.' He grimaced, looking down. 'I do not sleep. If I could only sleep, then I might wake refreshed.'

I was not going to get any more of the tale from him that night. He closed his eyes and began to nod there in his chair, his chest rising and falling. I didn't know what to do.

After some minutes, Bessie came in. I gestured at Myles, not speaking as I was a little frightened of waking him.

Bessie nodded and beckoned. She showed me to the stairs that led up to my room and gave me a candle. Before we parted, I whispered. 'Will he wake and go to bed?'

She shook her head and said, 'He never retires to his chamber at night. He sleeps downstairs. If he sleeps at all.'

'Do you look in on him?'

Bessie shook her head. 'Barnabas and I do not lodge in the hall but in one of the cottages nearby.'

So it seemed I was to be all alone with my morose cousin.

Bessie left me at the foot of the stairs, but just at the far door, in the flickering light of her candle, I saw her turn. Here she said, 'God Bless and Keep you, Mr Timperley. God Bless And Keep You. Don't stay too long at Calgarth, Mr Timperley; it is not a suitable place anymore for one of your blood.'

Then she left.

Despite the warning, the place was so quiet compared with the town with its yells and drunkards that I fell into a deep sleep within minutes of getting into my bed.

A shriek woke me in the dead of night. My candle was out, and the room was black as pitch apart from the fingers of moonlight that intruded through the wooden shutters. The shriek came again. I thought for a second it was a screech owl that had somehow got inside the house. That was not impossible given the state of the roofs. But I knew it was no owl. A scream of a different timbre than the first keened through the house. It had an echoing, otherworldly tone and was filled with anger and hate. I pushed myself up against the headboard of my bed and pulled the blanket around me as if such flimsy things would protect me.

The screaming built in crescendo. My mouth was dry, my heart beat as if it would jump from my throat, and my fingers curled in the sheets. I hoped the screams would stop, but they did not. And then I thought murderers had got in and were attacking my cousin.

But if so, surely the servants would rush to his aid. Then I remembered they did not lodge in the Hall itself. Though Heaven knew the screeching and wailing were loud enough to rouse the dead, and they must surely hear it from wherever they slept.

If no servants came, or even if they did, I could not leave my kinsman to suffer this terrible assault alone. I jumped from my bed, rushed to the windows to pull back the shutters and bring the moon-light flooding in so I could at least see where to put my feet. I ran to the door and yanked it open. Then I paused. Dark stairs loomed below. The screams arose from the floor below me. The floor Bessie had led me past at such a pace.

It was dim there, but I placed my hand against the wall and felt my way down. A tremendous din of crashing and smashing was coming from along the short passage. The flickering yellow light of candles shone from behind the open door. Great wailing rang out, and in answer, great hammer blows responded.

From where I stood, 'Cousin Myles,' I called. 'Are you well? What is happening?'

From behind the door, the rough voice of my kinsman responded, 'Get back to bed! You do not need to attend to this.'

'But the screaming. I thought you were being attacked.'

'As I was, as I am every night. But get ye back to bed.'

He surely could not expect me to return to my bed and sleep in the pandemonium. Despite his instruction, I hurried to the door and stared. My jaw fell open. It was the middle floor which I'd never seen before.

The room was unfurnished, with bare floorboards and a stone

fireplace and hearth in the wall. The fire blazed with hot, glowing coals. Myles kneeled there, a great iron hammer in his hand, and he brought it down again and again on two human skulls. No other bones lay there, no collar bones or leg bones, no hips or ribs, just two skulls. Then, with his massive hammer, Myles smashed them into pieces, each one, and as he did so, he grabbed the shards of bone and threw them into the heart of the red-hot coals.

And even as he smashed the skulls, they screamed. They screamed and wailed, and their anger and hate rang from wall to wall and echoed in every room in Calgarth Hall.

My hand gripped my throat. I had never seen such a thing. I had never before experienced the supernatural, but here and now, there was no doubt I was in its presence.

Myles dropped his hammer and scrabbled to gather the last fragments and crumbs of the two skulls, and these bones he pitched into the fire.

Clapping and rubbing his hand, Myles stood. 'There,' he said. 'That will silence them for a while.'

'For a while?'

Myles turned and gave a bitter smile. 'You ought to go back to your bed.'

I shook my head. 'I'll never sleep. You must tell me the story behind this strange visitation.'

'Aye, I'll tell you, but come downstairs, and we will have whisky rather than ale.'

And so I followed him downstairs. He had let the fire down there in the dining room die down, and the room was chill, so now he banked it up with dry wood, and soon it blazed forth again.

Myles poured me a glass of whisky, and I drank it to steady my nerves. The echoing screams of the skulls still echoed in my head.

When we had finished one glass of whisky, Myles filled another for us both, and without question, I drank it.

He said, 'I told you how my father lost this house in a bet on horses?'

'You did.'

'And it was won by a draper and his sister from Appleby?'

I shook my head. He had not given me that detail.

He said, 'Kraster Cook and his sister Dorothy were a loathly couple—come from nothing with no nobility in their blood, though they had money to spare. Even after they won the Hall, they only came to their new possession now and again, and when they did, they made a point of lording it over us, we who had the right to be counted gentlefolk but now lived as labourers. They cared nothing for Calgarth nor its land, and soon it fell to rack and ruin. They did nothing to keep out the rain, and as I grew to be a man, I watched powerless as the home of my ancestors became the haunt of owls and sheep. I think they did it deliberately to spite us. And then mother was dead, and I was alone.

One summer, the Cooks came, and of course, they couldn't stay in the Hall. It wasn't fit for human habitation, but they stayed in an inn nearby, ordering the best of everything and acting like lords of the manor, which in law, they were.

Kraster Cook came knocking for me at the poor tied cottage where I lived. And from where I laboured for them. I went to the door, but I wouldn't call him master, which was what he wanted. My lack of respect, as he saw it, enraged him, and he seemed determined to find a way to bring me even lower. His sister leered at me over his shoulder.

Then Kraster Cook nodded to his servant, who returned to his carriage and came back with a silver cup. At first, I didn't recognise it. It was many years since I'd set eyes on it.

'Recognise this, Myles philipson?' He brandished the silver cup right up to my face.

I said I did not, and he pushed it closer to me.

'I think you might if you just look closer.'

And then, as I studied the cup, a memory returned. I hadn't seen that silver cup since I was a boy. I narrowed my eyes, and Kraster Cook saw my recognition.

'Aye, lad. This is the Luck of Calgarth Hall. We had it from your father when his luck ran out.' He laughed.

The Luck of Calgarth Hall was this silver cup, and the legend said that if it left the Hall, then the Hall and the philipsons would fall to ruin. That is precisely what happened. Kraster Cook and his sister Dorothy had removed it from the Hall with the other valuables, looted the week after my father lost the place to them. And true to the legend, both the Hall and the philipsons had fallen low and stayed low ever since. I had known of the cup, but the misery I had lingered in since my father's death had driven memory of it from me.

'That is mine by rights,' said I speaking with a hot temper.

Kraster Cook waggled his finger, and his sister sniggered behind him.

'It is ours by winnings, and because we have it, you and your family and this hall....' He gestured behind him at the sorry state of Calgarth Hall, 'will never rise again above the ruinous state it is in.'

I reached to snatch the cup, but he struck my hand away, and his servant stepped up to protect him, or I would have knocked him down with my bare knuckles.

And Kraster and Dorothy Cook took the Luck of Calgarth with them, turning away, laughing at me.'

I sat forward, whisky glass in hand and said to Myles. 'And did you believe the superstition of the Luck?'

He nodded briskly. 'Aye, I did. The evidence of its loss was plain around me.'

I gestured at the new furniture and the windows and doors here, which were in good repair. 'But clearly, that is not true, for look how the Hall, and, I may say, yourself, have gained again in status since that day.'

'Not true, you say?'

'Obviously not.'

Myles nodded and went over to a cupboard I had not paid attention to. It was a sturdy oaken cupboard, and he took a black key from his pocket and unlocked it. Then, in the glimmering firelight, he pulled out a silver cup. 'This,' he said, 'Is the Luck of Calgarth.'

I said, 'So the Cooks had mercy and gave you back the Luck, and eventually the hall, it seems.'

His face was sour. 'The Cooks had no mercy in them,' he spat.

'Then how is it here? How are you back here?'

Myles returned to his seat by the fire and now in his hand was the silver cup, which he stared at, twirling it idly.

'I took it,' he said.

'And they let you?'

He laughed. 'They had little choice once they were dead.'

I waited, and he told me the tale. 'That night, the night the Krasters taunted me with the Luck, I went to where they were staying at Troutbeck Bridge and waited. It was a damp autumn day, and wreaths of mist hung on the lake's edge where the road runs. They set off early in their fine carriage, but I was waiting for them where the road is lonely. I had my father's sword, and I wore a mask like a common highwayman. The coach came from behind a tree. The driver saw me. He, the servant who had protected Kraster the previous day, pulled his pistol, but my sword was quicker. I leapt up at him, and at sword point, he dropped his pistol and fled. He realised his life was not worth spending to protect the Cooks who surely did not treat him well, as they knew not how to treat any man well.

With the carriage stopped, I found the Cooks.'

'But surely they would know it was you?'

'Surely they did. But that availed them nothing.'

I sat incredulous. 'You killed them?'

'Aye, more quickly than such curs deserved.'

I shook my head. 'Then why are you not hanged?'

He smiled, the Luck of Calgarth still in his hand. 'Because no one saw me. I took their money and the cup, and it passed as a robbery. It was the news of the district for a long time, but then interest moved on. There were other robberies to talk of on other roads.'

'But surely when you returned to Calgarth Hall, someone would have said something?'

Myles shook his head. 'The philipsons belonged at Calgarth. My father, for all his faults, was well-liked and besides, the Hall was a ruin. No one wanted it. I took it back, and with the money I took from the Cooks, I repaired it as much as I could.'

A strange horror dawned on me. 'Then the skulls....'

'Aye, they are the skulls of Kraster and Dorothy Cook. Every night they come, and every night they scream their lust for revenge.'

Myles pressed his hand to his eyes and said with a tired smile. 'I am weary. I never sleep. They come every night, and I try to destroy them. I smash them; I bury them. I have thrown them in the lake. I have hurled them in the River Eden and the River Kent, the River Mint and the River Leven. I have taken them to Maryport and buried them in a coal mine. I have taken them to Whitehaven and put them on a ship for America, but still they return.'

'But I saw you smash them into the tiniest pieces and burn the bone in a red hot fire.'

He nodded. 'Aye, but still they return.' He looked broken, on the edge of madness.

'Have you told anyone else this story?'

He sighed. 'The keeping of the story to myself has cost me dear. I thought if I now told it to you, I might get some relief. Unburdened of the secret, I thought I might at last sleep.'

'But aren't you frightened I will report your crime to the authorities?'

He shook his head. 'You are of my blood. This Hall will be yours when I am gone. This cup is the Luck of Calgarth and the luck of your own family. You will not betray me.'

We sat in silence until fatigue overcame me, and I said, 'I will go to my bed. I am setting off for Whitehaven tomorrow morning.'

He nodded. 'Call in to see me on your way back.'

I was in my bed when the screaming began again. The screaming and the hammering rang through the house, the infernal din rising up to Heaven and reaching down to Hell.

I rose at dawn and left Calgarth Hall without speaking to Myles. He had fallen finally into a doze, and Bessie let him sleep on. Truth was, I would not know what to say if he were awake. He was right. I would never betray his secret. He was my kinsman, even though he was a self-avowed murderer.

When my business with the Lowthers at Whitehaven was done, I took the post coach to Carlisle and then to Lancaster without going near Calgarth.

At the end of that year, I received notice that Myles was dead and Calgarth Hall was left to me. He had drowned in Windermere, allegedly by accident.

I travelled to the Hall with a friend, and we were met there by Barnabas, the servant, who handed me the key without a word.

However, it was Bessie who told me that Myles had taken his own life. She muttered, 'And I do not wonder, sir, Not with the terrible things in that Hall.'

Whether she knew of the Cooks, she never said.

I inherited the Luck of Calgarth and Calgarth Hall. I stayed at the Hall until the screaming began in the middle room the very first night. I left then, even though it was full dark and walked back to the village. I took the Luck with me, but I sold the silver cup when I returned to Lancaster, and I never went back to Calgarth Hall again.

CHAPTER 14

THE MILK WHITE CHILD OF RAVENGLASS

I wanted to get away from it all. I'd had it up to my back teeth with work, and the boss said to take some time, lower the stress levels and when I felt better, to come back. He gave me a month. That was generous of him, and I appreciated it, and I thought he must think something of me to cut me the slack.

Scrolling through Trip Advisor, I thought of the Scottish Highlands or Wales or Ireland, but in the end, while I had abandoned the computer and was flipping through a road atlas one night at home, the endless traffic on the North Circular buzzing outside my window, I saw Ravenglass. I liked the name, so I thought I'd go there. It had the added bonus of a railway station and I wouldn't have to drive. My nerves had been shredded that past few months, and I don't think I could have taken the motorways, heading round the M25, then feeding myself into the pasta maker at Spaghetti Junction in Birmingham. Ravenglass allowed me to escape all that. Ravenglass seemed to be calling me.

It took ages to get there on the train. After reading *The Guardian* and then *The Spectator* (I like to be contrary) and finishing both and flipping through them again to see if I'd missed anything, then eating two packets of crisps, gazing a long while out of the window, staring blankly down the carriage and finally heaving down my bag from the overhead rack, I alighted from the train at the empty railway platform and saw an adjoining miniature steam railway at the station over the line. That was the one that ran down the valley between the mountains.

Ravenglass is by the Irish Sea, in case you didn't know. The smell of salt and seaweed invaded my nose as I took the path from the station. I checked the directions to my B&B—'The Old Church House' it was called. My landlady was a Mrs Nelson. I found it quickly enough.

Ravenglass is basically two rows of houses that run along the seafront with a cobbled street between them. The street starts not far from the railway station and ends at the beach.

When I saw it I knew it was exactly what I wanted. The Old Church House was a prominent building that looked Victorian made of red sandstone. It had a shallow front garden where summer flowers bloomed madly: roses and geraniums and iris and lupins.

Mrs Nelson had a bird-feeder out front. My opening the green-painted wooden gate scared off the greenfinches and blue-tits that were feeding there.

There, amidst the blooms I stopped and breathed in, filling my lungs with a mixture of sea air and the sweet stocks. It was still light even at eight o'clock that night just slightly before Mid-Summer.

I rang the doorbell, and Mrs Nelson opened it. I had imagined an old lady in a frock wearing a pinafore, but a completely different woman opened the door. She was about forty with auburn hair and freckles and cool, blue and red-framed designer spectacles. She wore denim shorts with sparkly sandals and a loose summer blouse white with blue and yellow flowers printed on it.

She reached out a hand. 'Mr Jones?'

I smiled awkwardly. "Call me Owen.'

'I'm Sally. Want a brew?'

She boiled a kettle on her gas hob. She got out a blue teapot with a golden dragon design. It looked Chinese, I thought perhaps Jing Dezhen, though I'm not up to the mark these days on Chinese ceramics. Then Sally grabbed a silver spoon in her left hand, a 1920s-looking, gold and red decorated tin tea-caddy in her right and took out three heaped spoonfuls of black, aromatic tea, which she popped into the dragon teapot.

'One for you, one for me and one for the pot,' she said.

When the boiling kettle whistled, Sally poured the steaming water into the teapot and then, after giving it time to mash, as they say up here, made me a cup of tea in a Claris Cliff teacup that sat on its saucer in front of me.

'Milk?'

I nodded. Sally poured the milk from a Portmeirion milk jug. None of it matched, but in some way, that added to the charm. I felt suddenly strangely relaxed, almost serene. It was as if I was being treated to a special Cumbrian Tea Ceremony.

She tipped the jug, dropped several drops and a gulp of milk into my cup then lifted the milk jug's spout, holding it poised in case I said I wanted more. 'Enough?' she said.

I smiled. 'Thanks, Perfect.'

'Sugar?' She stood ready with silver sugar-tongs, about to lift an irregular lump of white sugar from a Portmeirion bowl. It was the Moss Agate design—never produced in large numbers but which received high critical acclaim when Susan Williams-Ellis designed it in 1961. It was very valuable, and here was my B&B landlady, Sally Nelson, using it every day.

'You're a collector?' I gestured to the jugs and bowls.

Sally smiled. 'I'm an art teacher, but my love is ceramics.'

'Weird.'

'What is?'

I sat back. "I'm a ceramics designer. I work in a commercial pottery in London. I design plates and jugs and things.' I grinned. 'Nothing as special as those you have here. These are valuable, yet you use them every day.'

Sally said, 'Their beauty comes from their function. If you don't use them, you rob them of their purpose.'

Movement in the hall outside caught my eye. I glanced and saw a child peering round the door—a girl, I think. It must be Sally's daughter. She was very pale and darted her head back when she realised I'd seen her.

I went back to studying the tea dishes. "We both love ceramics. What a coincidence that I ended up booking here.'

Sally smiled and finally sat. "There are no such things as coincidences, Mr Jones.'

Of course, she was a hippy. You could tell that from the clothes she wore and the Buddha on the window sill and the book on Mandalas, open face down on the sideboard near the yew-wood chopping board with its loaf of artisan bread and pat of yellow, organic Cumbrian butter.

I'm not a hippy. I'm more practical than that. I work with my hands—worked with my hands—mostly it's computers now. But I am a down to earth man. If I can't touch it or at best see it, I doubt its reality. A coincidence is exactly that; there's nothing mystical or meaningful to it.

The child in the hall flitted across the doorway again as if she were playing hide and seek.

'She can come in if she wants," I said. "No need to be scared of me."

Sally smiled again. 'Who can?" She saw I was looking into the hall. 'Oh, the cat? He's a tom: Marmaduke.'

'No, the girl.'

Sally frowned. 'Girl?'

I gestured. 'The little girl in the hall. I thought she was your daughter.'

She shook her head. "My kids are at school.'

I sat back. I was sure I'd seen a little pale girl. When I thought of her, she came more vividly to mind as if she flourished and grew in my imagination, becoming more present and luminous than the brief glimpse of her in the hall.

Sally stared at me.

I laughed. 'Now you're going to tell me the house is haunted. A big old ex-vicarage like this is bound to be haunted.' I didn't know why I'd said it. I didn't believe in such things, but I bet she did.

Sally said, 'You're pulling my leg." Her smile, at first hesitant, grew broader. "You are a wag, Owen.'

'So it's not haunted?'

She shook her head. 'I've never seen anything. No guests have ever reported anything, and the kids have never talked about ghosts. So much as I like the idea of it being haunted.' She put her hand over her heart. 'I can't honestly say it is. Sorry. Did you want it to be haunted?'

'God, no. That's the last thing. I don't believe in ghosts.'

'But you just saw one.'

My jaw tightened. 'I saw a girl.' I shrugged. No point getting annoyed. 'I thought I saw a girl.'

'I don't think so. The only living thing in the house except you right now and me is my big ginger tomcat, and he's very likely asleep on my bed.'

I slept and saw no ghosts, but that picture of the pale young girl with hair like silver and eyes huge and full of moonlight and cobwebs drifted through my dreams. The girl didn't speak, only stared, and I thought she wanted something. Then I awoke.

It was a beautiful morning. Sparrows chirped outside my window. I opened it so I could listen to them and the sound of the waves' murmur. A slight breeze shifted the gauzy curtain. I lay until I thought I'd better get a shower then breakfast. I had nothing to do that day, and I thought I would get up early and enjoy doing it.

There was another man in the breakfast room sitting on his own table. He looked up and nodded to me, knife and fork in hand, knife lifted smeared with egg, fork raised ready to spear a piece of black pudding. 'How do?' he said.

'Good. Thanks.'

I sat. Sally bustled in. 'Full English?'

'I'm vegetarian. Should have said.'

She smiled. 'No problem. Ovo-lacto?'

I nodded. She brought me slices of farmhouse bread cut thick, toasted golden brown, with curls of organic butter and Cumbrian heather honey dribbled on and spread with the big silver butter knife. The coffee was organic, fair-trade—Guatemalan. The milk was local, organic, naturally. Then I had porridge with more local milk, a drib more honey swirled in. The oats were Scottish. That was fine— not too many air miles, especially if they came by boat across the Solway Firth.

The man at the other table wanted to talk. He was looking at me, waiting for me to meet his eye. Eventually, I did.

"I'm Taffy.'

'Owen.'

He sported big whiskers and watery blue eyes. He wore a brown tweed waistcoat with a broad check and a yellow tweed jacket that didn't match—nearly but not quite. His shirt was white, and I saw he had silver cufflinks, visible as he waved his knife and fork while talk- ing. 'On holiday?' he asked.

' Taking a break.'

'I'm a storyteller.'

I'd met plenty in my time, but I guessed he meant that was his job, not merely his inclination.

'Nice," I said.

'Doing the schools roundabouts. Contracted by the County Council.'

I smiled and said, before biting my toast, 'Sounds interesting.' Then I bit. It was delicious—a mouthful of Paradise as the bread crunched with melting butter and gooey honey, and I chewed while listening to the Storyteller.

He said, "I do Cumbria mostly and festivals, and of course, North Lancs, North Yorks, the closer side of Northumberland, National Park centres, et cetera.'

I swallowed my toast and took a sip of coffee. 'What kind of stories do you tell?'

'Folk tales. Fairy tales. Embellishments on the truth. Twists of History. Unrealities and make-believe, all with a strong moral element.'

'A moral element?'

He looked serious. "It's important that the little buggers know how to behave.'

'The kids?'

He laughed out loud. 'That's a good one. Of course the kids! Who did you think I meant—the fairies?'

I sat quietly.

He jerked a thumb as if the wall was invisible. "I'm at Ravenglass school later. I know Sally. Knew her husband, poor lad.'

'Oh.'

'He died. Was drowned.' He pointed at the unseen sea through another wall. 'Out there. It's treacherous to walk on these sands. Three rivers come to the sea here: the Esk, the Mite and the Irt. This confluence creates a lot of channels and currents. Of course, this area is isolated. It sits on a promontory sticking out into the sea. Muncaster Castle at the high bit facing inland. The old Roman port was up there.' Again he pointed through a wall.

'Romans?' I said.

Taffy nodded vigorously. "Romans, Celts, Vikings, Anglo-Saxons, Irish pirates, Manx fishermen—lots of tales. I'm doing King Eveling today.'

I smiled in polite interest. 'Eveling? Never heard of him.'

'He was a Dark Age king of the Britons. They had lots of little kings, sub-reguli Gildas called them. He appears in the Arthurian stories as King Evelake of Sarras, most probably. I'm telling a story about him, anyway.'

'You seem to know your stuff.' I bit more toast.

'I have to, old boy. It's my living: stories.' He raised a finger. 'But the legend says Eveling was King of the Fairies —that Ravenglass was then part of fairyland, or at least fairyland broke through into the real world here. Its old name was Renglas, which may mean The Green Promontory: *Rhyn Glas* in old Cumbrian.

As if he suddenly remembered something, he got up. 'Sorry, old lad, time and tide and all that. Well, they don't wait for me. Don't know about you. Hah!' And he left in a great bluster of tweedy waves to Sally and brisk nods at me.

After he'd gone, I reflected that in Ravenglass, time, if not tide, would wait for me. I had all day to do nothing much, and I loved it. It was the freest I'd felt for years.

Sally stood drying knives with her tea towel by the kitchen sink, door open to the breakfast room. 'Off anywhere nice today?'

I shrugged. 'It all seems nice.'

'Yes, it is. You could go on the La'al Ratty.'

'The what?'

'The steam railway.'

'Ah yes, I saw that.'

'Or up to Muncaster Castle.'

'Yes, that sounds nice.'

'There's a footpath. Go over the footbridge over the railway line, past the Bee Garden on your right and strike up through the woods. It's a lovely day for it.'

So that's the way I went. I fetched my boots and knapsack from my room, put on my shorts, got onto the landing then remembered my sunglasses and cap. I went back and got them, but as I locked my room and stood there, I had a strange feeling that I was being watched. I spun round and saw nothing, but as I stepped down the stairs, I thought that with some inner ear, not the natural worldly one, but one more attuned to things mostly unheard and mainly unspoken, I heard a soft voice say, 'Past is in future, and future is in past. What you do for us today. We do for you tomorrow.'

I shivered like someone had run a peacock feather up my spine. It was the strangest sensation and, pleasant as it was, it made me quite anxious, but I stood there, hand on the polished bannister and told myself I didn't believe in such things. It was only the stress being lifted from me. It was simply a relief that I didn't have to face my life for a while.

The walk up to the castle through the cool woodland was a dream. I strolled along the long drive after buying my entry ticket. The rhododendrons were all out in their glory, and blackbirds warbled from the bushes. Muncaster Castle itself was ancient, massive and hewn from dark sandstone. With all due respect to the National Trust, who do a great job of preserving the nation's heritage, their places can feel samey and regimented: a sort of corporate version of heritage, but Muncaster was gloriously independent, and even a little eccentric. I enjoyed the human touches and the humour and the fact that the same family lived there who'd founded the castle in the 1200s.

And then I walked back.

Sally had offered to cook, and she made a vegetarian tagine, and she and Taffy and me drank organic wine—French, not Cumbrian. 'I get it from a bloke in Penrith. He has a company called Black Hand wine. He's an organic winemaker—no sulphites, so no hangover.'

Of course, that wasn't true, but the wine slipped down like fruit punch. Taffy went upstairs to his room to do some work, and that left me with Sally.

'Would you like to see my studio?'

I said I would. The wine added to the day added to my pleasant company made me feel agreeable indeed.

She was good at pottery. She had a kiln and a potter's wheel and all the other bits and bobs a ceramic artist needs in her brick shed in the long garden on the landward side of the house. It was simple, but I had become over-sophisticated and arrogant. When you live in London, you come to believe that nothing worthwhile can originate from anywhere else. Maybe New York or Paris —Berlin or Tokyo at a push, but everywhere else must be second rate because it's not London. Except Sally's work wasn't second rate. She wasn't world-shattering, but she was very competent and her work had real charm.

She hitched up and sat on a bench. She motioned for me to sit on her stool. I looked around me, taking in the range and quality of the items she'd made.

'You could sell this,' I said.

She shrugged. 'Not fussed.'

'You don't want to sell it? I've got contacts in galleries in London. I could get you an exhibition.'

'Why?'

'So more people would see your work. So people would buy your work. So you'd be properly rewarded for your talent.'

She grimaced and took a sip of her organic Tempranillo. 'I do it for me. Because I enjoy it.'

I nodded rapidly. "Yes, of course. But even so. You could make a name for yourself.'

'I have a name: Sally Nelson who lives in Ravenglass. Part-time art teacher, part-time B&B lady. You know her?'

I smiled. 'Yes. It's just....'

She cocked her head. 'Tell me, Owen. Do you like *your* job?'

"Like it?' I sighed. I stopped. I ran my hand through my thinning hair. 'I used to. I used to love making things.'

'But not now?'

I said, "Now, I don't make anything. I come up with designs. We put them through the team. We do market research and focus groups, and in the end, we come up with saleable items. We get them into the best stores.'

'But you don't make them yourself.'

'No, how could I? It's a multi-million-pound enterprise— world-wide. We ship tens of thousands of items. We have factories in China and Brazil.' I laughed. 'If I had to throw each bowl on the wheel", I gestured to her potter's wheel. 'I'd never finish.'

She said, "Would you like to make things again?'

I exhaled. 'I wouldn't like to make the shit we produce.' Then I corrected myself. 'No, that's not fair. Our products have very high production values.'

'Yes, but the production values aren't high enough to touch your soul,' Sally said. 'You should try making something that isn't designed to position it in the market. You should make something with your hands just because you want to.'

And she was right. That was why I was burned out. I'd sold my art to the machine, and the machine gobbled it all up and spat out the pips.

Sally nodded. 'Let's go back to the house. It's more comfortable.'

We sat down on the sofa, and Sally put on some Nick Drake and then some John Martyn, and we talked about colours and clay and what it felt like to form things and mould them with your fingers until something inside told you that you had the shape right and then you could stop.

That night I dreamed of the milk-white child again with her long wisps of hair and her eyes like mother of pearl and her lips the colour of chalk. I woke with the moonlight flooding my room. I'd left the curtain undrawn, and an illumination of ivory spilled in. It came over the carpet and up to the end of the bed, lighting up the chair in the room's corner. And there, sitting in the chair, was a child the colour of snowflakes and moonbeams, blinking at me with eyes like selenite through eyelashes fringed with crystal clear as quartz.

I watched, amazed, horrified, unable to believe what I saw was real, and the girl-child leaned forward and said, 'Your future is my past. I recall what you will do and I give you thanks. I will not remember to ask you in future, so what can I give you now in repayment?'

As I sat, trying to think of an answer, a dream answer, for surely I must be dreaming, the child was gone. She had slipped away like a story when the page is turned and the plot only half remembered. But the page can always be turned back if you know how to do it.

I lay awake until dawn which came early with birdsong and

always the slow shushing of the waves on the sand out of sight behind walls. Then I slept.

I was late for breakfast. Taffy had left already. I walked alone again.

I found myself in the woods behind the village, climbing the hill through dense rows of trees. This was *Rhyn Glas* —the Green Promontory indeed. At times, I saw the sea behind me, the estuary with its sandbanks and bobbing yachts. But as I went further, there was no more sea, no more mountains to the east, only trees. The trees went on forever like an ocean, and the paths grew wilder and criss-crossed with briars, rosebay willow herb, mugwort and wild rose until I realised I was lost.

I heard the thin reedy notes of the pipes long before I saw the piper.

In my vision it was as if the curtains of a theatre were drawn back for the show to begin and behind the red velvet hangings, were painted scenes of far countries.

The wood rippled and then everything was more ornate, more vivid, more vibrant. The flowers were huge and alien. Incredible insects buzzed on iridescent wings from orchid to orchid, pollinating them. Strange, bobbing birds trilled and hooted from a canopy of unfamiliar foliage.

But it was the people that amazed me. A procession wove through this extraordinary English woodland, made so strange and new by their presence. At their head was a king with long white hair and a crown of pearls. He walked with his queen, a stately, tall woman, with a face as white as alabaster. Her gown was pale, but silver rings studded with gems—yellow and red as fire—sparkled on her fingers. Behind the King and Queen, a graceful troupe followed, laughing among themselves, pipers playing on fine fairy pipes, others clicking fingers to strike tiny cymbals that rang out sweet and clear through the glade. There were perhaps twenty adults and ten or so children, playing and frolicking behind as their elders walked on.

I thought that somehow I was seeing the Court of King Eveling and that I had been granted a vision of the other world where the fairy folk still walked abroad.

Instinctively, I had crouched when they appeared, but my stance was painful and needing to stretch my calf, I moved. That was all it took. My movement attracted the attention of twenty heads and all the milk-white eyes.

A cry of alarm went up, and the fairies disappeared, melting into the leaves, and within a second, they were gone. The children were less adept, but they too ran from me, though I meant them no harm. With shrieks of alarm, they vanished. And then a cry of pain went up. One of them was injured. I ran to where I'd heard the sound.

And there, sprawled among the undergrowth, was a fairy child, only four or five years old if it had been human. It was pale-skinned with pale hair and eyes lustrous and empty as pearls. A metal snare such as some leave out to catch rabbits was twisted round its ankle, and where the taut wire dug into its flesh was a ring of red. I saw that despite their pale skin, the blood of the fairies was as red as ours.

As I reached to help, the child backed away in terror from me, but with gestures, I tried to show I wanted to free it and tell it that the snare was nothing to do with me.

The child pulled away as far as it could, but that made the wire dig deeper and made it scream, and crystal tears ran hot down its cheeks. Eventually, it lay still and allowed me to release the snare. It seemed not to know how they worked and had been unable to release it itself, whether from ignorance or through pain, I did not know.

I was sure this was the child I had seen in Sally's house that said its past was my future. It had spoken to me then, but it did not talk now. It merely looked at me with its empty white eyes and blinked tears from its crystal eyelashes onto its lily-white cheeks.

And then I picked up the child and held it against me as it sobbed. It was light and limp, and I thought I would need to seek medical attention.

I carried the milk-white child slumped over my shoulder, my

shirt and trousers smeared with blood from its cut leg. I got into Ravenglass, but there was no one close, and no one paid me attention, and I hurried to Sally's house.

I found her in the kitchen.

'Who's that?' Sally said, her eyes wide.

I put the child down on the wooden kitchen chair.

'A child. She had her leg caught in a rabbit snare in the woods when I found her.'

Sally stared at the pale child, and it looked back at her with pearly eyes that were devoid of any pupils.

'What's the matter with her?' Sally said. 'Is she an albino?'

At that moment, attracted by the commotion, Taffy, the story-teller, came into the kitchen. 'Oh my God!' he said.

We both turned around. The milk-white child stared at him impassively.

Sally said, 'Owen found the girl in the woods. Unfortunately, she had her leg caught in a trap.'

Taffy said, 'That is no human child.'

I said, 'How do you know?'

Taffy said, 'Because I know the stories of the White Folk. She is fairy kin.'

Sally said, 'You believe that? She's just an albino girl. Her leg's hurt." She stepped over. "Here, love, let me look.'

'We can't treat her. She needs to go back to her own kind,' Taffy said.

Sally shook her head. "She's not a fairy, Taffy. You've got confused with your own tales.'

But I nodded my head. 'I saw them,' I said.

Taffy turned his eyes on me. 'Who?'

I rubbed my forehead. 'I think I saw the Fairy King, Eveling, in the woods. It was like a door opened, and I saw another world.'

Sally stared bemused as if she thought both Taffy and I were drunk or drugged, but then she looked at the white-skinned girl. The girl was ethereal and strange. No human child had ever looked like this.

'If that's true, then you need to put her back,' Sally said.

'Where?'

'In the woods.'

'She'll die,' I said. 'We can't leave her there.'

'She's dying now,' Taffy said. 'She can't thrive in our world. The snare trapped her and brought her here with its iron. Iron and steel are poison to the fairies. She's sick.'

'Then what can we do?'

'We have to wait until they come to fetch her,' Taffy said.

I looked at the girl. Already she was languishing. She lay back, weak, with her breathing shallow. 'Can we feed her?'

Taffy said, 'Well, according to the stories, the White People can only eat white food.'

“White food? How strange. Like what?'

'Egg white and milk.'

Sally got a glass of milk from the fridge, and I held the beaker to the girl's mouth. At first, she pushed it away, but she was weak and getting weaker. Some drops of milk fell onto her lips and tentatively, she licked them. Taffy cheered. Then she started to drink though only sips, but enough so that half the glass was soon empty.

And so we spent the summer night, waiting with the fairy child on the sofa in the living room, feeding her milk while Taffy ate egg yolks.

The night stole on us unseen. One minute daylight lingered, and then the pale blue of the summer night fled the sky, stars appeared, and a great ivory moon rose. The moonlight came in through the window and bathed the child in its wash of light. She stirred as if revitalised by its cold white glow. But still, no King of the Fairies came.

And it grew very late, and first Taffy and then Sally went to bed, leaving me with the slumbering child. I nodded and dozed, my chin on my chest and then I opened my eyes to see her staring at me.

For the first time since I rescued her, she spoke, 'My father will come soon.'

The moon illuminated the room, and everything it touched grew mysterious. Though I had not left Sally's house, again, I entered an otherworld, and I heard the soft jingle of bells, and the child looked to the door, and the door opened and in stepped Eveling, King of the Fairies and with him his fairy wife, Vivienne, and Vivienne bent down, and the red and yellow gems in her silver rings gleamed in the pale moonlight, and she scooped up her daughter.

King Eveling turned to me and said, 'Thank you for saving my daughter. Trapped with iron in the day world, she would have wasted away and died if not for you.'

I said, 'It was the least I could do.'

He studied my face. 'What gift would you have of me?'

Beautiful as he was, I feared him. Stepping back, I shrugged. 'I don't need a reward.'

Eveling, King of the Fairies, said, 'But you shall have one nevertheless.'

He bent forward and whispered in my ear.

And I dreamed on and my dream twisted and changed and only when I woke did I realise that I had slept for several hours.

Sally came down in her dressing gown. 'She's gone,' she said.

But I had seen something on the seat where the girl had been. So I went over and saw it was a beaker made of porcelain, but porcelain so pale and silvered that it looked like mother of pearl and moonlight had been mixed into it.

'What's that?' Sally said.

'It's for me,' I said.

'It's beautiful,' Sally said, staring as I turned the beaker in my fingers.

I gazed at it in silence. I was so quiet that Sally studied me, frowning, but also faintly smiling.

Finally, I said, "I can make something like this."

Sally put her hand on mine. 'Then you should.'

CHAPTER 15

THE HAUNTING OF UNIT 409

You never know what's behind a locked door. And the romance and mystery of all those locked doors was perhaps what attracted John Shaw there in the first place.

He'd worked security up at Kingmoor and down at a site in Whitehaven. Before that he was on a merchant ship for a while. Something about the job at the Storage Depot attracted him more than all of his previous engagements—what could be behind six hundred and twelve locked doors, all of them neatly padlocked, all of them hiding somebody's secret behind their green metal faces.

The storage units came in a hundred and twenty-five square foot, or seventy-five square foot, or smaller. And there were hundreds of them: so plenty of room for mysteries.

John Shaw had settled down to mainly work night shifts. Perhaps it was the darkness or the quiet of the place in the dead of the night that drew him to those hours. Sometimes he worked nights with Billy Laidlaw from Harraby, sometimes with Polish Dan from Dowbeck, and sometimes with Ian McGuirk from Annan. But mostly on nights he was on his own.

The storage units can be found in an old leather factory on a half-deserted industrial estate that nestles not far from the city centre but you wouldn't find it easily because it's buried in a wasteland of pulled up railway tracks, disused Victorian gas holders and abandoned caravans.

And at night, it was very quiet. So quiet that you might think the building sucked in the silence, drinking it into its old bricks, and making it ooze thickly, dropping drip by drip by drip in the wee hours of the night.

You could get mesmerised by that quiet. And then, your meditation might be disturbed by the bark of a fox, or the shout of a drunk, or the yee-yaw siren of a speeding ambulance. But they were normal and all out of sight behind the big walls and chained iron gate.

So this night, in October, John Shaw was going to be working alone. It wasn't supposed to be that way. Polish Dan was rostered on to be with him, but Polish Dan hadn't turned up, and Scotch Ian wasn't due till 7 am.

So it was just our man John Shaw from Currock. All alone with the six hundred and twelve locked rooms and the six hundred and twelve secrets they held. Their contents might be mundane or mysterious, but they were all secret, and what they hid was out of sight, sitting quiet by itself, settling in.

At least that's what John Shaw thought. John Shaw on his own, and the night and the long hours draining by and the shifting silence.

And the whispering. Not that he heard it at first.

Like I say, it was a Friday in October, not long after 9 p.m. The boss, Julie, had been in on the backshift, and Dan was supposed to come in, so there would be two on nights.

'If he's sick, he should have called in,' Julie said. 'Dan, I mean."

'Was he on nights last night?'

"Yeah, and Ian said he was all right this morning.'

John shrugged. 'We often don't have two on nights.'

She sighed. "Billy was supposed to be on tomorrow, but we're so short-I've shifted Billy till Sunday.'

Julie grimaced. John guessed she didn't like paying for the extra staff much.

She said, 'We've had word that the place is being targeted by someone who thinks there's something worth nicking in here.'

'Well,' John said, 'They're not supposed to lock anything valuable up in their storage units.'

'Exactly,' Julie said. 'No foodstuffs, no dangerous chemicals, no weapons, no explosives. Especially: no valuables.'

She pointed to the poster on the wall and in the contracts the customers had to sign. Still, who knows what they ferreted away in these units away from the prying eyes of the staff.

John said, "They've only got padlocks on them, so they'd be stupid to store anything valuable here."

The lights flickered.

"Wind's getting up,' Julie said.

John shrugged. It didn't matter to him. He wouldn't be going outside. He had his flask of coffee and sandwiches, crisps, tins of pop and a ready meal from Lidl that he would microwave about 3 a.m.

They couldn't see outside directly from the office because it had no windows, and pigeon shit and moss covered most of the skylight.

On the desk, two large monitors sat, not so high resolution, but good enough for general surveillance. Both monitors were squared into four screens. The right showed four views of the empty corridors. The left showed four views of the empty night outside.

The funeral director opposite was shut. The antique dealer closed. The town and country interiors warehouse over the way sat in darkness. All locked up. None of those businesses had night staff.

So on this whole business estate—the old leather factory in other words-there would just be John on his own that night. The nearest other humans would be the delivery drivers from the pizza shop across the railway tracks and over the grimy, soot-stained eight-foot wall and past the brownfield development land beyond.

The storage depot itself was cocooned by a wilderness of roads, industrial units, briars, bindweed and rats. John didn't like to think about the rats. He hoped the owls ate them all, because there were owls too and on still nights they hooted all night long. But it wasn't still tonight; it was windy, and the owls would be taking shelter and keeping quiet.

Inside the storage unit, traps with rat poison were positioned along corridors and in corners. Folk weren't supposed to store food in their units in case it attracted rodents. Some did. But also maybe the rats came out of simple curiosity, wondering what was locked up behind all those metal doors with their shiny, flimsy padlocks.

Then Julie was gone, and John was glad. Not that he didn't like her, but he preferred being on his own. Now it was quiet, he poured himself a tea from his thermos flask into a mug that said: 'John: The Man, The Myth, The Legend.'

The tea steamed, and he sipped it and watched the monitors. Nothing moved on the outside screens to the left. Nothing moved among the myriad blank corridors to the right. He sipped more tea. Then he looked at the paper. He was a Liverpool fan and read the report about the game against Stoke City. He'd read it before, but it was nice to read about wins more than once.

He glanced at the clock on the wall—9:15 p.m. He was here until 7 a.m. He might watch Netflix on his phone, but his eyes weren't as good as they used to be, and the screen was small. He'd been enjoying The Expanse on Amazon Video, but Series Four wasn't as good as Series Three, so far anyway.

John finished his tea. The wind rumbled round outside the storage unit. The monitors showed more blank silent pictures like still lives, or still deaths or stillborn loves and stillborn dreams and hopes behind the still iron doors, standing sentry over all those put-away possessions.

Time for a wander around.

Maybe later, he'd switch off the strip lights that ran along the long passages to save money for Julie, but for now, he let them burn —long tubes of glowing gas that flickered in tip-tap time, and if you spent too long in their luminous company, you ended up with a banging headache.

John stepped out of the office with its bare desks and curling invoices and the friendly peeling false-leather computer chair and took one last look at the twin monitor screens unchanging, unenlightening, unmoving, unmoved.

His footsteps echoed on the concrete floor as he strolled past rat traps and padlocks and door after door after door, all green, all metal, all locked, and John was relieved when he turned the corner because that at least gave a change of scene, but soon the new scene was as familiar as the one he'd walked out of: more doors, more locks, more secrets, more things locked away.

He laughed. Why did his imagination run riot like this on night shift? Probably normal. Secrets, eh?

Most peoples' secrets weren't much and ordinary lives didn't interest John. They were like his: boring. He went to work, watched the football, went to the Howard Arms with Maisie, and the William Rufus for a good meal with Pete, rang his lad who lived in Sunderland, talked to his mates, most of whom he'd known from school forty years before. Proper Carlisle lads they were and lasses: chavas and buwers.

John's footsteps tapped out on the floor. He'd almost done an entire circuit now. He was on the four hundreds, which weren't the furthest. Weirdly the two hundreds were further away from the entrance than them. The numbering made little sense until you realised that the storage unit had taken over the disused leather factory piecemeal, elbowing out others who'd previously staked a claim. Storage was big business, and it hungrily devoured smaller weaker businesses that had occupied the old leather factory. The auction house business would be next. The storage units would take over that in their turn and fill it with blank metal units and their silent metal mouths.

In fact, they weren't mouths—they didn't have tongues for one thing. He laughed for thinking such a thing. It was then that he heard it.

It sounded like whispering. At first, he thought he'd pocket dialled someone, or his walking had pressed play on Amazon, and *The Expanse* was muttering its interstellar secrets to his leg. He checked. But it wasn't his phone. His phone was silent, showing gleaming icons but saying nothing.

But the whispering went on.

Had someone left a radio on or something in one of the units? He stopped and tilted his head. The voice—it was a voice—came from just ahead. It was faint, and it didn't sound like a radio programme. It sounded like one of the old boys who sit in pub corners talking to themselves.

John walked along the passage, curious now, listening at each door. It was ahead and left. He counted the numbers on the doors: four hundred and six, four hundred and seven, four hundred and eight, four hundred and nine.

That was it: 409. The muttering came from unit four hundred and nine. John put his ear to the green metal door. It was cold. He listened and heard: a voice came from inside, but it wasn't speaking to him. It must be a radio or something. But it didn't sound like a radio programme. It was a voice talking in a language he didn't understand. What was it-Polish? Urdu? Welsh? He shook his head.

It was like a tape of someone, maybe like an old home movie where grand-dad is telling a story and nobody is listening, but they taped it because it was Christmas or summer holidays in the caravan.

But it didn't sound quite like that either.

John shuddered. The wind was louder outside now, while the voice prattled on. It was a little voice. He didn't know why he'd said that: a little voice. But it was.

He guessed the battery on the tape recorder would die eventually, and the voice would stop. He smiled. He walked on, completing his lonely circuit and arriving back at the office.

This time, for some reason, he locked the office door from inside, and he went to the monitors and scanned them, just in case something might be moving outside the storage warehouse. Or even inside.

They had been targeted, Julie'd said that.

And then John flicked his eyes from the left screen over to the right, to the cameras that showed the empty passages with their faceless, windowless, featureless green metal doors, all the numbers adding up until they got to six hundred. Six hundred and twelve to be exact. No one moved there either, not even a rat.

He drank more tea, had a packet of XL Cheese crisps, flicked through the paper and, letting the page drop from his thumb, went back to the monitors. The branches that showed on the screens were swaying about crazily: the wind.

John's mind wandered. When he came back to himself, it was past midnight. Where did the time go? He sighed, rubbed his eyes. Night shifts numbed your brain. He squeezed his face. He'd go for another wander to stretch the legs and pass the time.

He unlocked the office door and stepped out. It was cold, suddenly cold. There was an odd smell too. He couldn't place it—something like sweat and leaves mingled.

John had forgotten about the voice in unit 409 until he got into the three hundreds. Then he remembered, and he was mildly curious to hear if it was still prattling on, or if the battery had died and it was silent.

Before he turned the corridor into the four hundreds, he heard it. It was louder than before. How could that be? The battery should be draining and the sound fading. And the wind was louder, rushing about the storage depot, so how could this muttering, whispering, whatever it was, sound louder?

For the first time, John Shaw realised he was scared. He was alone. The bunch of keys that jingled from his belt as he walked along went silent as he stood, listening. That smell was more pungent too: old sweat and old leaves, like an old tramp who lived in the fields, or something that's burrowed up from the ground.

Instead of completing his circuit, John turned on his heel. He walked quickly back to the office and locked the door. Imagination, it was pure imagination, but it's funny what imagination could do to you. It was just the whispering and the smell together and the fact it had got louder when it should have got quieter and then the wind going wild outside and the fact it was the middle of the night and he was on his own and all of that.

Settling in the office, John took up his paper.

He caught the movement out of the corner of his eye—from the right-hand monitor, but when he glanced over, all was still. It showed the internal corridors—where nothing should be moving at all. But something was. To be fair, he sometimes saw rodents. There was nothing there now. It was probably just a rat.

The fluorescent light flickered. Damn this wind. And just when his nerves were shaky. He'd have his microwave meal soon. It wasn't properly time, but it would take his mind off things. John stood from the peeling computer chair that always seemed such a comfort and stepped over to the office door to check he'd locked it.

He hadn't. He twisted the key and felt it clunk round: locked. He breathed in relief and pushed his hand through his sandy hair.

What was the need to lock it? There was no one here. The external doors were all bolted tight. He patted the bunch of keys at his hip. He was the only one who could get in or out.

The microwave pinged. He ate his meal. Watched TV on his phone, straining his eyes. He didn't like to look at the monitors now. But every quarter of an hour or so, he forced himself. There was nothing. Of course not.

He should go for another walk around. Not that anyone would know if he didn't. But *he* would know. John was a conscientious man, not a dosser or a shirker. He should go. He looked at the door with its black key turned. And he didn't move. He moistened his lips. He swallowed. That's what she was paying him to do. Finally, he stood, walked to the door, turned the key, pulled the handle, yanked the door open and stepped out.

That odd smell was stronger. The wind pummelled the building. He imagined the old leather factory where thousands of hides had hung. All those slaughtered cattle down the hundred and fifty years it had been open.

And he walked, but quickly, and not paying attention. There was nothing to pay attention to. And then he reached the end of the three hundreds.

The smell soaked the place now, and it stunk. He put his hand to his nose. It was more organic, deeper, older, stranger. Two steps before John turned into the four hundreds passage, he nearly retched. He slammed his hand over his mouth. Had something broken open—some container and liquid leaked out?

He should go and check. 409.

He turned into the four hundreds and stopped and stepped back, hand to his throat. The door of Unit 409 hung open.

It *had* been padlocked, and the padlock had been on the outside. The door was not forced or bent, though even from here, he could see stains on the inside at the bottom like something corrosive had spilled onto the door. The door swung wide. It looked like someone had opened the door, and if someone had opened it, that meant someone was in here with him—locked in here with him. But John had the only keys, and the outside doors were bolted shut, which meant that someone had been in here with him all this time.

Bullshit. Not possible. He tapped the keys. He'd seen no one. But then there had been that movement on the monitor, just a flicker, maybe a glitch, almost certainly nothing. It was undoubtedly nothing, just an electrical jitter. The lights had been flickering all night with this wind. It was just that. There was no one in this old warehouse with him. There couldn't be.

Just John and the skins of all those dead animals.

He breathed out. He shook his head. He didn't approach Unit 409.

The whispering was going on still. It came from inside Unit 409, and he knew it wasn't a tape recorder or a radio. Something was in there.

The padlock hung around the hasp four feet away, lying on the floor, and it was still clicked shut, locked. It couldn't be taken off without the key. Only the renter of this unit had the key. Their name would be in the books in the office. He hadn't checked. He never checked who had which unit. It wasn't his job. He didn't normally care.

He tip-toed close enough to see into the unit. It hung in shadow and the voice whispered from inside, unseen.

John's phone had a torch function, so he pointed the light into the gloom. There was something there. What the hell was all that? He saw now it was half full of mouldy boxes. The boxes were made of wood but old. They had mildew and moss growing on them. And the whispering came from inside one. They weren't big boxes, not coffin-sized or anything. Most people kept things in cardboard boxes, but these were wood, old wood, and damp and stinking. They smelled of leaves and mould but also sweat, animal sweat, or human sweat; he didn't know which: or maybe something that was sometimes an animal and sometimes a man.

The wind moaned outside. The lights flickered. John did not step into Unit 409. He would report it to the morning shift. Now he would go back to the office and lock it and wait until it was day and someone came. Scotch Ian was on earlies. Scotch Ian was daft. He joked about nowt. He prattled on about less than nowt. But he was human. John wanted to see Scotch Ian. Or Polish Dan, big Polish Dan, all six foot three of him.

John Shaw looked one more time into Unit 409, and turned. Whatever was in there making that whispering wasn't a normal thing. Whatever had come out of those old, damp boxes wasn't a person like him.

John didn't close the door of Unit 409.

In fact he didn't go within six feet.

In fact, he turned and ran.

All the lights in the storage unit died before he was halfway back. And now he got lost on those long corridors with all their doors: six hundred and twelve doors. John Shaw stood in the absolute pitch black, and he heard something coming, whispering, crawling down the passage towards him.

John fumbled for his phone. He stabbed at the touch screen. The torch wouldn't go on like that. You had to long press it to make it work and he couldn't do that because his hand shook so much.

The sound crawled closer and closer, and the smell oozed nearer and nearer, trailing like invisible slugs along the corridor walls.

Finally, the torch beam snapped on. John turned and shone it.

There was somebody there. Somebody small. Somebody who stared round the corner of the passage, long thin fingers on the wall, black-blinking eyes, teeth like needles. And when John's beam fell on him, he darted back as if he was shy. But he wasn't shy. He was playing a game .

John screamed and ran down the corridor, his heavy work boots thudding on the concrete floor. He got to the office door and saw the monitors were off. There was no light except the light of his torch. He pushed the door. It didn't work. He dragged the door open and behind smelled that stink of grime and wet, and blood and death somehow inside the smell and inside that whispering in a language older than time, someone small with teeth like needles came to eat him.

And John thought: who had brought those boxes here? Or had they brought themselves?

With a shaking hand, he slammed and locked the door behind him.

He was safe in the office.

But the small person was in the office already, playing peek a boo from behind the chair—playing funny games with its human friends. John saw it and stepped back, and then the small person jumped at him.

. . .

Scotch Ian unlocked the doors at seven. He scratched his head. John should have unlocked them before now. And then Scotch Ian couldn't find John Shaw, so he rang Julie.

'He's been here because his paper's here and the remains of his meal,' Ian said. 'But he's not here now.'

'Well, he's not getting paid, if he's nicked off," Julie said.

'One other thing, boss,' Ian said.

'What?'

'Unit 409 is open.'

Julie didn't speak. Then she said, '409?'

"Yeah," John said. "You said we should never open that one."

"No," Julie said, "But sometimes it opens itself."

CHAPTER 16

THE SHADOW MAN OF KENDAL

It was in Kendal, in a cafe up one of the little alleys that run off Stricklandgate, one afternoon in Autumn some years ago when Sam Davies was given the book. It was his friend Mark who gave it to him. The cafe they met in that day was organic, where they had oat-milk chai with chia seeds and were playing Nick Mulvey over the speakers.

Sam arrived first and got the table. But only two minutes later, the door opened, letting in the cool air and tousle-haired Mark entered. Mark hung his canvas messenger bag carefully over the back of his wooden chair and sat opposite. He gave a cheesy grin, then was quiet. Three minutes went by with no one speaking.

"Are you all right?" Sam said.

"Sure."

Sam studied him. "You're being odd."

Mark beamed back at him. "No, I'm fine."

"You seem..."

"What?"

"Anxious."

"Why would I be anxious?"

Sam said, "I have no idea. But then I forgot —you've always been weird. This is just another example."

They both laughed. Mark looked around the cafe. He wouldn't meet Sam's eyes.

"Busy here," Mark said.

There was hardly anybody in. Sam said, "Not really."

Mark stood abruptly. His hand going to his pocket. "Want a coffee?"

"Sit down. It's table service."

"Oh," Mark sat.

Sam studied him. What was going on?

The waitress came and took the coffee order. They fell into silence while they waited for her to return with the drinks.

Sam was a photographer. He'd wanted to be a wildlife photographer when he'd trained for it at Newton Rigg, but now he mainly did weddings —some food photography for websites too. It wasn't the career he'd dreamed of, but it was okay.

Sam met Mark three years before at the Kendal Comic-Con that always happened in October. The next one would be in three weeks. They both planned to go. Sam wanted to meet Gary Spencer-Millidge, who'd written and illustrated the mysterious and beautiful graphic novel *Strangehaven*. He didn't know if Mark wanted to meet anyone in particular.

"How did your job go?" Mark asked.

Sam chewed his thumb. "Simon Havers never paid me."

Mark raised his eyebrows. "What a swine."

"Yeah. That's what I thought, though I didn't use the word swine when I was thinking it."

"But Havers promised you."

Sam nodded. "But now he says I'll need to take him to court to get the cash."

"Oh man, but Havers has got loads of money. He owns a hotel for Heaven's sake."

"Aye, yes, but he made loads of moncy by ripping people off."

"I'm sorry, mate. Bummer."

Simon Havers owned a boutique hotel in Kendal and had other hotels in Cartmel and Fellfoot and Skelwith Bridge. Havers lived in a designer house on the way to Hawkshead. He was a wealthy man.

Sam said. "In your message, you said you had something for me."

Mark nodded. He shifted in his seat. "I wanted to give you something."

"A present?"

Mark rummaged through his bag and pulled out a big, A4 sized book.

Sam grinned. "That's for me?"

"Yes. For you. This book changed my life, Sam," Mark said. He had a serious look on his face —an earnest, wide-eyed look.

Mark was a soft-hearted, lazy charmer. You couldn't help but like him. He didn't work. He believed in The Law of Attraction, and, Sam thought, if what he'd wanted to attract was a crummy flat and a string of unreliable girlfriends who weren't much interested in him and soon departed in search of better pickings, then The Law of Attraction was working.

Sam turned the book over in his hand. It was heavier than it looked and had a lurid cover with bad type-setting and appeared to be a facsimile print of an out-of-print book — the sort where someone scans each page on their phones, makes a PDF and prints it. It always depended on how good the scanning was because sometimes the pages were skew-whiff, or the type went off the edge of the page.

The blurred, printed letters on the front cover of this one said: *The Grimoire of Asmodeus*. Apparently, it came from the ancient Middle East, but a man named Austin Yeats edited this edition. A black-and-white photo of a severe man with big grey curls stared up from the back.

Sam riffled the pages, looked up, uninterested. "What's it about?"

"Magick," Mark said.

"Magic — like conjuring?"

Mark shook his head. "No, magick with a k."

"Magik?"

"No—Magick. It's spelled like that to set it apart from stage magic and conjuring. It's so not magic. Magick with a k is serious."

Sam put the book down. His latte was half drunk. He said, "I need to get off soon. I've got a shoot at twelve up in Windermere."

Mark pushed the book across the cafe table to Sam. "Take it. It'll change your life too."

Sam smiled but kept his hands where they were, the right holding the white ceramic handle of the mug that contained the chai, the left tapping gently on the tabletop. "For the better?" he asked with a grin.

Mark frowned. A funny look came over his face. "Everything has a price, yeah?"

Sam peered at him. "Really? Have you been on the mushrooms again?"

Mark sat back defensively; the attitude of the born liar caught. "No. It's nothing to do with that." He touched the cheap gloss cover of *The Grimoire of Asmodeus*. "This is different; it's philosophy. It's deep."

Sam sat back. "You look jittery."

"You should take the book."

Sam noticed how bloodshot Mark's eyes were and they had dark rings smudged under them.

Mark sat forward. "Please."

Sam sighed. "Well, it's not my normal reading material."

Mark whined, "Please take it?"

Sam's brow furrowed. "Well, if it's a present."

"It is."

Sam shrugged, picked up the paperback grimoire, and thrust it into his camera bag. He liked Mark for all he was a dosser. He didn't have to read the book. Probably wouldn't.

Mark looked pleased, relieved, almost. He suddenly smiled, got up. "Thanks, mate. I've got to rush. I'm off to see Sarah now."

Sam nodded. "Give her my regards."

At the door, Mark turned and stopped. "Thanks for taking the book."

"Thanks for taking my present?" Sam grinned. "Sure."

Still, Mark hesitated. There was something he wanted to say. Clearing his throat, he blurted, "I like you, Sam. You're my mate, but I couldn't think of anyone else, you know? I mean, I couldn't give it to Sarah now, could I?"

Sam shook his head. "You're weirding me out, mate. What do you mean?"

"Nothing." Mark waved Sam away. "But make sure you give it to someone. Maybe Simon Havers?"

"Give a present to the bloke who never paid me? I don't think so."

"Well, anyone. But maybe him."

Mark hurried out of the cafe, leaving Sam to pay, the little bell on the door jingling like he was a departing angel who'd just got his wings.

THE DAYS ROLLED ON BY. Sam found the grimoire in the bottom of his camera bag on the Thursday after Mark gave him it. He didn't want to be lugging it around with him in his camera bag, so he slapped it a coffee table in his living room and soon a Council Tax bill, and his Vodafone bill covered it — he must go paperless with that — and a copy of the *Kendal Courier* free magazine he hadn't got round to reading, that, in fact, he never got round to reading.

The grimoire was half-buried. Only the corner of its poorly printed cover peeking out from under the paper. It looked harmless enough like that, but it was watching.

. . .

SAM HAD A BUSY DAY. It was the Saturday, and he'd been shooting a big wedding at Crook. He got home, reached for a bottle of Lancaster Blonde ale from the fridge, cracked the top off with the bit on the end of his tin opener and sat and watched a replay of the football, but fell asleep.

He woke to find the football had finished and there was an old horror movie playing, something from the 70s: *Psychomania* or something? Anyway, it was about Satanic Hell's Angels in the South of England and something about a locked drawer, or was it a locked room?

Sam's head had lolled on the sofa while he slept and his neck was stiff. The beer was half drunk and flat, and there was someone in the room with him.

The realisation he was not alone arrived with a slither and a jump. First, the idea slithered along the floor, barely noticed, then it jumped fully into his consciousness. Sam shrieked, slammed his back against the sofa and stared.

'It' sat in the chair opposite. It wasn't smoke, though it was grey. It wasn't paint, though it was wet-looking. It couldn't be a shadow because if it were a shadow, where was the creature that cast it?

Instead, it sat like something emerging, a moth from a pupa, a chick from an egg, a parasite from the dead, eaten body of its host.

The thing emerged into the room, squeezing itself into this space, feeling its way out of the place it came from with shadow hands. A shadow without a man, but shaped like a man. The thing blinked, and Sam swallowed, and swallowing was hard, when his mouth was so dry. And the shadow man whispered like the sound dirt makes when you slide the sole of your boot over it on a stone floor, a grinding, swirling sound at once both hard and soft: gritty, but breaking down too. And it smelled. It smelled like an old box where grandmas keep letters forgotten until they go old and yellow, and those who write and read them are both long dead. The smell had the tang of vinegar. It had the aroma of overcooked meat.

The shadow man blinked and rose from its seat. It flowed and rippled across the space between the chair and where Sam sat, knees drawn up to his chest, one hand to his mouth, the other raised in flat-palmed protest.

"No!" he yelled, but the shadow man did not listen. The shadow man came closer and closer and closer until it was close enough for Sam to smell its burned-meat breath and its bathroom-mould soul and its burial-shroud hair.

The shadow man reached out to touch him, and Sam feared that if the shadow's spindly fingers caressed his own sweet skin, it would pull him into itself, and it would consume him, swallow him down inside itself like a drink of milk.

Sam yelled "No!" again, and this time he woke to the same room, the same flat beer, the same flickering television, but there was no shadow, and his beating heart slowed. He exhaled heavily, and he grinned and said out loud, "It was just a dream. Thank the Lord," and he reached and took and sipped his warm beer, even though it was flat, and he rubbed his sweaty forehead with the back of his hot left hand, and said again, "Just a dream," and those words seemed to calm him.

But though the shadow had vanished, the fear remained, and hung in the room like the hint of perfume. But this was not a pleasant fragrance, instead it reeked of sackcloth and ashes and funeral flowers redolent of desolation and decay and unquenchable grief at the graveside.

As Sam looked around the room, beer glass still in hand, he swallowed, and though he saw nothing, his terror rose again like the tide flooding in because although he saw nothing unusual with his eyes made of flesh, his eyes made of memory could not forget the shadow man with his spindle fingers and his worm-tail hair and his garbage breath and his cobwebbed eyes.

Sam moistened his lips and stared. He stared at the chair, but now nothing sat in it; no man made of shadows. It had all been a nasty dream. And then his eye alighted on the grimoire given to him by Mark that had lain there unthought of and buried by bills, with only one corner peeping out, and Sam had the horrible idea that the book was watching him. But it was only an idea brought on by fatigue and overwork and waking in the middle of the night in your clothes on the sofa.

Stretching with a hesitant hand, he took the grimoire and pulled it out from under the envelopes. He flexed it in his hands and it was an ordinary book, ill-printed, inelegant, written by Austin Yeats, gazing with a wicked grin from his black and white portrait on the book's back.

Sam flicked through the pages. For the first time, he took an interest in it, and, as he read page after page, an idea blossomed in his brain. The idea was this: that the book had been watching him while he slept, and it was from the book that the shadow had come. But these were three a.m thoughts, worth nothing in daylight — mere imagining. But he read on.

This grimoire told of the conjuration of things from other realms. It spoke of creatures that lurked unseen out there but could not get inside into our world. In his helpful commentary to the grimoire, Austin Yeats explained all they needed to break down the doors between their world and ours was an invitation and an offering, and this offering was a libation —a sacred drink. The Ancient Egyptians had offered them barley beer; the Phoenicians had given them blood, but any liquid would do. It seemed these extra-dimensional crea-tures, these demons, were thirsty.

Among these creatures was an order of wraiths with unpro-nounceable, barbarous names. Sam's trailing finger caught one, and he stopped. The engraving in the book looked like the thing he had seen. This was Barbatel, a shadow thing that sucked out human life. The sorcerer had to summon the creature, offer it a libation, then when it came he would give the shadow demon a task, and it would set forth and feed on a victim, bringing home the victim's energy and giving it to the magician himself.

But this was pure imagination. Sam knew that because such things did not exist. They could not exist because if they did, that would mean that the world was unsafe and all rules of physics and science and everyday certainties were insecure and could swing open like a flimsy door on broken hinges.

He rubbed his eyes. Why was he thinking such things? He snapped the book shut, and it lay face down on the coffee table, this time on top of the pile of bills and from its back cover, the dour face of Austin Yeats stared out.

This was so much tosh. So you were supposed to summon one of these things by saying its name and giving it a drink? It made no sense. Sam was a rational man. He believed in science and progress, and he voted for the Green Party. He was an optimist, and so he pointed his long finger at the book and laughed scornfully. "Come on, Barbatel, do your worst." And when nothing happened, he took a sip of the Lancaster Blonde ale, but didn't finish it, and went to bed.

NOTHING MORE FOR TWO DAYS, not even a bad dream. The following Monday, he was walking down Finkle Street. It was just before lunch, so a few people were walking up and down and looking in shop windows. He sensed that something wasn't right, but he didn't know what it was at first, so he snapped round his head, stopping mid-stride, sniffing the air.

The old panic rose in him. He smelled the thing like ashes on the wind: like decay and dissolution, and though the sun was shining, he still shivered. He saw it. He zeroed in on it, shaking. There it stood behind a trio of friends, like a photo-bomber, taller by half than any of them, faceless and flickering, made wholly of shadow even though there was nothing there to cast a shadow. It came at him, pouring through the passers-by, sliding straight between them, coming fast. It was Barbatel. He had summoned it with his foolish invitation to do its worst, that and the libation of undrunk beer.

Barbatel slid across the ground, and Sam ran. The surrounding people looked startled, and they jerked round like chickens to see if there was a robbery and whether he was the thief or the victim. Sam fled in his panic. He ran onto Stricklandgate, sprinted along the road that led to the river and out of the town centre, but before getting that far, he panicked more. This was no good. It was too empty. He needed people. Surely it couldn't hurt him while shoppers surrounded him. Surely, ordinary people could prevent it from swallowing him down like a drink of milk.

But when he stopped and turned, breathing hard, leaning on a wall, the eyes of alarmed pedestrians studying him disapprovingly, working out if he were some kind of threat, and when he dared to glance behind, Barbatel had vanished.

THE THIRD TIME Sam saw Barbatel was in a dream. The shadow man swirled in the corner of a Hall of Mirrors. There were mirrors everywhere —big mirrors, small mirrors —mirrors that distorted and mirrors that gave an accurate reflection. The shadow man flowed out from one mirror and into another, in and out and in and out, from one shining glass into the next: silver and shadow a fume of boiling, swirling, black vapour. Not realising he was dreaming, Sam found his courage and stood.

"What do you want?"

But the shadow man spoke not, merely curled his way across the floor towards Sam like a page turning, and flickered and fluttered like the flame of a candle that was about to die.

"Leave me alone!" Sam shouted.

The shadow man crept closer, and as he got closer, Sam smelled sourness and dampness and realised he didn't have a sense of smell in dreams and woke. He jumped bolt upright in bed, heart hammering, sweat soaking the sheets, but he was alone.

Another dream.

· · ·

THE NEXT DAY he Googled Austin Yeats. Yeats had been an occultist, a friend of Austin Osman Spare and the author Arthur Machen. He'd died years before but specialised in shadow magic.

Sam followed the link to Shadow Magic and then a reference to the Shadow Plane and in the end landed up at a website that claimed that a sorcerer could indeed send out shadows, even after death. He could prevent his total end by feeding off the living by sending out his shadow to drink down their souls like a draft of refreshing water and digest their life. This energy would not give enough life to bring the sorcerer back from the grave, but enough to keep him from drifting into the whirlpool known as hell.

Sam knew what he'd seen.

He rang Mark Jones. The first three times, the call got rejected, but when he tried later, about 8 pm sitting with all the lights on and the television blaring out, he left a voicemail.

ANOTHER SLEEPLESS NIGHT.

Mark phoned him the next morning.

"You bastard," Sam said.

"Sorry, mate. I couldn't give it to Sarah. It crushed me that I had to give it to you, but the shadow was getting closer to me. The next time it was going to get me."

"But now it'll get me."

"No, no."

"How not?"

"You've got to give it away. Someone has to accept the grimoire willingly from you."

"What? I have to give it to someone else, knowing what that means, that this shadow thing will turn its attention to them and hunt them down instead of me."

"Yes."

"What kind of person would I be if I did that to someone?"

Mark said, "A live person —a person who wasn't going to be drunk down by a demon like a glass of milk."

SAM WENT to Paperchase and bought the prettiest wrapping paper, that was for wrapping up the *Grimoire of Asmodeus* and he bought a red ribbon to be tied in an attractive bow round the book. He stopped off at the supermarket and picked up a bottle of cheap brandy. In Photoshop at home, he designed a label for the brandy bottle and stuck it on after he'd steamed off the original. It said:

"Barbatel, Vintage Spirit."

Then he drove to The Old Lakeland boutique hotel and rang the bell. The attractive receptionist, because Simon Havers only employed beautiful people —both male and female, answered. "Can I help you?"

"I'm here to see Simon."

She yawned. "He's busy."

"Tell him it's Sam, the photographer."

Her pretty face twisted in a scowl. "I told you he's busy. He won't see you."

"Just tell him I want to see him because I want to tell him face to face that I am dropping my legal case for the money."

She hesitated.

"Please," Sam said.

The pretty young thing turned on her heel, and Sam waited nervously, the wrapped grimoire in his hands. Havers had to take this of his own free will, or Sam would never escape the Shadow.

Eventually, Simon Havers came to the door. He didn't invite Sam in, but kept him outside on the threshold. Havers sneered. "So, little boy, you've seen the error of your ways."

Sam nodded.

Havers grunted. "Taking me to court would cost you more than you'd get even if you won."

Sam said, "I know."

Havers shrugged. "And I've got no money, anyway."

Sam gestured to the plush exterior of the hotel.

Havers laughed. "Well, let's say as far as the taxman is concerned, I've got no money. Clever accountants have their uses. Technically, I'm broke. So no money for you little photographer."

"No, Simon. I realised that you're an influential man in this community."

"I am."

"And your word can make or break my career."

"So right."

"With all your friends, it would finish me if you blacklisted me."

Havers smirked. "Glad you see sense."

"And I thought maybe if I came and saw you and told you I now see it your way, maybe in the future you could give me some more work."

Simon Havers sneered. "Let's not get carried away."

Sam dropped his gaze. "But I want to be in your good books."

Simon Havers said, "You're smarter than you look, which wouldn't be too hard. See, son? No one crosses me and wins." He jerked a spade-like thumb at his chest. "I am the man."

Sam saw his chance. "Listen, as a gesture, I wanted to give you a present."

Simon Havers took the gift-wrapped book with magisterial pomp as if getting gifts was what he expected as his due. He shook it, snorted, tapped it, and said, "A book? I don't read books."

"No, but it's a special book, and I wanted to give it as a gesture from me to you."

"Hmm. But you think this is enough to win me round? What a loser you are."

Sam produced the bottle of brandy. He gave that to the swaggering hotel owner.

"Barbatel, Vintage Spirit? Never heard of it."

Sam started to smile. "It cost me a lot. It's strong."

Havers shrugged. "I like strong drink. This is a better present than the book. Your Barbatel is welcome in my house. I'll take this and the book as your apology."

Sam grinned. "Thank you, Mr Havers. I think you'll really like that Barbatel."

Simon Havers looked at his big gold watch. "Listen, I'm a busy man. So thank you for grovelling." He waved the book. "But piss off."

"Sure. Thank you, Mr Havers."

Havers snorted. His pretty assistant sniffed, and they closed the door in Sam's face. But at least *The Grimoire of Asmodeus* went inside with them, willingly accepted and gift-wrapped.

It was the perfect gift, and Simon Havers was a man who deserved to have his soul drunk like milk if ever there was one.

ALSO BY TONY WALKER

Christmas Ghost Stories

More Cumbrian Ghost Stories

Further Ghost Stories

Haunted Castles

London Horror Stories

Horror Stories For Halloween